"Are you ready for a walmfully bu_____... so, visit Walmland—a magical place . . . where you can forget about all your worries and meet many fantastic creatures. They will take you on a journey full of warm light, sweet scents, joyful laughter, and good deeds. *Bunky and the Walms* is a cheerful Christmas tale and a must-read for all brave little Bunkies (as well as other nice children)."

—EWELINA PRAŻMO

Maria Curie-Skłodowska University

"This is a true Christmas Story! Those who do not believe in the story should read it twice. The second time loud so their ears can hear it, and with their eyes open so they can see it. It is only then that they would realize that this is an amazing, true story. I really enjoy it, especially the story with Santa Claus."

—GREGORY PAPANIKOS

Athens Institute for Education and Research

"In *Bunky and the Walms*, Aleksandra Tryniecka invites readers, regardless of age, to enjoy reading an interesting Christmas event in the life of the restless yet adventurous little Bunky, who, guided by senile Santa Claus, roams the world distributing gifts and learning lessons about Christmas values. Interweaving other interesting narrative threads into the fabric of the fable, Tryniecka skillfully creates out of Walmland a setting for her story, where fairy-tale elements embrace reality."

—IBRAHIM A. EL-HUSSARI

Lebanese American University

"As warm and fulfilling as gingerbread and cupcakes . . . on Christmas Eve, *Bunky and the Walms* is a book about the joys of reading, writing, holidays, and striving to be a better person. . . . *Bunky and the Walms* is not just a magical Christmas story but a guide for how to live a good life, an adventurous life, a Bunky life, as we all struggle through life's challenges to become the heroes of our own stories."

—BRUCE GATENBY

Author of *The Kingdom of Absurdities*

"Christmas would be no fun without any presents. In the exciting and suspenseful story of three Christmas heroes who help repair Santa Claus's sledge and deliver gifts around the world, Aleksandra Tryniecka tells of love, friendship, mutual understanding and affinity. The tale introduces the reader into a delightful world of Christmas magic where dream and reality intertwine. This beautiful book . . . will appeal to children and adults alike. A perfect family read for the coming Christmas!"

—ANNA KĘDRA-KARDELA
Maria Curie-Skłodowska University

"*Bunky and the Walms* is an exciting and heartwarming tale of self-discovery. Narrated in a playful yet emotional and affectionate style, Aleksandra Tryniecka's book entices us to follow its uniquely crafted characters in their attempt to realize their dreams. As the magic of Christmas touches all, this beautiful narrative is a must-read for children of all age groups who wish to find the strength to be themselves and lead the way for a better, more tolerant, and more inclusive world."

—MARIA PIRGEROU
Ministry of Education and Religious Affairs, Greece

"*Bunky and the Walms* assails the reader's imagination. . . . Tryniecka invites the reader to understand holiday conundrums with thoughtfulness and love. Ultimately, the characters are taken on an inter-dimensional journey of thought form and going beyond what may seem possible into reality, showing readers young and old that it is important to dream."

—CHRISTOPHER R. STERN
Senior Spectrographic Technician, EVRAZ Pueblo

Bunky and the Walms

Bunky and the Walms

The Christmas Story

Written and Illustrated by
ALEKSANDRA TRYNIECKA

RESOURCE *Publications* · Eugene, Oregon

BUNKY AND THE WALMS
The Christmas Story

Wipf & Stock
An Imprint of Wipf and Stock Publishers
199 W. 8th Ave., Suite 3
Eugene, OR 97401

www.wipfandstock.com

PAPERBACK ISBN: 978-1-6667-1865-2
HARDCOVER ISBN: 978-1-6667-1866-9
EBOOK ISBN: 978-1-6667-1867-6

09/29/21

For my Bunky and my Walms –
Thank you for always being such a ray of joy in my life

Contents

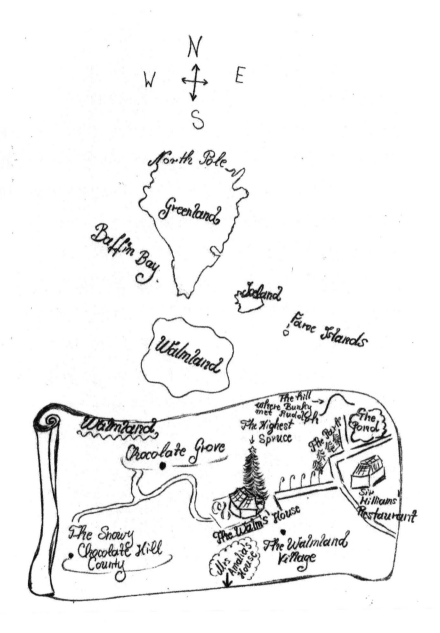

I

Bunky Winter

It was pleasantly snowing outside when Mr. and Mrs. Walm returned home from a little Christmas shopping. It was already very close to Christmas and their little nephew Bunky Hippo was in the living room making efforts to decorate a huge Christmas tree. He carefully distributed colourful socks all over the branches and stared critically at his enterprise.

"Hello, dear Bunky!" said Mr. Walm, "Why did you decorate the tree with socks?"

"Merry Christmas!" answered Bunky wryly, "And why not?"

"I don't know," said Mr. Walm, "Perhaps you'd prefer to use our Christmas decorations from the last year?"

"No," said Bunky, picking up a newspaper from a nearby sofa and moving with it to a table.

"That looks exceedingly nice," said Mrs. Walm peaceably, "such an original style!"

"Yes, yes," agreed Mr. Walm, "The neighbours will be even jealous, I dare say."

"Rubbish," said Bunky Hippo, unexpectedly tearing the first page of the newspaper in two, "Obviously, they didn't publish my poem!"

"Oh please, do not feel upset, my dear!" said Mrs. Walm, giving Bunky Hippo a hug, "You can recite your poem for us on Christmas day next to the fireplace!"

"We love your poems," agreed Mr. Walm, "I especially like the one about chocolate cookies."

"We've got you a Christmas sweater!" Mrs. Walm rejoiced, hoping to improve Bunky's mood.

The sweater worked its magic, as Bunky's face quickly lit up. In truth, he was a good-natured, little creature with a sharp disposition but a very big and loving heart. Everyone in the Walmland Village loved Bunky Hippo, even though he was slightly grumpy at times, but who isn't?

"Is it with a squirrel?" he asked with some hope in his voice.

"With a squirrel and snowflakes," smiled Mrs. Walm, "Here it is!"

Bunky Hippo smiled too and started dressing in front of the mirror. In this moment, he was quite happy, forgetting all about the newspaper and the ungrateful association of poets who ignored his imaginative mind and creative work.

"I look really nice in red," he decided while critically examining his reflection in the glass.

"You do!" confirmed Mrs. Walm, unpacking her shopping in the middle of the cosy living room. And it was such a cosy, magnificent living room! If only you could see it, Dear Reader! But anyway, you are truly here with us now, in the Walmland Village, in the Walms' house, next to Mr. and Mrs. Walm, and next to our little, slightly grumpy but quite friendly Bunky Hippo! In the living room, Christmas lights were glaring all around, soft red armchairs were inviting one to sit down and take some rest after a long day, and a fluffy grey carpet was constantly encouraging home dwellers to walk on it barefoot. Beautifully framed windows revealed an enchanting winter landscape with delicate snow quietly settling on the ground in the Walms' garden.

The Walmland Village was located in Walmland—a beautiful land one thousand miles away from the North Pole, west of the Faroe Islands and east of the Baffin Bay, and I ensure you, Dear Reader, that not everyone could get there but only those who believed in Bunky Hippos with all their might.

"Will there be more Christmas presents this Christmas?" inquired Bunky Hippo, curiously glancing at Mrs. Walm's shopping bag, "I do love Christmas presents, and reindeer, and snow!"

"Certainly," smiled Mr. Walm, "Santa Claus will not forget about us!"

"I've been good this year. At least I intended to. The results don't always reflect my deepest intentions," Bunky Hippo wondered, "Will Santa place presents underneath our Christmas tree?"

"Yes," Mrs. Walm confirmed. She was quite sure about it and there was plenty of free space underneath the tree: enough for any possible presents!

"Then," Bunky Hippo continued, "what if the *Mouses* get hold of them and hide gifts in the Mouse Hole?"

"*Mice*, not *Mouses*," corrected him Mrs. Walm.

"I was talking about the *Mouses* specifically," Bunky Hippo huffed, "not about the *ordinary Mice*."

"Is it a different species?" Mrs. Walm knew how stubborn the little Hippo was.

"Absolutely," said Bunky Hippo, "But yes, I admit I was wrong. Perhaps the *Mouses* are not officially discovered and classified as a species yet. So what will happen if the *Mice* get hold of our gifts?"

"I am sure they would love them!" Mrs. Walm smiled, wondering what was the intention behind Bunky's questions.

"I would be glad then too," decided Bunky Hippo, resolving to have an open heart and delight in others' joy—even though it was so difficult—oh, how difficult it was!

"I would be absolutely thrilled if the *Mouses* took the gifts and loved them!" repeated Bunky, trying to convince himself as well.

A little Mouse stuck out her nose from the Mouse Hole, listening carefully to Bunky Hippo's assurances. It was snowing outside still, with elegant snowflakes subtly swirling around in a happy pre-Christmas dance. Mrs. Walm sat in a rocking chair in order to prepare a list of ingredients for her famous Christmas chocolate cake, and Mr. Walm began arranging Christmas lights and wreaths around the living room. Bunky's socks on the Christmas tree were very mysterious, yet they looked homely: these were all kinds of fluffy, colourful socks one wears on a cosy winter evening while having a cup of warm tea. Bunky Hippo gazed at his work with satisfaction and then went to his bedroom. He sat at a mahogany desk and began writing the Most Important Letter of the Year—the letter addressed to Santa Claus!

*From the Walmland Village
and Bunky's bedroom (clean and well-ordered before Christmas)*

Dear Santa Claus!

How are you? Christmas is coming again and I am writing to reassure you that I have been trying to be good as much as possible. As you know, it is not easy to be good. I was naughty at times, but I stopped. I would like to be good like you Santa, even though it is very hard, but please know that I am trying. For instance, this Christmas, I would like to ask you to remember about the Mouses living in the Mouse Hole in uncle and aunt Walm's living room. Please bring them something they dream about. I do not know what the Mouses might possibly like, but I know that you do because you are Santa Claus. I also wanted to greet your Reindeer and ask about your plans for Christmas? I am planning to spend Christmas with uncle Walm and aunt Walm whom I love very much. This will be the best Christmas ever, I feel, as it is already snowing! I was wondering if you could bring me some skating boots because I like dangerous sports. I promise I will be careful while ice skating. Dear Santa, if you think that I should receive something else, it is up to you. I have been trying to be good and I will try again after Christmas. When you will be around with the skating boots, please take a look at our Christmas tree—I decorated it in my own way which reflects my individuality and deep artistic inclinations. Please remember about aunt and uncle Walm, and maybe my cousin Rodney Williams will join us this Christmas, so if he arrives, please remember about him too. I don't know what he would like to receive, but I am sure that you do. I send you the best Christmas wishes and hugs! I really hope to meet you because I'm sure that you would appreciate my poetry. Ho ho ho!

Affectionately, your Much Improved and Constantly Improving,
Bunky Hippo

ॐ

Bunky carefully re-read his letter, drew with a pencil a beautiful Christmas tree surrounded by hearts and stars, and placed the letter in a red envelope. He opened one of the desk drawers and found a golden ribbon to decorate the envelope. *"To Santa Claus—from Bunky Hippo"*—he wrote on the envelope. The Most Important Letter of the Year was ready.

"Was I good this year?" wondered Bunky Hippo, gently placing the letter on a windowsill in his bedroom. The windowsill was a magical spot—Santa Claus would pick up all the letters addressed to him from here. At least this is what always happened in the Walms' house.

The afternoon continued in a peaceful and carefree way. Mrs. Walm was sweeping the floor in the living room and you could hear her broom making these comfortable, homely "shh, shh" sounds. Mr. Walm donned his apron with orange tigers and quietly moved to the kitchen. He was a great, diligent cook and, just after a while, a delicious smell of tomato soup started circulating around the house.

Bunky Hippo stared through his bedroom window and saw those beautiful, distant, gentle hills of Walmland covered with a fluffy layer of fresh, Christmas snow. Barely audible voices indicated that many inhabitants of Walmland were spending their day outside, playing in the snow, building snowmen or running around in the characteristic Christmas hurry, trying to purchase Christmas lights, find products for these once-in-a-year Christmas cakes or send Christmas greetings in festive, red envelopes tied with golden ribbons. These days all the inhabitants of Walmland awaited good news—loving, hopeful news from relatives and friends meaning so much to one's heart, especially on the approaching Christmas Eve.

Mrs. and Mr. Walm's house was placed a little aside from the noisy main road and surrounded by tall pine trees and spruces which swung gently with every winter breeze. The most beautiful, sturdy spruce with vividly green needles grew just opposite the front door of the Walms' house, very close to the terrace. It was the Walms' idea to decorate the spruce each and every year with colourful Christmas ornaments.

Bunky leant on his elbow and began dreaming about Christmas and his cousin's, Rodney Williams', arrival, and about all of them joyfully singing "fa la la la la" while sitting around the fireplace, awaiting presents and Mrs. Walm's chocolate cake! What a joy!

The smell of tomato soup was irresistible, but Bunky knew that uncle would announce dinnertime exactly at 3:00 p.m. and not before this special hour. It was one of his habits. Uncle would often repeat that habits and schedules are important to Organise Oneself but Bunky, as a budding artist with a romantic spirit, could not understand the magic of Organising Himself and living in a complete order without a charming spark of chaos or those neglected socks found from time to time underneath his bed. Yet, he thought, he still tidied up his bedroom before Christmas—was it a sign that he began Organising Himself? Bunky hoped that the cleanliness of his bedroom would impress Santa Claus.

The clock struck 2:00. The Creative Hour arrived—Bunky Hippo's personal, creative time! Dear Readers, here you need to know that Bunky had a secret. And what a secret it was: a mystery dearest to Bunky's heart! Underneath Bunky's bed, hidden in the furthest corner, was his Very Personal Notebook with a blue cover (Bunky's favourite colour). In this notebook Bunky was writing a novel. His biggest dream was to become a published writer.

The notebook had one hundred pages—enough for a future published writer, Bunky thought. The novel, entitled *Happy Ever After*, was about a Hero who hoped to win the Princess's heart. The Hero's name was Bunky Hippo and the Princess's name was the Bunky Princess. The Hero was a courageous nobleman with a big heart and, partly, a sharp disposition—so needed in such novels, especially in those moments of trial, when the Hero is meant to show all the possible bravery and wit!

The Bunky Princess was a gentle, sweet creature with fluffy ears and an enchanting smile. She was wearing pink slippers and a pink, gauzy dress. Every morning, when birds would finish their sweet songs, she would play the harp in front of her Bunky Castle and sing with a delightful, melancholy voice. The Hero, Bunky Hippo, would listen patiently while hiding behind a rosebush. He would smell the roses and his heart would be filled with eternal love. Whoever saw this unearthly smile of the Princess would fall in love with her immediately. Whoever heard the Bunky Princess's singing would be under her magic spell for eternity! Whoever recognised the noble mind and loving heart of the Princess would never forget her!

However, only Bunky Hippo, the courageous nobleman and the distinguished Hero of this novel, truly possessed the qualities which the Princess desired. Only he fully deserved her heart, as he was truthful, noble, and wise enough to become her Knight. Most importantly, he loved her. The only problem was that she was probably not in love yet, as they had not met in person through the first twenty pages of the novel dedicated to the descriptions of the Princess's castle and the Hero's armour. Or, maybe, she had already loved him for a very long time, but they were merely meeting in her dreams . . .

The time arrived in Bunky Hippo's novel for this Important Moment of Revelation: the Hero was meant to abandon the rosebush and introduce himself! Bunky Hippo the Writer felt that this scene in the novel should take place before his Christmas in Walmland. He assumed that the characters in his novel were very real—almost like his friends—and he realised that he would enjoy Christmas much more knowing that, in the novel, the Princess recognised the Hero's noble heart.

He found the notebook underneath his bed, wiped the dust away from its cover, as the floor was not perfectly clean (even though bedroom, in general, as indicated in the letter to Santa Claus, was perfectly tidy), sat back at his mahogany desk and continued writing. His mind was filled with romantic ideas intermingled with a delightful smell of uncle Walm's tomato soup . . . Bunky began writing:

> . . . *The time arrived for this Moment of Revelation! Hidden behind the rosebush, the Hero decided that he could not be anonymous any longer. He longed to introduce himself to the Bunky Princess—the gentle creature who completely took possession of his noble heart! Her song was about a merry tea party in her castle and joyful hours spent in the garden among birds and flowers, and Bunky Hippo felt that he needed to introduce himself immediately, as in the song neither did he appear at the tea party, nor in the garden. Finally, he did not appear in the entire song which, he felt, wasn't right. He longed to see the Princess's smile! At last, he regained his usually endless courage, picked up his rucksack from the ground, stepped outside the rosebush and, finally, was honoured to address the Princess in these dignified, bunkyful words:*
>
> *"Oh Gentle Creature, may I be allowed to introduce myself as Bunky Hippo, the Hero of this novel!"*
>
> *The Bunky Princess stopped singing and remained quiet for a moment. She gently turned her head towards the speaker and gazed at him with her soft, pleasant, bunky eyes. After a minute*

and thirty seconds of a delightful and meaningful silence, she addressed Bunky Hippo in the following manner:

"Is it you?" she asked (and her words were like music to the Hero's fluffy ears), "I've been waiting for you all this time, meeting you only in my dreams!"

"I knew that!" exclaimed Bunky Hippo most happily, "I knew that you would recognise me!" However, he could hardly believe in his own happiness (it often happens to such fortunate and brave Heroes).

"Of course," said the Princess, abandoning her harp and directing her gentle steps towards Bunky Hippo, "In this novel in which we are living in, all that I've ever done was waiting for my Hero and in you I immediately recognised the One—my One and Only Bunky Hippo! My courageous, wise, and loving Bunky Hippo—you finally arrived! Where have you been for so long?"

"Behind a rosebush," admitted Bunky Hippo with unconcealed shame, "I have never fully supposed that you might be waiting for me! I was concerned that you may not like me. But how do you know my name, oh beautiful Princess?"

"All the past, the future, and the present is here," the Princess said, taking a small book out of her pocket. She loved dresses with useful pockets and decorative ribbons which combined practicality with elegance.

"Do you recognise the book?" she inquired. It was in a blue binding and had one hundred pages. It was a little dusty as if removed from underneath a bed. Bunky the Hero had to admit that the book was new to him. The Bunky Princess smiled gently and said:

"This book is entitled 'Happy Ever After.' I have learnt from it all about my Hero."

"How truly unthinkable and how very delightful!" Bunky Hippo exclaimed. He knelt in front of the Princess and said: "Oh, Noble Princess, can I become your Knight?"

The Bunky Princess placed her delicate hand on Bunky Hippo's shoulder and uttered these solemn words: "I, the Bunky Princess of Bunkyland, choose you, the noble Bunky Hippo, to be knighted as my Hero until the end of this novel and beyond its one hundred pages. May the final chapter not divide us and may we go hand in hand beyond the final page."

Bunky Hippo felt that his eyes filled with tears of true, bunky happiness.

"Rise, my brave Hero!" the Princess exclaimed and Bunky Hippo noticed that the garden filled with a sweet smell of roses,

while thousands of pink, gentle butterflies began circling above their heads. They fell into each other's arms and the world became even a better, brighter place than it had been before, although Bunkyland had always been the land of goodness and nobility, not to mention bravery (represented by Bunky Hippo himself).

"I would like to offer you a gift," he said, as soon as he could contain the rare tears of happiness, "Watch this!"

Bunky the Hero reached for his rucksack and opened one of the compartments. There he found a lasso. (It is only natural for the Hero to carry around various useful objects so that he can use them when the Right Moment arrives.) The Right Moment arrived and Bunky Hippo threw the lasso up into the sky!

"Oh!" the Princess exclaimed with deep admiration in her voice. Bunky Hippo pulled the rope and it came down to the ground with a little, shiny Star.

"It is a shiny Star from the sky for you, my Princess!" said the Hero, placing the Star at the Princess's feet. It had the glow of a thousand sunrises, the elegance of the brightest diamonds, and it shimmered with delicate, silvery lights like winter auroras.

The Princess could not find the right words to thank her Hero. She told Bunky Hippo that his heart was all that mattered to her. The Princess carried everywhere with her a small, pink bag, as it is usual for women to carry small, useful bags whenever they go. In the bag, she kept a very convenient enchanted wand by means of which she could create anything she wanted, from the stars to castles. It made her feel like an independent woman who did not require gifts from anyone, apart from the priceless gift of love. Yet, she felt deeply moved by the daring deed of her noble Hero, as she had read in her book that, when he arrives, he shall offer her a Star from the sky and this would be the sign of his truthfulness. This deed convinced her even more that Bunky Hippo was her True Hero. They went towards the castle holding hands and smiling at each other, while butterflies were singing delightful songs . . .

Here Bunky Hippo stopped writing and re-read the last sentence. He frowned, crossed out the word "butterflies" and substituted it with "birds." After that, he crossed out the word "delightful" because he felt that "delight" already appeared in his writing too many times:

. . . ~~butterflies~~ birds were singing ~~delightful~~ amusing songs . . .—wrote Bunky Hippo and still did not quite like it. Perhaps he meant *amazing*

instead of a*musing*. After all, these songs were not meant to be *amusing* but *delightful*! Bunky frowned: the word *delightful* crossed his mind again, but there was no better word, he thought. His novel was meant to deeply move the reader and portray a grand, genuine feeling between the main characters! *Delightful* had to appear at least once again—by all means! Thus thinking, Bunky corrected the sentence in a following manner: . . . *the ~~butterflies~~ birds were singing ~~delightful amusing~~ delightful songs* . . .

The clock struck 3:00. The smell of uncle Walm's tomato soup invitingly wafted up to Bunky's bedroom.

"Dinner!" uncle Walm proudly announced from the kitchen.

"Dinner—what a beautiful word!" Bunky thought. He instantly imagined his favourite tomato soup. He kissed the precious notebook and secretly hid it underneath his bed. Suddenly he was struck by an unexpected thought followed by a rare feeling: it was the first time when he realised that he, Bunky the Writer, might be in love with the Bunky Princess of Bunkyland . . .

2

Christmas is Coming!

No one, but no one could cook so perfectly like uncle Walm! The heavenly tomato soup was already waiting for Bunky in the living room and delicate rose pancakes were also there and, to Bunky's joy, even those little, creamy chocolate muffins were carefully placed on a silver tray! Aunt Walm was just preparing her favourite lavender tea while planning on hanging the colorful Christmas stockings—at last!

"What a bliss!" Bunky Hippo thought, reaching for his cup with the aromatic lavender tea. He also drew near a huge bowl of sugar with the intention of placing a full spoon of white sugar in his cup. Hopefully, aunt Walm might not notice!

"No, my dear!" aunt Walm immediately exclaimed, " So much sugar is definitely not good for your health!"

"But aunt!" Bunky Hippo cried in dismay, "How can I have my tea without sugar?"

"Yes, you can," she insisted, taking away the sugar bowl and placing it somewhere far, far away, in the furthest corner of the cupboard. Bunky followed his aunt with a gloomy look.

"My dear Bunky, it is not only detrimental for your general health, but may also contribute to a visit in Mr. Beaver's office!" aunt Walm continued. Mr. Beaver was a local dentist.

"Mr. Beaver is very nice!" argued Bunky, still with a look of dismay on his face, "It cannot be *that* bad!"

"He is very nice, my dear, but I'd prefer you to meet him in other circumstances than in his dentist's office," calmly observed Mrs. Walm.

"Ah," Bunky sighed looking towards the furthest corner of the cupboard and then staring at his cup filled with aunt Walm's lavender tea. Perhaps not every tea was meant to be sweet. He clearly remembered that he swore in the letter to Santa Claus to remain good as long as possible (hopefully even forever!) and decided to keep his promise.

With all these solemn, gloomy, and courageous thoughts swirling in his mind, Bunky left his place at the table and bravely approached a cabinet where Mrs. Walm kept dietary supplements.

"I will take magnesium with water instead," he announced, "It will positively influence my health and offer me inner peace."

Aunt and uncle Walm looked at Bunky with surprise, but they were fully aware that Bunky was the most unique creature one could possibly imagine, so they decided to allow him to have his slightly eccentric ways.

Indeed, deep inside, Bunky Hippo experienced some vague unrest. Christmas was drawing near and, with every hour, he felt more and more restless and impatient. It was generally so in Bunkies' nature.

"An admirable choice of magnesium!" aunt Walm praised Bunky in order to cheer him up.

Bunky thought about his resolution. "Be good, be good, be good . . ..," his Thoughts kept telling him.

"Of course I want to be good!" Bunky pondered and smiled, forgetting all about the bowl of sugar.

"Uncle Walm is such a great cook!" he observed kindly, trying to make up for his previous highly *unwalmful* behaviour. This remark brought a blush to uncle's cheeks.

"This is what happens when men start cooking! They always do well in the kitchen—as soon as they are willing to try!" Mrs. Walm noted with pride. She was always proud of Mr. Walm. Now she could finally concentrate on hanging her favourite Christmas stockings.

The sun used to go to sleep quite early during these winter days and Bunky Hippo would go to sleep just after the sun. Today he had found himself in bed even before the sun announced its nightly departure, but he could not think about sleeping: there was a bottle with hot water placed comfortably at his feet and a novel written by his favourite author, Sir Bunky of Walmland, by his side—each page waiting to carry him to distant times and those forgotten places inhabited by *bunkyful* dragons and unicorns joyfully hopping around!

The title of this intriguing literary masterpiece was: *When Dragons and Unicorns Inhabited Walmland.* ("When was it?" Bunky wondered.) The second chapter was entitled: *Blessings of Unicorns and Thunders of Dragons.* Bunky found it especially beautiful to call a group of unicorns a "blessing." He also found it particularly intriguing that a group of dragons would be referred to as a "thunder."

"It fits them well," he thought and, immediately, imagined a group of Bunkies.

"*A thunder of Bunkies* sounds courageous," he kept musing, "but I would still prefer *a blessing of Bunkies.* *A blessing of Bunkies* means that they are good, helpful, and kind. Everyone would like to have them around."

And then he came up with other phrases: *a wisdom of Bunkies, a brilliance of Bunkies, a genius of Bunkies* and *a flair of Bunkies.*

Bunky yawned and returned to his book. "*Many of us were not granted an encounter with a unicorn or a dragon,*" he read. How would it feel to meet one? "A little scary," Bunky thought, but still he longed to encounter a blessing of unicorns and a single dragon.

"A tiny dragon, as tiny as a butterfly," Bunky reflected, "and definitely not a thunder of them."

Many of us find comfort in reading in bed during the winter months: what a pleasure it is to find yourself in bed with your favourite book and no other cares in the world! As you have already learnt, Dear Reader, Bunky Hippo was quite a secretive figure and here he also had a new little secret: beneath his bedclothes, he stored a little chocolate cookie, planning to enjoy eating it while reading Sir Bunky of Walmland's novel. It is always nicer to have both: a book and a cookie. Mrs. Walm would criticise the habit of eating in bed but, Bunky Hippo thought, it was only a little, innocent pleasure. Nothing so concerning as having appetizers, an entire dinner, and dessert in bed just because one would enjoy it.

The whole neighbourhood outside seemed to be sleepy and, yet, it was ringing with mysterious winter voices muffled by the snow. The weather was perfect for Santa Claus's arrival! Bunky Hippo glanced from bed at the calendar.

"One more day!" he thought in anticipation. His beautiful Christmas sweater with the squirrel was hanging on the back of the chair and Bunky

admired it from his bed. He always dreamt about such a sweater. In a minute, he was fast asleep, with Sir Bunky of Walmland's novel by his side and
the secret chocolate cookie underneath his pillow, his dreams filled with
blessings of unicorns and thunders of tiny dragons with butterfly wings.

Bunky woke up at 8:00 a.m. next to his secret chocolate cookie and
Sir Bunky of Walmland's novel. He jumped out of bed and looked through
the window. The snow was still there. It was a very good sign before Christmas, he thought and began dressing vigorously. As soon as he was dressed,
he quickly approached the windowsill only to discover that the letter for
Santa Claus was gone! Santa collected his letter at night! What a joy! Bunky
smiled victoriously and carefully stored the cookie (for the evening) in his
mahogany desk.

He ran to the living room where he encountered Mr. Walm in his
old, striped, winter scarf. Mr. Walm was preoccupied with collecting boxes
filled with Christmas decorations. At present, he was lifting the boxes one
by one, carefully placing them on the terrace. How many curious Christmas trinkets they contained—only Mrs. Walm knew! Mrs. Walm was a
very knowledgeable person who specialized in details: she remembered
what was inside each cabinet in the living room and how many socks there
should be in Bunky's wardrobe.

When Bunky entered the living room, she was laying the breakfast
table, singing her favourite Christmas song. This is what she truly enjoyed:
a peaceful, cosy living room on Christmas and her family, relatives and
friends all around. Of all the things in the world, Mrs. Walm cherished a
loving family and a clean household.

"Good morning!" said Bunky Hippo, abruptly sitting down to his cereal. Practising patience as much as he could, he was still very impatient
to eat his cereal. Then, it occurred to him that he was wearing his sweater
inside out. "Ah, it's for good luck!" he thought, quickly rearranging his attire
so that he could admire the winter squirrel with cotton snowflakes. Bunky
was really keen on squirrels.

Suddenly, there were footsteps outside.

"Ding dong!" the doorbell rang.

"Ah!" groaned Bunky, putting aside his spoon.

Mr. Postman appeared in the front door, encountering uncle Walm
with his boxes.

"Merry Christmas!" exclaimed uncle Walm, putting the boxes aside to shake hands with Mr. Postman.

"A letter for Mr. and Mrs. Walm!" Mr Postman announced in his elegant, official voice, placing the correspondence on uncle Walm's boxes, "And one letter addressed to Mr. Bunky Hippo!"

Bunky Hippo banged his spoon on the table and jumped excitedly to receive his letter. In his mind he already pictured a letter from Santa Claus inquiring after his exact shoe size so that he could make sure the skating boots would fit him well.

"Merry Christmas, Mr. Postman!" exclaimed Bunky and returned to the table holding in his paws the precious envelope. *From R.W., Cousin, to Bunky Hippo, Cousin*—the envelope announced.

"Ah, it's from my cousin, Rodney Williams!" Bunky sighed. But then, why should he complain? In truth, the letter was not from Santa, but Rodney's news was also exciting!

Rodney was meant to come for Christmas with aunt Barbara and uncle Bill. He was a little younger than Bunky and not as interested in dinosaurs and planets as Bunky desired that he could have been, but still, he was a great companion and a trustworthy friend. In fact, Bunky was very affectionate towards his cousin and wished to see him.

He impatiently opened the letter and leant over the correspondence, temporarily abandoning all the thoughts concerning cereal.

> *Dear Cousin Bunky Hippo!*—the letter began, *I am writing to announce my arrival with aunt Barbara and uncle Bill, so that you can get ready and know that I am coming.*

"That's very thoughtful and true," agreed Bunky Hippo, thinking about neatly folding all the clothes in his room.

> *I hope that this Christmas we can build a snowman and I truly can't wait to see you!*
> *Ho, ho, ho!*
>
> > *Your Loving Cousin,*
> > *Rodney Williams*

Bunky folded the letter and carefully placed it in the envelope. Then, he carried the letter to his mahogany desk and only afterwards returned to his cereal. Aunt Walm fondly patted Bunky on his fluffy head.

"Eat, my little Bunky," she said, "Aunt Barbara and uncle Bill are coming today with cousin Rodney!"

"I'm getting ready!" announced Bunky, eating his cereal in the fastest possible way, fidgeting with impatience around the table.

It was decided that just after breakfast they would all go outside in order to decorate the Christmas tree and the entire front yard—the exciting time was coming! Bunky hoped to impress Rodney with decorations, so it was necessary to begin all the decorating process before his arrival, meaning: right now!

"Ho, ho, ho everyone!" cried uncle Walm through the half-open front door.

"Ho, ho, ho!" loudly responded Bunky. He wrapped himself up in a woollen scarf and found his favourite blue mittens. Blue, by all means, was his favourite colour—the colour of his own fur!

"Ho, ho ho!" sang aunt Walm, thrilled at the prospect of decorating their Christmas spruce.

Mr. Walm managed to gather outside the entire tower of boxes with family decorations and ornaments, some of them decidedly remembering the times of dragons and unicorns from Sir Bunky of Walmland's novel.

"The yellow and silver ones first," Mrs. Walm instructed her husband, "They are from the earliest years and thus the most important ones."

"They belonged to Grandma and Grandpa Walm!" Bunky Hippo exclaimed.

"I found the Christmas star!" proudly announced uncle Walm and hurried to bring a ladder. Year after year, it was his task to bravely climb to the top of the spruce and attach the Christmas star to its highest point. Then, Christmas in the Walms' house would officially begin and, as Bunky believed, Christmas would also start in the entire Walmland Village!

Bunky Hippo looked around and realised that it had been snowing at night more than they all expected. He thought that it might be a good idea to shovel sidewalks before their guests' arrival. There was a special winter shovel in uncle Walm's shed and Bunky proceeded to work with it, swinging the shovel cheerfully, as the snow kept surging up into the air and falling down again! He worked untiringly, hoping that Santa Claus might be hiding behind a bush, thinking: "Oh, what a hard-working little Bunky he is!"

To give Bunky his justice, he was mainly shovelling because it was making him happy and he simply enjoyed helping his aunt and uncle. Only partially he wanted to be noticed and praised by Santa Claus. I guess, Dear Readers, that we all do.

"One, two, three, ho, ho, ho!" sang Bunky Hippo but, suddenly, he stopped and carefully gazed at the pavement.

Apparently, there was something mysterious that had not been there before: a footprint on the snow which looked as if someone had been running around the house a while ago. Bunky stared at the footprint cautiously, trying to find out whether it resembled a hoof or a paw. The Walms' garden was fenced from all the four sides. Who was here a while ago?

Bunky frowned in an attempt to gather his thoughts, wondering about a mysterious creature who had crossed the fence and run around the house. At first, Bunky thought about unicorns; then—about dragons (but definitely not the entire thunder of them). At last, Imagination aided Bunky with a vision of a big, portly, dignified Deer with mellow, brown fur and silvery, twinkling antlers. In Bunky's Imagination, the Deer gracefully leapt over the fence, followed by a magical glow of stardust. Then, decidedly, he took a brief look around the garden. And then . . . yes! Bunky Hippo knew: this very special Deer began looking for Bunky's bedroom window and there, on the windowsill, he saw Bunky's letter . . . The Deer must have collected the letter and he must have carried it to Santa Claus!

Bunky leant on the shovel, dreaming about the Christmas Deer for a while more, but then he heard an actual rustle in a boxwood.

"Who is it?" he asked tentatively. After all, the bush was too small to contain the Glorious Deer of his Imagination. Something tiny and grey flitted behind the bush, but Bunky could not see who was hiding there.

"Strange and mysterious!" said Bunky and continued shovelling. However, now his thoughts were preoccupied with the Glorious Deer and the Mysterious Creature in the bush. After all, it was winter and just before Christmas—the time of the greatest magic, mystery and suspense.

Step by step, Bunky Hippo bravely shovelled all the sidewalks around the house and, in the meantime, he encountered numerous traces of the Mysterious Creature's presence. Apparently, the Mysterious Creature loved bouncing around.

The garden was quiet—nothing like in the summer time. However, Bunky adored this tranquillity! He cherished this particular silence and the magical expectation of Christmas—the feeling that the world slowed down for a while—at least for this winter season—beginning its elegant, quiet dance with delicate snowflakes. And what a joy—he could finally wear his cosy scarf and his delightful Christmas sweater!

Bunky was often tired of the hustle and bustle of the summer season: only a thought concerning all his distant relatives arriving for the summer holiday to run around in swim rings, jump to the pool, and scream at the top of their lungs exhausted him. Oh, how tiring it was! No, Bunky longed for peace and quiet. Bunky was a writer at heart. A romantic writer who delighted in quiet winters when he could dream about his Bunky Princess. He enjoyed shovelling and humming his Christmas tune. He even came up with the following verse:

Mysterious creatures behind every drift,
So discreet, gentle, puzzling, and swift!

"Peace and quiet!" exclaimed Bunky with satisfaction and took a deep breath after finishing his short song. He heard steps coming from the front yard and this time he was sure that these were not any Mysterious Creatures, but his aunt Barbara, uncle Bill, and cousin Rodney. Being an orderly person (at least when it came to gardening, sheds, and shovels), he did not forget to place uncle Walm's shovel back in the shed. Then, he directed his steps towards the front yard. While passing nearby the boxwood, he could swear that he heard some gentle rustling. However, his courage gave way to anxiety and he decided not to investigate the matter any further. Instead, he tiptoed cautiously past the bush and ran to the front yard.

"Cousin Rodney, uncle Bill, aunt Barbara!" he cried.

"You grew up quite a lot!" exclaimed aunt Barbara excitedly, just like aunts often do, but it was not a very fortunate remark, as Bunky did not want to be tall or grown up at all. Not even a single bit.

"I didn't," he answered wryly, " I actually feel that I am slightly shorter."

Uncle Bill gave aunt Barbara a mysterious look. Sometimes uncle Bill understood Bunky Hippo much better than aunt Barbara did. Maybe it was so because he was not in a hurry to grow up himself. In fact, most probably, uncle Bill was not fully grown up yet, as he still loved surrounding himself with train sets and rubber ducks. It had nothing to do with responsibility though, as uncle Bill was, next to Mr. Walm, the most responsible uncle in the world.

"Actually, I also feel that Bunky became shorter," declared uncle Bill, "I can see it very clearly."

"It is so true!" eagerly agreed Bunky. He never understood all those little Bunkies and other children who wanted to grow up fast and become taller and taller. It was so upsetting for his spirits!

However, Bunky knew that Rodney wanted to be a grown up person as soon as possible. Bunky had no idea how anyone could be a grown up without a deep interest in dinosaurs so, according to Bunky, there were actually no signs of Rodney Williams becoming an adult, but he decided to compliment his cousin anyway.

"Oh, cousin Rodney," he said, "I see that YOU are actually much taller than before! And so grown-up!"

Rodney's eyes sparkled in delight.

"Do you really, really think so, cousin Bunky?" he asked with hope in his tiny voice. Rodney Williams was a decliate, brownish creature with big, fluffy ears, mousey nose, and soft, glittering eyes. He took Bunky's paw in his and shook it gently, waiting for the reply.

"I do think so," replied Bunky to Rodney's satisfaction (in fact, he really thought now that Rodney was a little taller), "Actually, I feel that the next year you will be as tall as this Christmas tree!"

Here Bunky pointed at the spruce growing in front of the house. The spruce, taking on the role of the Christmas tree each winter season, was the highest tree in the garden and probably one of the highest trees in the neighbourhood. It was a slight exaggeration to suggest that Rodney would be so tall, but Bunky thought that everything was possible. After all, he never saw a grown up Rodney. Who knew how grown up he could become?

"Aw, our little Bunky has grown up so much since last year, what do you think Barbara?" cried aunt Walm who suddenly joined the conversation or, rather, made it unbearable again.

"No," said Bunky Hippo wryly, "Nothing of this sort."

"He didn't grow up *at all!*" pointed out uncle Bill and winked at Mrs. Walm.

"Indeed, now I noticed that I must have been mistaken," quickly corrected herself aunt Walm and patted Bunky Hippo on his fluffy head. Then, she patted Rodney Williams on his fluffy head too because she did not want him to feel excluded in any way. Mrs. Walm always wanted to pat and hug everyone equally.

"Our Christmas has just begun!" Mr. Walm proudly exclaimed from the top of the ladder.

Everybody looked up: on top of the spruce there was the most charming, bunkyful Christmas star one could ever dream about! Mr. Walm performed his annual ceremony of placing the Christmas star in its celebrated spot and slowly climbed down the ladder.

"Now that we are all back on the ground, we can start celebrating!" said aunt Walm cheerfully, the Christmas star reflected in her eyes.

But before everyone even moved from their places, there was a very familiar sound of the doorbell again and they saw a very familiar figure of their neighbour, Sir Williams, waving to them in a friendly manner from behind the gate.

Bunky got especially happy on seeing Sir Williams—it was their old neighbour, probably as old as the neighbourhood! At least this is what Bunky thought, even though, Dear Readers, I have to point out that, in fact, Sir Williams wasn't that very old. However, it was true that Sir Williams had inhabited this place long before anyone else did. He lived next door, close to the Walms, in a tasteful house with walls painted in an equally tasteful colour of yellow cheese. His favourite word was "delicious" and it should not be surprising, as Sir Williams owned a small restaurant situated next to his yellow abode. He prided himself on knowing more recipes than anyone else in the whole Walmland and enjoyed cooking for customers himself.

Sir Williams was a bachelor which meant, as Bunky heard, that he was living in his house completely alone and there was no one to tell him to vacuum the house, wash teeth three times a day or behave well. It would not be necessary anyway, as Sir Williams was the most elegant and orderly creature Bunky Hippo knew—perhaps apart from aunt Walm. Bunky believed that Sir Williams was saying all these important things to himself in a kind of imperious, decided voice: vacuum the house, wash teeth three times a day, and behave well! It wasn't so bad to be a bachelor, Bunky thought. He was able to live in this way too! He even wondered for a moment whether he and Rodney would become bachelors one day too. It sounded like a perfect possibility of having a chocolate cookie in bed every evening. On the other hand, if he could choose, Bunky would still prefer to live in his house with the Bunky Princess (even though she might possibly instruct him to wash teeth). If only they could also have a pet dinosaur!

"Hello, hello!" cried Sir Williams, "The Christmas star is shining bright! Do we have any good children here?" He had such an elegant, operatic, pleasantly ringing voice.

Bunky's ears perked up. Sir Williams stepped through the gate and reached into his bag. He was wearing a very fashionable coat with a long Christmas scarf. He leant over the bag and reached for some colourful lollipops, swiftly distributing them among everyone.

"I prepared them on my own," he explained with a wide grin, "A very old family recipe!"

"It is so kind of you!" said Mrs. Walm, who truly admired every man on Earth who would make any effort in the kitchen, "And since it is such a special day, everyone can have a lollipop before dinner!"

"And a chocolate cookie in bed?" quietly inquired Bunky, but so quietly that aunt Walm did not hear. After all, what was the chance that aunt would agree? Bunky knew that he had to act independently in the matter of chocolate cookies in bed.

"Awww!" cried Rodney Williams, who really loved sweets and lollipops.

"He's not an adult," thought Bunky, "Adults would pretend that they are not that interested in lollipops and would not jump high on receiving one."

"Awww!" said uncle Bill, reaching for a lollipop as well. Bunky looked at uncle Bill in surprise.

"Is uncle Bill a child too?" Rodney inquired.

"Yes, he is," explained aunt Barbara, "especially on Christmas, when everyone is like a child!"

"How are you doing, my dear neighbours?" kindly inquired Sir Williams, shaking hands with everyone and giving Bunky and Rodney a friendly hug, "I'm sure you are looking forward to Santa Claus's arrival! If he appears, he shall receive a lollipop as well!"

"Before dinner?" inquired Bunky.

"Whenever he wants to!" smiled Sir William, "I'm sure Santa Claus adores lollipops and I am sure that you can't wait for him!"

"Oh yes!" admitted Bunky and his eyes lit up with hope and expectations. Bunky hoped that Santa Claus already knew his shoe size.

"He will come," assured him Sir Williams, "I've seen his sledge last night through a telescope. Actually, I am not sure if it was Santa Claus's sledge, but I often see mysterious things through my telescope or even without it!"

"I understand," said Bunky, "It also happens to me!" He immediately thought about the mysterious rustling bush.

"Hot chocolate, everyone!" announced aunt Walm, unexpectedly appearing on the terrace with a tray of red Christmas mugs and thus breaking all the "not-to-do-before-dinner" rules. Hot chocolate outside in a wintry garden, accompanied by Sir Williams' lollipop, was a dream turning into reality.

Bunky thought that it was the best afternoon he could possibly imagine: the scent of chocolate, fluffy, swirling snowflakes, their festive Christmas tree with the enchanting star, the presence of his family, Sir Williams' amazing Christmas stories and his cousin's laughter all contributed to his happiness. Bunky tried to count snowflakes but, after a while, he decided that the number of snowflakes was endless. Instead, he devoted himself to dipping his nose in the red Chrismas mug in order to delight in the vibrant scent of chocolate.

These are the carefree, happy pictures which, afterwards, after many, many years, always return when one is older and spends long afternoons knitting in a rocking chair. Being older definitely has many highlights, but Bunky was still very young and could not imagine yet what these would be. However, he was sure that every age carried a special value and included a very special adventure.

Dressed in fluffy jackets and thick scarves, Bill and Barbara were sitting on a tiny snowdrift near the terrace, holding hands and sipping chocolate in the same way they used to do every Christmas since they were at school. They were weary after a long travel from Chocolate Grove to the Walmland Village, but nothing could prevent them from enjoying this peaceful afternoon. Their old car was parked at the Walms' gate in the same manner as years ago when they arrived here for the first Christmas. Everything was still the same. Neither Barbara had changed, nor uncle Bill had grown to be any different. None of them lost this secret, the magical ability to embrace every little happy thing in their lives, including their favourite hot chocolate. This sameness was truly beautiful and endearing—if one could remain unchanged at heart, it was much easier to remain so on the outside too.

Bunky's little cousin, Rodney Williams, already knew this secret: he quickly drank his chocolate and hurriedly began building a snowman.

"Cousin Bunky!" he shouted, "We must have a snowman immediately, so that Santa Claus would be pleased wih us!"

"Yes, yes," answered Bunky, still preoccupied with his Happy Thoughts and also some other more Mysterious Thoughts concerning the Rustling Bush. As a very traditional Bunky Hippo, he aspired to roll the biggest snowball in the garden, if not in the whole town!

"If not in the whole world, if not in the entire universe!" Bunky began forming these competitive thoughts as soon as he started his work.

"Do they have snowmen out there, in the universe?" he wondered.

He was rolling a snowball, patiently circling around the house, while the snowball kept growing and growing. After fifteen such circles, Bunky finally felt tired. He placed the snowball next to the terrace and thought that he truly felt as if he moved the entire universe. Rodney was standing aside, admiring his cousin's work and hoping to become that strong and patient one day.

"Phew," said Bunky, trying to appear quite rested, "It will be a magnificent snowman!"

"Hooray!" Rodney squealed with excitement and clapped his little paws. His eyes glistened with admiration.

"Now, I will place one snowball on top of the other," said Bunky knowingly with a tone of voice of somebody who devoted all his life to building snowmen.

"Yes!" agreed Rodney.

It turned out to be quite difficult though, as the snowball was huge. Bunky frowned and decided to use a ladder.

"Children, please remember not to block out the light in the living room with your snowman," said Mrs. Walm, "If you place your snowman in front of the window, we will not have enough light in the living room during daytime."

Mrs. Walm was engaged in a lively conversation with uncle Walm and Sir Williams, but kept watching Bunky and Rodney out of the corner of her eye. Mrs. Walm always worried that someone would fall, have an accident, or require her help.

Bunky scratched his head. "At present, in order to lift the snowman up and change his location, we would have to eat three jars of cookies!" he exclaimed.

Aunt Walm gave Bunky a knowing look.

"No, no, I don't think the snowman will block out the light!" cried a more adventurous Sir Williams, waving his Christmas mug in the air. He always gestured with passion while speaking. "Let me help you at once!"

He put the cup aside and lifted the snowball. Mrs. Walm raised her eyebrows but did not say anything. She was already prepared to have a *snowman view* from her living room window.

"Hooray!" shouted Bunky and Rodney, dancing around Sir Williams.

Sir Williams had more strength than Bunky and Rodney together, as he used to spend many days stirring soups with big ladles in pots as big as the entire snowman himself.

"One, two, and three!" said Sir Williams, gathering all his strength and placing the snowball on top of the other one, "Here you are!"

"Magnificent!" exclaimed Mr. Walm.

Even Mrs. Walm had to admit that the snowman was very shapely and pleasant, even though his presence endangered the brightness of her cheerful living room.

"But the snowman is cheerful too so, perhaps, we can manage without all the light!" she thought and went to their little basement in order to find a carrot for the snowman's nose and small pieces of coal for his eyes and smile. She also gathered some pine needles for his eyelashes. In few minutes, the snowman had a joyous and slightly mischevious expression on his round, cheerful face. It was a good-natured kind of mischevious: a face expression which Bunky usually had while placing a chocolate cookie underneath his pillow. The snowman was dressed in a colourful poncho made from Mrs. Walm's old tablecloth (Bunky found it in a laundry basket and insisted that it should belong to his snowy friend).

From now on, Dear Readers, he shall be our Snowman spelled with the capital "S"—a new inhabitant of Walmland brought to life in this Christmas tale! It has to be sincerely admitted that everyone praised the Snowman, even aunt Walm. Bunky gave Rodney a high five and dipped his nose in the Christmas mug. Hot chocolate was gone, but the Christmas scent was still there.

Faintly shining on the background of the rosy, evening sky, the star on the top of the spruce was a perfect prelude to the Christmas Eve. The star seemed to invite everyone to remember that Christmas was truly here—very, very close: just around the corner, almost on the doorstep! Bill and Barbara looked up at the sky to see the first delicate, shimmering stars glaring up there, far above the spruce.

The night of Christmas Eve is always mysterious—it is the moment when the world stops and awaits beauty and peace. Each year there is hope, but only in Walmland it is truly peaceful, especially thanks to its inhabitants. Now it was the right time to go home, have an evening meal, sing carols together, and dream about Santa Claus arriving in his silver sledge. It was the right time to talk at the table, play board games, laugh, and do all the precious little things one could never find time to do on any other occasion.

"Would you like to see my collection of stamps?" asked Bunky, who currently was in high Christmas spirits. He had a delightful collection of stamps with kangaroos and dinosaurs and thought that he would love to show them to his cousin. Rodney said that he would be very glad to see the stamps, even though he was very sleepy.

"I have no doubt that you were good this year," estimated Bunky, carefully looking at his little cousin. He could not imagine Rodney being naughty. Rodney smiled and nodded his head.

"I hope so," he said.

Even though he had no idea about dinosaurs, he was amazing—this is what Bunky thought. They stepped into the living room but, as it often happens during a busy Christmas time, as soon as they all found themselves indoors, somebody rang the doorbell again! Mr. Walm tried to look through the window in order to greet the newcomers, but the Snowman prevented him from seeing anything. Instead of the newcomers, uncle Walm saw the Snowman's wide smile and his rich eyelashes. Mr. Walm decided to open the front door and gazed into the darkness.

"It's us!" he heard two voices in the vicinity of the gate.

"Who?" responded Mr. Walm.

"Us!" the voices replied.

"Ah, it's Mr. Elk with Mr. Meow!" rejoiced Mrs. Walm, who had a great hearing and recognised the voices immediately, "Come in, please!"

"It's Mr. Elk and Mr. Meow," said Bunky to his cousin, " I guess they will be singing Christmas carols. We may see the stamps later."

It was very true. All the Walmland Village knew that Mr. Elk and Mr. Meow were very passionate about music. It was their usual habit to appear every Christmas Eve in the Walms' house, play the Walms' family piano, sing their hearts out, and try Mr. Walm's Christmas muffins.

Mr. Elk entered the living room wearing a long, woollen scarf wrapped several times around his very long neck. Mr. Meow appeared in the door wearing an elegant black hat which he would always find in his wardrobe just before Christmas.

"Welcome, neighbours!" cried Sir Williams from the sofa, immediately reaching for his coat in order to find some additional lollipops.

Bunky and Rodney politely shook hands with the guests and went to the kitchen, planning to help Mr. Walm with ordering muffins on an ornate tray. Mrs. Walm was all smiles, eagerly inviting her newly arrived guests to find comfortable seats in the living room. She had a big, white cotton rose pinned in the collar of her woollen dress. It was her endeavour to look more festive and now she resembled a snowflake.

As soon as the guests were comfortably seated and Mr. Elk's scarf, as well as Mr. Meow's hat were placed on a hat rack, aunt Walm started a fire in the fireplace. The living room instantly lit up with warm colours, revealing its every nook and cranny so that everyone could see how carefully Mrs. Walm had vacuumed the carpet on the previous day. The Walms' ancestors were smiling good-naturedly from their portraits, as if watching the company gathered in the living room.

Leaning on his elbows, Bunky traced the quiet snowflakes dancing and swirling behind the kitchen window. When the sweets were ready, he reached for the tray and, hoping to impress Rodney, constructed a small tower of muffins.

"Be careful, Bunky!" said Mr. Walm.

But Bunky was still daydreaming about Santa Claus, skating boots, and his Bunky Princess. He was wondering how would it be to spend Christmas with the Bunky Princess, but in the real world and not on the pages of his literary masterpiece. He was also debating with himself whether it would be a good idea to share his secret with Rodney. There was such a need in him to have a confidant but, on the other hand, it was also truly delicious to have such a great secret all to himself, especially on Christmas! Bunky was still hesitating, wondering what would Rodney say on seeing his book. He lifted the tray carefully and directed his steps towards the living room. Rodney followed his cousin almost like a shadow.

In the living room, Mr. Elk sat gracefully at the piano, tossed his hair, and coughed in an artistic way indicating that he shall begin, while Mr. Meow grunted, situated himself on a nearby stool and began singing. He had a soothing, mellow voice perfectly fitting for the peaceful winter scenery.

"Oh!" exclaimed Mrs. Walm in delight and clasped her hands, as she truly loved music performances.

Bunky, Rodney, and uncle Walm proudly entered the room with the tower of muffins. They saw Sir Williams quietly sitting on the sofa, listening to the song with his full attention. Barbara and Bill were sitting nearby, holding hands and gazing in wonder at the Christmas tree. Even the little Mice looked out from the Mouse Hole in the corner of the living room and opened their mouths in wonder on seeing how charming and magical the room was tonight. The song lured them into the living room and, soon, they were occupying the best places on the branches of the Christmas tree, swaying back and forth in harmony with the music.

In the meantime, Bunky Hippo was proudly parading around the room with his tower of muffins, kindly offering them to everyone, having a sweet Christmas smile of somebody who decidedly was quite good the entire year and deserved a pair of new skating boots. Mr. Elk kindly denied, as he was in the middle of staccato[1], but he promised to have a muffin as soon as possible. Mr. Meow eagerly followed the muffins with his eyes but bravely decided to finish his part first and kept singing in a high, melodic voice. Bunky also decided to use his strong will and wait for the guests before he would have his own muffin, even though a tempting inner voice kept repeating that he could possibly try just one.

While passing with the tray near the window, he thought that he saw something moving outside—something which he spotted with the corner of his eye. There were too many mysterious things tonight, he thought, but, after all, it was Christmas. At first, he mused that it could have been Santa Claus, but then he realised that it was definitely too early for his visit. Bunky deliberately looked again towards the window and then he saw it—a pair of fluffy, grey ears! The Snowman was standing outside quite unmoved, not really surprised by this new mystery. Mr. Meow was just finishing his song about swirling snowflakes and little mice ringing their Christmas bells.

"Oh!" said Bunky and felt that he just got another secret, while the tower of muffins is on the point of collapsing on the vaccumed carpet. He quickly placed the tray on a table. In this moment, he felt curious, excited and slightly dizzy.

"It's Christmas time!! Ooooooooooooooooooooo!!" finished Mr. Meow, adopting the highest notes and dramatically waving his paws above his head, "OooooOOOOOooooooOOOOOooooooOOOOOOOOOO OOOOOOOO OOOOOO OOOOOO!!!"

---

1. "Staccato" means that the piece is played with each note separated from the other.

"This is delightful!" sighed Mrs. Walm and reached for a handkerchief, "Mr. Meow is truly improving every year!"

Each Christmas she was deeply moved by the neighbours' performance. Aunt Barbara nodded in understanding and also shed a tear. It reminded them of the olden days when they were little and played under a big table in the very same living room.

Uncle Bill looked at uncle Walm expectantly and then glanced at the tray with muffins, apparently wishing for something more than a spiritual feast.

Mr. Elk hit the keys with passion to indicate that it was the very culminating moment of the song and tossed his hair again, so that everyone would understand that it was the end of the performance. In a minute, Mr. Elk and Mr. Meow received a loud applause. The tiny Mice were also softly clapping their hands while still swaying on the branches.

"Bravo!!!" shouted Bunky, as he loved Christmas music and also wanted to be a part of the performance, and a part decidedly louder than Mr. Meow himself, even though he was still thinking about the mystery behind the window.

"Bravo!!!" shrieked Rodney, as he admired his older cousin and wanted to follow him in everything.

Mr. Elk and Mr. Meow bowed in an elegant manner and both reached for their well-earned muffins. Bunky jealously followed them with his eyes and hesitated between having a muffin and solving the outdoor mystery. Everyone was laughing and talking at present and it was uncle Bill who sat at the piano this time, even though he was holding a muffin in his left hand.

"Let me hold it for you," offered aunt Barbara, "You might get the crumbs on the piano."

Uncle Bill made a disappointed face. "Can I play the piano *with* a muffin?" he asked shyly, "The introductory part will require only one hand."

Aunt Barbara shook her head and reminded uncle how one time in the past he had an ice cream on a sofa.

On the other side of the room, Sir Williams was just in the middle of a witty anecdote. Bunky tiptoed unnoticed to his cousin Rodney. Only the ancestors saw his movement from their portraits.

"Now, Rodney," he said quietly, "I shall leave the room for a moment and go outside."

"Why?" asked Rodney curiously.

"I think," whispered Bunky, "that there is something behind the window."

Rodney squealed and put both paws to his mouth.

"Is it dangerous?" he inquired.

"Not really," said Bunky knowingly, although he hardly knew the right answer.

"We need to tell aunt Barbara!" observed Rodney, looking visibly scared.

"No," said Bunky, "This is the worst idea. It would spoil the entire fun."

"Oh," said Rodney, although he didn't understand. He knew for sure that he didn't like dangerous things.

"We are brave and independent," announced Bunky, "And also we have our own secret."

"Oh," repeated Rodney.

"Stay here," ordered him Bunky, "If I don't return in an hour, tell everyone to look for me."

Rodney felt faintly. It didn't sound like good news.

"It won't be that bad. I'm sure it's something good," smiled Bunky and proceeded to the front door. He was convinced that nothing bad could happen in Walmland, especially on Christmas Eve. He wrapped himself up in a scarf and quietly opened the door without making any noise.

Everyone was engaged in a conversation and no one noticed his quiet escape. No one apart from cousin Rodney who was standing motionless in the middle of the room. As soon as the door closed behind Bunky, Rodney ran to the window and pressed his nose to the glass to have a better view.

"I will save cousin Bunky if it is necessary!" he told himself. Deep inside, little Rodney was as brave as a warrior.

Bunky immediately felt the cold air and felt slightly grumpy, especially when he realised that he didn't take gloves, but soon grumpiness gave way to excitement. Also, he promised himself not to be grumpy for several Important Reasons: one of them being Santa Claus's approaching arrival; another—his desire to become a better Bunky. It wasn't too dark outside, as the Christmas spruce was all lit up with the most beautiful, enchanting, glistening colours. The Christmas star on the spruce reigned above the Walms' house and, probably, above the entire Walmland Village, filling the neighbourhood with a welcoming mellow glow. Bunky sensed a unique, aromatic scent of wood lingering in the air, as all the Walmland families gathered around their fireplaces. He always associated this scent with Christmas.

Suddenly, a tiny snowflake landed on his nose as if to remind him that there was a mystery to be solved. Bunky crept quietly towards the Snowman who was standing quite unmoved in his poncho, most probably quietly admiring the Christmas star. Apparently, the mysterious grey ears did not puzzle the Snowman. Or, perhaps, he knew everything . . .

"Mr. Snowman, you've got a secret," whispered Bunky, looking expectantly at the Snowman's face. Apparently, the Snowman was good at keeping secrets, as he did not reply. He did not even look at Bunky.

"Hmm, I understand," continued Bunky, "It is a very noble behaviour not to reveal secrets, especially when one made a promise not to do so. I hope you are not cold."

And he carefully examined the Snowman's poncho, making sure that he wouldn't be cold on such an important night. In the vicinity of the Snowman there was the very place where Bunky saw the mysterious ears. He tiptoed around the Snowman, but there was no one and nothing to be found, apart from the Snowman himself and Bunky's not-so-mysterious footprints.

"And Mr. Snowman does not have such grey, fluffy ears!" Bunky observed, "In fact, does he have any? Perhaps they are very tiny so that he can pretend that he does not hear whenever he does not want to reply to an uncomfortable question!"

Since there was nothing to be found in the front yard, Bunky bravely decided to explore the backyard. He kept moving quietly close to the wall and felt that the backyard was much more secluded than the front yard. He could no longer hear those comforting, cheerful voices from the streets of Walmland. Only the bush was rustling: "shhh shhh shhh."

"Hello?" said Bunky. He did not like the rustle.

"Hello?" repeated Bunky and felt uneasy. But then, like a typical Bunky Hippo, frustration took hold of him and, all of a sudden, his fear gave way to irritation.

"Hello!" screamed Bunky and angrily stamped his foot, hoping that the ground would shake.

After this ignoble deed performed just before Santa's arrival, he realised that he might be risking not receiving his Christmas present. Yet, there was a pause in rustling and, out of the blue, a tiny grey creature emerged from the maze of leaves. Boxwood is evergreen and retains its green leaves in winter too, so it is always a good hideout for all sorts of tiny, mysterious animals. The little creature probably thought so too. It was a very tiny creature indeed and it kept shaking in fear. Bunky immediately recognised the grey ears. He felt stupid and deeply regretted raising his voice. He often regretted doing *bunky* things. All the warm, kind, and very *walmful* emotions took hold of him once again on seeing this small animal. He immediately removed his scarf and placed it around the creature's neck. The animal stopped shaking and looked at Bunky with its big, blue eyes, and Bunky already knew that he would never let go of this creature, if only the creature somehow wanted to stay with him.

"Who are you?" he asked gently, hoping that the creature would forgive him.

"I am a little Wolf without a home," said the animal and looked at Bunky again, this time with more expectancy than fear.

Bunky noticed what a delightful, soft fur the animal had. If only he could take the Wolf home and keep him forever as his friend! He always dreamt about having a pet, but aunt Walm would usually remind him what a great responsibility it was—almost as if Bunky was an irresponsible person!

"I apologise that I shouted," said Bunky quite sincerely, "I didn't know that it was you and I was scared."

"I apologise that I was hiding," the Wolf remarked, " I didn't know you too and I was also scared."

"Nevermind," said Bunky decisively, "Would you like to go home with me and become my friend?"

The Wolf's eyes were reflecting the bright stars floating high above Walmland on the nightly sky.

"You have no idea how happy I would be!" he cried.

"What is your name?" inquired Bunky, "It is very important! I would like to introduce you to everyone at home and, especially, to my cousin Rodney!"

"Will they like me?" the little Wolf became visibly worried.

"Yes, I have no doubt about it!" assured him Bunky, "Who wouldn't like such a beautiful, kind creature?"

The Wolf blushed, but Bunky could not see the blush behind the fur. I am convinced, Dear Readers, that you would also find it difficult to discern this blush.

"I do not have a name," the creature sadly admitted.

"Would you like to be called Plum?" asked Bunky without much thinking, just as Bunkies usually do.

He loved plums—plums in chocolate cakes—sweet and special– and he thought that it might be such a charming name for this enchanting creature encountered in the backyard. It is not every day that one makes such discoveries. The Wolf nodded and smiled and it was the first time in his life when Bunky Hippo saw a smiling Wolf. It was also probably the first time in Plum's life when he saw a smiling Bunky.

3

Little Plum Finds Home
and Adventures Begin!

"Taking care of others is the greatest responsibility of one's life," aunt Walm instructed Bunky in a solemn voice.

She noticed that Bunky's fur was even more bluish and shiny from joy and excitement of the evening. He was sitting on the sofa next to her, cuddling the little grey creature wrapped up in a soft blanket. The creature was fast asleep. Plum was breathing quietly and peacefully.

"I know, aunt," said Bunky, glancing towards the mirror, "Do I *look* irresponsible?"

"On the contrary," Mrs. Walm opposed, "I think that you are a *very* responsible little Bunky."

"Cousin Bunky isn't that little," observed Rodney who was sitting underneath the Christmas tree, anticipating the appearance of Santa Claus. The Mice gazed at him quietly from their hole, probably also looking out for Santa.

"I am *still* very little," answered Bunky with a deep sigh. He greatly disliked being called "tall," "grown up," or "no longer little."

This time Mrs. Walm was ready with a perfect answer. "Oh, Rodney," she said, "You and Bunky are still little, but being little does not have to do with responsibility."

"See?" Bunky grinned.

"I'm growing up very fast," announced Rodney from underneath the tree.

Bunky Hippo rolled his eyes, but in such a way that no one could notice. At least no one apart from the ancestors residing in their portraits. And probably no one apart from Santa Claus, Bunky thought in fear and decided to improve himself and act nicely, even if others would not.

"Knowing that being responsible is the greatest and most difficult task of one's life, I have no doubt that you will be a very responsible Bunky while taking care of Plum," aunt Walm finally declared.

"Yes, aunt," said Bunky as his face brightened up, "I love Plum. I will be his friend for a lifetime."

"When one decides to invite a little wolf, dog, cat, guinea pig or any other animal into one's life, one has to remember that it is no shorter than for a lifetime and one can never let this creature down," continued Mrs. Walm.

"Yes. It is forever," said Bunky quite simply, looking at Plum who, at the moment, began smiling in his sleep.

Honestly, Bunky knew that he wouldn't like it any shorter. At least they would have "forever"—hopefully it was long enough. Plum was warm and cosy. It was the first time since many days when he had a proper supper and a bowl of milk.

"Forever," echoed Rodney from underneath the tree and the Mice nodded their fluffy heads.

"Unfortunately, there are still those who don't realise it and treat animals like toys," observed Mrs. Walm.

"They don't deserve Christmas," said Bunky angrily, "You don't ever leave a helpless friend behind."

"Happily, there are many responsible owners out there, just like you are," Mrs. Walm stated.

"I won't be an *owner*," explained Bunky, " I don't own Plum but I am his best friend *forever*."

Aunt Walm smiled and gave Bunky a loving hug.

"Well said," she admitted, "I am so proud of you!"

"And so is Santa Claus!" declared Rodney, emerging from underneath the tree in order to receive his hug too.

"My little, precious ones," said aunt Walm, "Although I dare say that Rodney is growing up too fast! Happily, Bunky is still quite little!"

And then she winked at Bunky. Her words satisfied both of them.

"Merry Christmas!" said Mrs. Walm, kissing Rodney and Bunky on their foreheads, "Merry Christmas, little Plum!"

She patted the Wolf gently, as he was still dreaming about his new home, warmth and soft blankets. In his dream he also encountered a little Bunky who was very kind and loving and promised to become his friend.

"Merry Christmas, aunt Walm!" answered Bunky and Rodney in a choir.

"Shall you join others and go to sleep before Santa's arrival?" asked Mrs. Walm.

They looked around the living room. It was very quiet, as the guests went to sleep after singing, talking, and feasting together. The Mice disappeared in their hole and went to sleep as well.

Sir Williams was invited to stay overnight and it transpired that he had planned it before, as he secretly brought with him cotton pyjamas, an elegant comb, a disposable toothbrush, and a book to read before sleep entitled *Ten Renowned Recipes that Changed the Universe*.

Mr. Elk and Mr. Meow, tired but greatly satisfied with their artistic performance and uncle Walm's pastries, were fast asleep too in a special guestroom located in the most peaceful part of the house.

Barbara and Bill were sleeping as well, pleased with the beautiful memories which Christmas Eve brought to them once again. Mr. Walm went to bed just after Barbara and Bill, because he felt uneasy about going to sleep before his guests. The living room was quiet now.

Undoubtedly, the greatest sensation of the evening was the little Wolf Plum himself. In the beginning, Plum was quite overwhelmed with emotions, but soon he realised that there was only warmth and kindness awaiting him in the Walms' house. The first thing he saw in the living room was the Christmas tree throwing a gentle light on the walls, carpet, paintings, table, and sofa. It convinced him that he is back to safety. Everyone was taken by surprise when Bunky and Plum appeared in the living room and Rodney cried that "Bunky is the bravest cousin ever." Mrs. Walm, the most practical person of them all, immediately arranged a warm blanket for the unexpected visitor. But now Plum was no longer unexpected. He went to sleep loved and no longer homeless.

"What a *walmful* creature," whispered Aunt Walm while leaning over Plum to admire the soft fur growing on the tips of his grey ears. Plum was still smiling gently in his sleep.

Finally, Aunt Walm also went to bed, arranging beforehand her curlers for tomorrow. Bunky carried Plum to his room and gently placed him in a wide, comfortable wicker basket. Rodney tiptoed behind his cousin in a long, purple dressing-gown. It belonged to Mr. Walm in his youth and it was still too long and too big for Rodney, however, he insisted on wearing it in order to look grown up enough. Bunky thought that this grown up look might cost him a loud fall.

"Santa Claus will think that you are too old and won't bring you a present," he threatened Rodney.

"Santa Claus visits everyone regardless of their age and he knows everything," responded Rodney.

It was very true, Bunky admitted deep inside.

"He sleeps like a rock," noticed Rodney, pointing at Plum.

"He is very tired," remarked Bunky, "He was all alone outside on such a special evening."

"Does it make you more tired if you are alone outside during Christmas?" inquired Rodney, sitting on the edge of Bunky's bed. Half of his dressing gown was still on the carpet. Bunky paused for a moment.

"I do think so," he answered, "I think that being alone on Christmas makes you feel exhausted."

"But he won't be tired and lonely anymore," rejoiced Rodney.

"Absolutely no," smiled Bunky, "Will you go to sleep now? We can see the stamps tomorrow."

Rodney stared at the carpet.

"Are you thinking about Santa Claus?" asked Bunky quietly.

"I'm thinking about chocolate cookies," replied Rodney and looked at Bunky.

"What about them?"

"I'm *dreaming* about them," explained Rodney, "Uncle Bill and aunt Barbara do not allow me to have them every day."

"That's wise," estimated Bunky, "It will help you to preserve your teeth for a lifetime. You won't have to visit doctor Beaver."

"Really?" wondered Rodney, swinging his legs from side to side.

"Think about dinosaurs," continued Bunky knowingly, "They had terrific teeth! And you know why? Nobody offered them chocolate cookies!"

"Ah," sighed Rodney, "I have never thought about that."

"But you should have," insisted Bunky, "You are grown up now and you should take care of your health in a responsible way. It's also about not having chocolate cookies *too often*."

"What about *sometimes*?" inquired Rodney, "After all, I'm not *fully* grown up yet."

"*Sometimes* is good enough," admitted Bunky.

"If only I had one," despaired Rodney.

Bunky sighed. He looked at his cousin and then marched decisively towards his desk, quietly opened one of the shelves and found his hidden chocolate cookie.

"Here you are," he said with a wide grin, "I am still not grown up enough to stop keeping these in my desk. I have only one though."

Rodney's eyes lit up with unexpected joy. He gratefully took the cookie and broke it in half.

"Here you are," he said, "Half a cookie for you."

If only Santa Claus could have seen them now! Bunky felt proud of his cousin and began struggling with the same thought—perhaps he could tell Rodney about his secret?

"Before we go to sleep," began Bunky carefully, "I would like to share with you the Greatest Secret I have."

"With me?" asked Rodney who, on hearing such words, was completely in awe. Sitting in Mr. Walm's purple dressing gown on Bunky's bed, he looked like a royal figure from tales about knights and princes.

"You are my Most Important Cousin," explained Bunky and blushed underneath his blue fur.

Rodney squealed quietly. "What is it, cousin Bunky?"

"You are sitting," continued Bunky ceremoniously, "on the bed which hides my Greatest Secret."

Rodney jumped to his feet in excitement and sat down again. Bunky became worried for a while that he would get entangled in the dressing gown, but Rodney was safe.

"I'm all ears," he said, pressing both paws to his mouth.

Bunky decided that it was the time to reveal his secret. He crawled underneath the bed and reached for the blue notebook. He handed it to Rodney in a profound silence. Rodney's paws trembled as he opened the notebook. The first page announced: *Happy Ever After: A Novel by Bunky Hippo of Walmland.*

"Oh!" whispered Rodney, "Oh, oh, oh! You've been writing a novel!"

"Yes," said Bunky in a whisper, "It's about the Hero and the Bunky Princess."

"Who is the Bunky Princess?" inquired Rodney, glancing at the notebook with curiosity.

"It's the most beautiful and talented Princess in and beyond Bunky-land," explained Bunky enthusiastically, "I think that I am in love with her."

Rodney opened his mouth but did not utter a single word. He knew that love was an important matter; almost as important as dinosaurs and chocolate cookies. Still, he wasn't quite sure what it exactly meant, but he felt that love was extremely meaningful. He imagined that the Bunky Princess would be the very person for whom Bunky would gather flowers or explain to her everything in detail concerning dinosaurs and, definitely, she would be all ears. After all, it was love—a grand, mysterious feeling combined with mutual understanding of dinosaur-related issues.

"Does she like dinosaurs?" Rodney inquired, as random pictures of dinosaurs kept running through his mind.

"Oh, I'm sure she does!" observed Bunky, 'she loves butterflies and flowers too, and she plays the harp in her Bunky castle!"

Rodney could not believe his ears. He had never heard about Bunky Castles before.

"Where does she live? Do I know her?" he asked.

"She lives in Bunkyland," explained Bunky.

Rodney was quite puzzled.

"It must be far away from here," he remarked.

"Not so far away," disagreed Bunky, "I don't think it's far from here."

"Did you meet that Bunky Princess in person?" Rodney gasped out.

"No," admitted Bunky, "But I will soon."

"Oh!" said Rodney. He started wondering if the Bunky Princess was real.

"But *you* described her in the novel, didn't you?"

"Yes," agreed Bunky, "I am the author." And he looked at the notebook with pride.

"So, if you described her in the novel, is it enough for her to be real?"

"Absolutely," said Bunky wryly, "And actually what is real and what is not? Every dream can be a kind of reality! Nobody saw triceratopses in *real* life, but everyone believes that they *are* real."

"I agree," said Rodney, feeling slightly confused, although he had to admit that he had never encountered a triceratops[1]; at least not around his house.

---

1. Dear Reader, I am convinced that you also have not encountered a triceratops feasting on local shrubs nearby your house. Triceratopses are the dinosaurs with three characteristic horns on their faces. Bunky is quite fond of them, but he also likes diplodocuses—the dinosaurs with very long necks—they were able to see everything from above

"I am sure she is *extremely* real," he added.

He looked at his cousin Bunky and started wondering how *real* the Bunky Princess *really* was. There was some lingering doubt in his heart and he worried that his cousin might be disappointed one day. What if she wasn't real at all but only existed in Bunky's novel? Maybe all this dream had its beginning and end in Bunky's imagination?

"Cousin Bunky, did you make her up?" he asked cautiously, "The Bunky Princess is a literary character, isn't she?"

"What do you mean that I made her up?," responded Bunky impatiently, but then he nodded his head, "I did make her up. But it doesn't mean that she does not exist. I thought a lot about the Bunky Princess and just wrote down everything that I know about her, so it *must* be true."

"Oh cousin," sighed Rodney, "I believe you and feel privileged to be your confidant. I would do anything I can to help you meet the Bunky Princess."

And Rodney was sincere. His cousin's face lit up.

"Please don't tell anybody," he entreated.

"Not in a million chocolate cookies," Rodney promised, "Goodnight, cousin Bunky!"

"Goodnight, dear cousin Rodney!"

Rodney marched out of the room in his long dressing-gown. Bunky felt good about having a confidant. He carefully placed the blue notebook underneath his bed and returned for a moment to the wicker basket in order to take a look at little Plum. The Wolf was sleeping quietly, submerged in his blissful dreams. Bunky made sure that he is well tucked in and then he swiftly minced towards his bed. The night was starry and bright—undoubtedly, Santa Claus would find his way with ease.

"A perfect night for an early sleep," Bunky thought as he rolled over on his side to see the stars glancing through the window into his bedroom. He thought about the Bunky Princess admiring the very same stars in Bunkyland and hoped that she would not stay up late but get some good night's sleep.

"Sleep is very important for general well-being, healthy complexion and understanding decimals," mumbled Bunky and soon he was fast asleep too.

---

without climbing a mountain!

Rodney Williams did not go straight to bed, but secretly returned to the kitchen. He found a pen and a spare piece of paper left on a dresser and, then, quietly sat at the kitchen table and began writing:

Walmland, Christmas Eve

Dear Santa Claus,

I know it may be too late, as it is already Christmas Eve, but I have something important on my mind and cannot go straight to bed without telling you all about it. I apologise for writing to you so late. It is very important. My cousin, Bunky Hippo, whom you know very well—I am sure of it, dreams about meeting the Bunky Princess whom he has described in his novel. I am not sure if the Bunky Princess is real, so I thought that you could make her real or bring her here to Walmland. My cousin said that she lives in Bunkyland in a castle with butterflies. I am not well-acquainted with maps and geography, but I suppose that you are because you must be already at least a graduate student. Dear Santa Claus, please help my cousin if possible. It would be the best gift for me this year, as I am grown up and responsible and do not need other gifts. Merry Christmas, dear Santa Claus! I hope that you will be able to rest too!

Your nice (and not naughty) all year round,
Rodney Williams

Rodney was very agitated while writing the letter, feeling that the task is of utmost importance. Finally, he tiptoed to the living room in order to dispatch his letter while placing it on a windowsill. Afterwards, he returned to bed, but still could not sleep.

Rodney was awake in his bed, quietly looking towards the window behind which the snow was gently dancing and swirling. He was thinking, thinking and thinking about his cousin Bunky and the Bunky Princess. How he wished that his cousin's dream would come true!

Rodney sat on his bed again and turned on the light. He found his cozy slippers from aunt Walm and dressed in his uncle Walm's purple dressing gown. Then, he directed his steps towards the living room.

"It is fortunate that the door does not creak," Rodney thought. Just one glance at the letter to make sure that it was still there and he would return to bed to sleep soundly!

The living room was fully submerged in a magical glow of Christmas lights. The Mice, apparently, went to sleep for good, as it was completely quiet in the vicinity of their Mouse Hole underneath the Christmas tree. And what a tree it was! It reigned above the room, twinkling with mellow lights like a giant, blinking cat; a homely kind of cat one wants to pet and admire. It was quiet all around, but there was a palpable anticipation in the air—nothing anxious or uncertain, but rather exciting and ceremonial. Rodney lingered at the door for a while and quietly stepped in. His slippers prevented him from making any noise. The twinkling lights of the Christmas tree were brightly reflected in his eyes as he was tiptoeing through the carpet. There were still tea cups and Christmas napkins left on the table—a clear evidence that the whole company had a very pleasant time. Mr. Meow's notesheets were still on the piano and Sir Williams' reading glasses were left on the green armchair. Colourful stockings with embroidered names decorated the mantlepiece, while joyful flames were still jumping up and down in the fireplace. There was a sweet, comforting scent of gingerbread cookies, hot chocolate and pine needle tea floating in the air. The Walms' ancestors did not go to sleep: instead, they were carefully watching the room, gazing at this serene scene from their portraits in wooden frames.

Rodney thought that he loved the living room on Christmas night. He carefully approached the Christmas tree and touched one of the flickering lamps—it was so beautiful, like a tiny star, but it was also unexpectedly hot. Rodney quickly removed his paw. Dear Readers, you should never touch hot Christmas lights.

"They are just to be admired," Rodney thought and he was right.

He also realised that the living room was different by night. Even the ancestors looked more impressive than usual. For instance, Great Grandma Walm was beaming with joy—Rodney was sure of it.

"Everyone is happy tonight, even the ancestors," thought little Rodney in delight.

And then he stepped on something—something rustling and delicate. He looked down and saw them—all the amazing presents underneath the Christmas tree! Rodney's eyes widened in surprise, while a sudden thought flashed through his mind. He looked around and carefully examined the room. The carpet underneath the tree was flooded with parcels and boxes in gift wrapping papers of different patterns and hues. Rodney threw a glance at the fireplace only to realise that the stockings were filled with sweets. His heart began beating fast. It must have been . . . Rodney ran to the windowsill to discover that his letter was gone. It must have been . . .

"Santa Claus!!!" shouted Rodney so loudly that the entire house almost began shaking. He entirely forgot that he was meant to be quiet. He pressed his nose against the window and saw him—the *real* Santa Claus trudging through the snow towards his silver sledge! The sledge was overly shiny and polished, as if Santa Claus cleaned it thoroughly before his all-night venture around the world. Even though he was carrying a huge sack with gifts and even though he was wearing numerous winter clothes, Santa Claus hopped gracefully through the Walms' fence and comfortably placed himself in the silvery sledge. He must have been practising this stunt all year round in order to be ready for Christmas! A glorious, shiny brown deer led the way, once in a while shaking his rich mane which continuously produced golden sparks.

"It is soooo fortunate that Bunky shovelled the pavements!" thought Rodney in amazement. He pressed his paws against the glass in order to see better.

"These are the obvious advantages of going to sleep late," he observed.

Santa Claus took the reins and glanced towards the Walms' house, as if planning to say "goodbye." And then he saw Rodney with his paws and nose pressed against the glass. He immediately raised his gloved hand and waved, sending Rodney a heart-warming smile. Then, he winked—Rodney could swear that Santa Claus winked at him—and nine magic reindeer swiftly ascended into the sky, climbing through invisible surfaces and leaving behind them a pink aurora and glistening stardust. Rodney was standing in the window quite motionless. He knew that it was not merely his imagination. Santa Claus was here *in person*.

"What happened? I had been sleeping blissfully until I heard your screams!" grumbled Bunky who just entered the living room, "Did you have nightmares?"

Rodney turned around towards his cousin. His face was so bright and animated that Bunky stopped grumbling and looked cautiously into his sparkling eyes.

"Oh, if only I could convince you that it *was* real!" Rodney gasped out, "Please, look through the window—a beautiful pink aurora is *still* there!"

Bunky's grumpiness gave way to an adventurous feeling. He looked through the window as advised by his cousin and saw the remaining tiny flickers of stardust and captivating pink colours stretching through the nightly sky.

"What happened up there in the sky?" Bunky asked carefully, "Did you play with fireworks, cousin Rodney? I think that you were meant to sleep early."

"Oh," blushed Rodney, secretly thinking about his letter to Santa Claus.

"It's ok," smiled Bunky, who immediately forgot that he had ever felt grumpy. Bunkies always act in this way—they are a little short-tempered but always loving.

He was glad to be here with Rodney. He suddenly realised that there was a pleasant scent of gingerbread cookies lazily floating across the room and that the ancestors staring from their portraits looked even more cheerful than in the afternoon. Something good, pleasant and warm reached his heart and he felt comfortable and happy with it. The fireplace was so inviting that he desired to sit next to it with Rodney and listen to his story.

Rodney looked at Bunky with glowing eyes. He was always a kind, good-natured creature but, at present, there was also something new and magical in Rodney's appearance—as if he had been very close to some source of goodness and peace. The whole living room resonated with this special, almost tangible feeling.

"Santa Claus was here," Rodney whispered, "I saw him. He waved to me."

Now it was Bunky's turn to say "oh." He wanted to impress his cousin by saying something like: "naturally, I saw him a million times," or "of course, he had knocked at my bedroom door before coming here," but he decided that it wouldn't be fair to deceive Rodney in any way. Therefore, he remained quiet.

"Words failed me," he thought.

"Do you believe me, cousin Bunky?" asked Rodney.

Bunky took Rodney's paw in his and finally said: "I do believe you. One hundred percent. Please tell me all about it."

There was no reason not to believe his little cousin. They found a comfortable spot next to the fireplace and Rodney told Bunky about his adventure in the living room, skipping the part about writing the letter.

"You are very lucky," said Bunky truthfully, "and you deserve to meet Santa Claus several times a year. I don't think that there was anybody kinder than you this year apart from our aunts and uncles."

"Do you think that he will return?" inquired Rodney, "We could invite him for a cup of tea."

"Sooner than you might think," estimated Bunky, although he wasn't quite certain yet. He needed to make calculations and analyse the situation in order to know better.

"He left presents," whispered Rodney, "underneath the Christmas tree."

And only then did Bunky see all the presents underneath the Christmas tree and stockings filled with sweets!

"Shall we take a look at them?" he asked.

Suddenly, they heard quick steps and Mrs. Walm appeared in the living room dressed in a nightgown and with a maze of curlers in her hair.

"What happened here? Why don't you go to sleep, my dear ones?" she asked.

Mrs. Walm looked concerned, as she always worried about her family and friends and, especially, about those who stayed up late at night while they were meant to be fast asleep in their bedrooms. In a few seconds, all the guests gathered in the living room. Apparently, Rodney woke up the entire house.

"I heard someone shouting," said uncle Bill, stretching and yawning in his blue pyjamas.

They all looked expectantly at Bunky and Rodney. Mr. Meow looked over Mr. Elk's shoulder, wondering if this unexpected event would possibly end with some singing and playing the piano. The little wolf Plum also woke up and, at present, he was sitting on the carpet close to Bunky. Bunky patted Plum and kissed his forehead. He did not respond to aunt Walm's question, as he wasn't sure what was meant to be the official version of the events, but then Rodney explained everything truthfully and in detail.

"Truthfully and in detail—always the best way!" Bunky thought.

"I came to the living room and saw Santa Claus," said Rodney with excitement in his tiny voice, "He was already outside and waved me goodbye; and even winked at me! If I counted correctly, he had nine deer and one of them was sparklingly brownish and looked so dignified!"

Indeed, Rodney learnt how to count really well and he wasn't mistaken. Last year, Rodney would have said: "eight and one," but this year he knew how to count up to ten, therefore he was able to count all the nine deer correctly.

"The Glorious Deer!" uttered Bunky. His imagination began working fast.

Everyone listened earnestly and everyone believed Rodney. After all, it was Christmas and, most importantly, Rodney never lied.

"What a great event!" sighed aunt Barbara and aunt and uncle Walm nodded their heads.

"Unbelievable, unbelievable!" Sir Williams kept repeating continuously. He wanted to indicate that he believed in every single word. Right now he was a child at heart. Everyone who feels young at heart is able to appreciate true miracles of life. Only sometimes Sir Williams slightly doubted the existence of Santa Claus and his enchanted reindeer, but that was only sometimes . . .

"How did Santa enter the house?" inquired uncle Bill. Wrapped up in a woollen blanket which he took from the sofa, he was standing near the window, looking quite animated and interested in all the practical details related to Santa Claus's visit.

"I do not know," admitted Rodney, "but definitely he had a magical way of doing it."

Aunt Walm nodded her head again and smiled.

"I guess I will prepare some hot raspberry tea for everyone and we can see the gifts!" she said good-naturedly, being as practical and resourceful as only aunts could be.

But everyone, including Bunky, wanted to hear Rodney's story again. They all gathered around the fireplace and Rodney began discussing his adventure over and over again, secretly skipping the part concerning the letter. Bunky was sitting next to his cousin with Plum on his knees. Mrs. Walm returned to the room with a tray of mugs filled with raspberry tea. Going back to sleep was out of question—they were too enthusiastic about Rodney's story and Santa Claus's gifts. Even the Mice gathered in front of their Mouse Hole, looking curiously at the gifts and perking up their grey ears whenever they heard Rodney's words. Uncle Bill loitered around the window for a while, hoping that Santa Claus could reappear, but it was generally agreed that Santa must be too busy to return. Uncle Bill appeared to be a little upset on hearing that Santa might be gone for good this year.

"He has to visit the *entire* world!" Sir Williams reminded him, stretching his arms to show what a huge place the world was; even bigger than Walmland itself!

"What a busy, busy man!" admitted uncle Bill, returning to the fireplace and reaching for his mug. Then, he sighed heavily. Rodney wondered for a moment about uncle Bill's sadness.

"Poor uncle Bill," he thought, "definitely he wanted to meet Santa Claus too!"

"The gifts . . .," whispered Bunky and gave aunt Walm a meaningful look.

The Mice, who heard Bunky, began giggling and dancing around the Mouse Hole, waiting for the big moment to arrive.

"My little Bunky is right," smiled aunt Walm, 'shall we unwrap the gifts? It seems that everyone was quite good this year!"

"I was, I was!" exclaimed uncle Bill, jumping to his feet and rushing towards the Christmas tree. Rodney felt relieved that uncle was finally in better spirits. They followed him: Rodney—with diffidence and Bunky—with hope. Sir Williams approached the Christmas tree in a rather reserved way. He longed for a gift from Santa Claus, but didn't want anyone to see how great was his longing for a Christmas present, so he pretended indifference.

Bunky felt that his heart was beating fast again. He imagined himself skating gracefully around a frozen lake and the Bunky Princess clapping her hands in admiration. To tell you the truth, Dear Readers, Bunky had been dreaming about his skates all year long. Little Plum lovingly licked his face.

"Thank you for being here, my little friend," said Bunky, "I am sure that Santa Claus did not forget about *you*!"

It was snowing outside again and Santa Claus's footprints disappeared in the snow . . .

4

The Northern Star is Rising and Bunky Unwraps his Gift

Santa Claus felt weary. He didn't really feel like leaving his cosy armchair or facing snowstorms outside. These were the early hours of twilight and Mrs. Santa Claus began preparing delicious sandwiches which were meant to sustain her husband during the coming night. It was a very important occasion—Christmas was coming! Mrs. Claus went to the stable to see how were the Reindeer doing. Clearly, they were in fabulous moods, dancing, singing and impatiently awaiting the night. The most fluffy, shiny and brownish of all, with a beautiful reddish nose, informed Mrs. Santa Claus that everything was ready. It was Rudolf the Reindeer—the fast and agile one who always led the way.

"If only my husband was ready too," sighed Mrs. Claus and returned to the house in order to see what Santa Claus was currently doing.

As she entered, Santa Claus was changing from his pyjamas into a more representative attire. Finally, he dressed himself in a red, majestic winter coat with a matching cap. He also selected some earmuffs, in case his ears got extra cold, and placed them in his spacious pocket.

"I feel so sleepy," said Santa Claus, "I wish Christmas Eve could have been tomorrow so I could rest a little longer."

"The soup is ready," said Mrs. Claus, who was as practical as Mrs. Walm, "and I feel that you should exercise more and care for your health in order to stay in a better shape for Christmas. What all the children in the world would say?"

"It's probably the age . . .," tried to explain himself Santa Claus, "Mrs. Claus, you know that I love my job. It's not even a job—everything I do during Christmas is from my heart. It is not even about offering gifts, but rather about bringing magic and happiness to those who need it the most."

"You know very well that Santa Claus is ageless," Mrs. Claus reminded him, "I feel that you weren't gardening and jogging enough during the summer and now you are not in the best shape."

"We went for a swim several times during the last summer," Santa Claus reminded her, alluding to the summer days on which he, Mrs. Claus, Elves and all the nine Reindeer visited the Arctic Ocean in order to swim joyfully in a very cold water, "It was very refreshing and quite healthy, I dare say."

"Swimming was very healthy," agreed Mrs. Claus, "but what happened to you today? It's the most important day of the year!"

"Perhaps air pressure is decreasing," wondered Santa Claus, sitting down to his soup and gathering all his strength to appear refreshed and fit, "Naturally, we will make this night the most beautiful night in the whole year for all those who were good: both children and adults! Ho ho ho! Mrs. Claus, I love your cucumber soups!"

"Thank you," smiled his wife and looked affectionately at Santa Claus. She started wondering that maybe he was not so ageless as she always thought him to be. In fact, he had been working for over two thousand years! It felt like infinity. Others retire after thirty years of work, but not Santa Claus. What would the world do without her husband? What kind of place would it be? Santa Claus was this type of husband without whom the world could not exist—Mrs. Claus thought about it with a deep pride. She looked at him more gently and sympathetically than a while before and felt that, indeed, he had all the right in the world to feel a little exhausted. It wasn't that he gave up on his task—not at all. Mrs. Claus saw a familiar glitter in his eyes. She hoped that her famous cucumber soup would restore his spirits.

All of a sudden, there was a gentle knock on the door and a tiny Elf in a green satin livery appeared in a doorway carrying a huge scroll of paper.

"Good evening Mrs. Santa Claus, good evening Mr. Santa Claus!" he said courteously. The Elf had such a bright, cheerful voice that even the little golden bells on the Christmas tree began giggling and ringing on his arrival. Santa Claus immediately felt better on seeing his old friend. All the unearthly adventures they had lived through together and all the special memories were immediately restored in his heart!

"When there is a will, there is a way," Santa Claus thought.

Mrs. Claus also brightened up on seeing the newcomer, energetically waving to the Elf with her knitting needle. She was just beginning her afternoon knitting routine.

The Elf, whose name was Merino, smiled back and bowed gracefully. "Merino," an elegant and refined name given to the Elf by his parents, was in honour of Mrs. Santa Claus's warm Christmas sweaters from her excellent merino wool.

Dear Readers, you obviously understand that there is nothing like comfort and warmth when one lives in the North Pole! You should know that Merino had a brother whose name was also a tribute to Mrs. Claus's remarkable sweaters. His name was Shetland—in honour of shetland wool. As you can see, all the varieties of wool Mrs. Claus possessed could easily accommodate with fancy woollen names at least a dozen of Elves.

"Here is this year's updated list of good children and adults and their hopes, dreams and wishes!" announced Merino and bowed again.

He was very excited about tonight's trip and always waited for Christmas with a slightly growing impatience. Sort of like Bunky waited for his presents. He produced from his pocket a seemingly endless scroll of paper. An hour ago it looked quite creased and tattered—an apparent sign of an excessive use, as several little elfish hands had studied the list scrupulously in order to get well-acquainted with every single good person in the world. At present, the paper was faultlessly straightened out and, in truth, meticulously ironed. It was Merino's idea to secretly iron the nice list so that it would be restored to its previous splendour. Merino borrowed his mum's iron to perform this demanding task and used his green livery as an ironing cloth so that the list would not be damaged. Dear Readers, if you ever have a similar idea, please ask your mum or dad, aunt or uncle, grandma or grandpa to perform this task for you (Bunky and Rodney decidedly would ask someone older for help).

"Thank you so much, dear Merino, my old friend!" rejoiced Santa Claus, "What I would do without you! And without Mrs. Claus!" Here Santa Claus blushed.

"I just love this cucumber soup!" he conintued, "I feel that it is restoring my old spirits! Merino, how can I thank you for your work?"

"It is not only my work, but the work performed by all of us," explained Merino politely, because Elves are always very polite, "For instance, Shetland worked hard on annual reports about good children and adults."

"Oh, I do appreciate the reports, even though I do not like diagrams and statistics," responded Santa, making a wry face, "I'd rather hope that this year everyone was good instead of seeing statistics again. I guess it's easier to be good than to draw a complicated diagram."

Mrs. Claus smiled. She comfortably nested herself in a rocking chair and began knitting a green Christmas sweater for somebody tiny and thin—presumably another Elf or one of those little, gentle Wood Fairies who inhabited enchanting forests of the North Pole and swiftly commuted on the wings of the North Wind, dancing from time to time on the magical background of colourful aurora. Those Fairies delighted in wearing delicate, airy clothes and Mrs. Claus constantly worried about their health.

"You should wear turtleneck sweaters in winter!" she would lecture the Fairies, but they were always complaining about it, insisting that a Wood Fairy in a turtleneck sweater is anything but a Fairy.

But Mrs. Claus was knitting all year round and, so far, she had already produced two thousand sweaters for the local Elves, Fairies, Gnomes, Reindeer and even a couple of Polar Bears. Everyone loved Mrs. Claus and you can easily imagine what kind of person she was if I tell you that she was very similar to aunt Walm or aunt Barbara: always caring for those who needed help, love, support, advice or a bowl of hot soup.

It is important to add here that Santa Claus was quite a talented cook too and his summer speciality was called "grilled vegetables with grated cheese." Winter was the busiest season for him and he could hardly think about cooking during the time when all the Elves and Fairies were constantly reporting who was naughty and who was nice. As much as he was displeased with diagrams and statistics, he still had to hear about them from his hard-working helpers. Santa Claus was the most impractical, jovial and good-natured person in the whole neighbourhood of the North Pole. Everyone loved him for his sense of humour and easy-going personality: from Polar Bears to local Elves. Enjoying his company for more than a thousand years—since the day he was born—Merino knew Santa Claus very well. At present, he produced from his pocket another well-ironed, shorter list.

"The list of adults and children who need some improvement," he announced and bowed.

Santa Claus searched for his glasses in innumerable pockets of his red coat and, finally, placed them carefully on the tip of his nose. He wasn't very fond of glasses, as he felt that they narrowed down his vision, but there were so many photographs and illustrations worldwide presenting his likeness with those famous glasses, so he decided that he should wear them from time to time in order to remain recognised as the true Santa Claus. Also, he had to admit, the glasses enabled him to see better when something or someone was too far away from him. When Santa Claus reached for his glasses, Merino realised that he was standing too far from him. He quickly moved towards the table with bouncy and gentle steps—very elfish steps.

"Thankfully, not such a long list," sighed Santa Claus, "I see plenty of improvement this year. It means less statistics. What are we going to do with those naughty ones?"

"Well, no gifts for them?" quietly asked Merino. In truth, he didn't know how to solve this problem.

Being good and gentle, Santa Claus felt a sudden pang in his heart. He didn't want to leave anyone without a chance. As he nobly believed, everyone deserved a chance to improve.

"Maybe some small gifts to encourage improvement?" he whispered, worrying that Mrs. Claus would disagree. Mrs. Claus didn't have such a high opinion about those who weren't trying to improve hard enough.

"Ehm ehm," grunted Mrs. Claus, indicating that she heard everything, "I think that tiny gifts will do just fine."

"Perfect, my dear," smiled Santa Claus, "I dare say that everyone on this Earth had a moment of naughtiness, myself including. Of course, it was when I was young and reckless. You, my dear, as I remember, were always well-mannered and polite. A perfect angel."

"Oh, not always," said Mrs. Claus and blushed, "I also had these moments of naughtiness I guess. I would skip Maths classes in order to skate on a frozen lake."

Merino and Santa Claus looked at each other and smiled meaningfully. Before they started their Christmas responsibilities, Mr. and Mrs. Claus had been attending school together. It was the place where they eventually got to know Merino's and Rudolph the Reindeer's parents. Believe it or not, Dear Readers, they were all in the same class! (If you don't believe it, you can see their graduation photo album—it is in Santa Claus's living room.)

"I think we all avoided Maths as much as we could!" rejoiced Santa.

"And now, these are the dreary effects of such conduct! Reluctance to study diagrams!" groaned Mrs. Claus, but she didn't mean to be strict, not being very keen on Maths herself.

"Oh my dear, do not worry," said Santa Claus, "I know precisely how many presents we have to distribute tonight."

"Here is an interesting report," remarked Merino, reaching towards his pocket again and presenting another neat piece of paper (Merino's mum had the best iron ever). At this point we can assume, Dear Readers, that Merino's pockets were simply magical and they could contain as many pieces of paper as he wished. In fact, this was precisely the case.

"*Bunky Hippo Report,*" read Merino.

"Ho ho ho!" smiled Santa Claus, "I hope that he is on the nice list!"

"Absolutely," confirmed Merino, "It is such an interesting case attesting to a complex inner struggle and tremendous power of a strong will."

"I always told you two that it *is* possible to obtain a strong will in order to improve oneself!" interjected Mrs. Santa Claus.

"What does the report say?" inquired Santa Claus.

Merino grinned from ear to ear and began reading:

> *Bunky Hippo, a young inhabitant of Walmland, distinguished himself this year thanks to his untiring inner struggle from which he emerged victorious. Inwardly balancing between the feelings of naughtiness and goodness, he attained a level of self-control allowing his goodness and beautiful heart to shine through all the previous months. Recently, just before Christmas, not only did he shovel the sidewalks, but also shared his last cookie with his cousin Rodney, not to mention him saving and befriending an orphaned little Wolf whom he named Plum. Moreover, during one conversation just before Christmas, Bunky Hippo expressed himself in a positive way about sharing Christmas gifts with the Mice inhabiting the Mouse Hole in the living room. From our observations, it is apparent that, although Bunky can boast a quick temper, his goodness and inner beauty could serve as an example for others. He is like a caterpillar transforming into a winged butterfly or like a bud turning into a rose!*
>
> *Observations by Rudolph the Reindeer, written down by Shetland the Elf before this Year's Christmas Eve*

Mrs. Claus nodded her head with approval. She really liked this particular Bunky. Santa Claus listened to the report with unconcealed pleasure. He immediately felt that he and Bunky could become friends. Indeed, he also liked this young, inwardly complicated, yet greatly victorious inhabitant of Walmland.

"How old is our friend Bunky?" he inquired.

"I am not sure," responded Merino, "but he is regarded in Walmland as *very little*."

"Admirable character!" said Santa Claus, "We shall visit Walmland immediately and then proceed further!"

"If you are planning to change the route, don't forget to take your Christmas compass!" Mrs. Claus advised her husband, abandoning all her knitting and jumping to her feet to make sure that Santa Claus would not forget about anything.

"Ho, ho, ho!" rejoiced Santa, who felt now as young and healthy as Rudolph the Reindeer.

"Also, the report states that Bunky Hippo has a noble and well-mannered cousin named Rodney Williams," indicated Merino.

"We will visit their house during our first stop tonight!" announced Santa Claus and began humming his favourite Christmas tune.

"Before you go, Merino, Shetland, and all the Reindeer should also have some soup!" ordered Mrs. Claus, "No one, but I repeat *no one*, will leave this house hungry—as long as I am ruling the kitchen!"

And she smiled with such kindness that it would have been impossible to oppose her. Merino immediately went outside to invite everyone to the warm, cosy living room. He left Santa Claus's cottage, glowing with yellow lights and smelling with gingerbread cookies mingled with chocolate cakes, and ventured out into the twilight. The nightly landscape greeted him with snow settling on his elfish ears and nose. Merino put his cap back on his head and stared into this mellow, moonlit glow. It was enchanting to live here, at the very north tip of the world: the sky at the North Pole was vast and spacious enough to contain all the northern stars which, at first glance, appeared quite lonely—randomly scattered across the vast heavens—but, after a while, it seemed that this northern universe was bustling with life. Innumerable constellations embraced the sky from east to west, while the universe giggled quietly with the Great Bear, Little Bear, Centaurus, Leo and many others. Above this merry party, next to the Little Bear, glowed the queen of the North—the Northern Star. It looked like a twinkling jewel placed on a pink cushion of the evening horizon. Somewhere out there, a little bit towards the south, Walmland was located and the Northern Star could probably see the land from above. Somewhere there in the distance

Bunky Hippo, Rodney Williams, uncle Bill, aunt Barbara and every good child and adult awaited the arrival of Santa Claus and the beginning of this year's Christmas. Walmland must have been very cheerful tonight: with glowing lights and lanterns, colourful Christmas trees, smiling snowmen and carefree skaters on a frozen lake.

The North Pole was very similar to Walmland—not only tonight but also every day: there was cheer and joy all year round here while, at present, one could see all the little and big creatures going about their Christmas routine: singing, jumping, talking, ice skating, dressing Christmas trees, shovelling front yards, baking cakes, going for walks and doing everything any happy inhabitant of a truly happy land would do. You may say, Dear Reader, that the North Pole is cold—that's true, but what a refreshing coldness it is to walk through those festive streets on a night like this when there is nothing but warmth in one's heart!

Merino was in a festive mood.

"Soup, everyone!" he cried, as the North Pole twilight painted the skies in navy blue colours.

Immediately, there was a noise coming from the stable, clip-clopping of hooves, whinny sounds and giggling. The Reindeer loved Mrs. Claus's cuisine, but who wouldn't? It was always magical—like the entire North Pole! Not only was Mrs. Claus's soup warm and healthy, but also it possessed a magic quality—everyone who had it would become happy even for one day! For this reason, it was famously called a "Carefree Cucumber Soup."

After the warming meal, the Reindeer, Merino, Shetland and Santa Claus cheerfully ventured outside into this cold, wintry twilight in order to commence the Most Important Night of the Year. On seeing Santa Claus, the sky lit up with a thousand bright Stars. They looked like a sea of twinkling lanterns, ready to safely guide Santa's magical Reindeer. You will probably not believe me, but as soon as Santa Claus appeared in front of the cottage, the Stars began to giggle. Their giggling sounded like hundreds of tiny hamsters squeaking cheerfully across the Milky Way.

"Take good care out there!" advised everyone Mrs. Claus in a loud voice in order to be louder than the giggling Stars, even though the squeaking sounds were very pleasant and gentle. As always, she worried that someone would act thoughtlessly, not wear a scarf while it would be cold outside or lean out of the sledge in a way which would be too dangerous. In this she perfectly resembled aunt Walm.

"Glasses!" she cried, running after Santa Claus who was already sitting in his dazzling sledge, "You can't forget the glasses! Do you have the compass?"

"I do, I do! Ho, ho, ho!" rejoiced Santa Claus, who was, by this time, fully awake and in a perfect mood for a sleigh ride. Merino and Shetland hopped into the backseat, holding the enchanted bag with Christmas presents. The bag was like Merino's pocket—it was practically bottomless and could contain innumerable gifts—provided that there were innumerable children and adults who deserved them! The bag was Mrs. Claus's original design. Mrs. Claus was standing outside the cottage in her red boots, thick, woollen dress and lacey evening cap, waving a white handkerchief with pink, embroidered roses—the very same one which Mr. Claus gave her at school on the day of their pre-graduation ball. She almost looked like a very young girl, as her face was full of youthful enthusiasm. Perhaps it was partly the effect of the cucumber soup. Yet, I am convinced, Dear Readers, that it was rather the effect of her youthful spirit. (Of course, the soup helped too.)

"One, two, three!" cried Rudolph the Reindeer as they set off straight into the sky with many cheerful shouts and "ho, ho, hos." The giggling Stars began dancing across the sky, as they could not contain themselves when they heard Rudolph. Christmas was coming once again! The jingling sounds of the bells resounded in the sky and intermingled with all the giggling.

"Wear your scarves everyone! Don't drive too fast!" cried Mrs. Claus in the most rational manner possible, just to make sure that she offered all the reminders and instructions she could in order to keep her extraordinary family safe and sound.

The sledge flickered in the sky next to the Northern Star and then it became very tiny, finally disappearing in the vastness of the nightly horizon, leaving behind a trail of stardust and silver sparks. Mrs. Claus sighed and returned to the living room. It was such an inviting living room; very warm and cosy, but it was not the same without Mr. Claus. She sat in her green satin armchair and found a collection of crosswords that would keep her busy until her husband's return. And then, she thought, they would have Christmas!

Meanwhile, the sledge was swinging high up in the sky, bouncing up and down through the Milky Way, carrying away its merry passengers.

"I feel so young!" declared Santa Claus, smiling from ear to ear like a child who was offered a longed-for present, swinging the reins in a carefree manner, since he knew that the Reindeer did not need any special instructions.

Each Christmas Eve he felt like a teenager playing truant. The Elves were giggling on the backseat together with the Stars. Needless to say, the Reindeer were overjoyed. The sledge wasn't heavy for them as, naturally, it was under a magic spell which made it light as a feather—or, perhaps, even slightly lighter. They were hurrying through the Milky Way with vigorous clip-clopping sounds, while sleigh bells accompanied them with light-hearted ringing. As it happened every year, Shetland began playing harmonica. Merino started singing and soon he was joined by all the nine Reindeer and Santa Claus himself. Merino raised his hand and gently touched the Milky Way. He loved the touch of this soft, sparkling, comforting haze and imagined that clouds would be quite similar. Still singing, Santa Claus was carefully searching for something in his travel bag and, finally, produced from it a red thermos bottle—one of Mrs. Claus's practical devices which he received from her on Easter. Then, after more searching, he found in the bag several red cups with paintings representing local Snowmen and even a Bigfoot trenching through the snow in some misty mountains. He began pouring hot tea for everyone, which was a challenging task when performed in the fast-moving sleigh. The Reindeer kept on speeding forward without any cares in the world. They knew that they would receive warm water during the first stop.

The sleigh was moving with a swift, almost uncontrollable speed, bouncing up and down in order not to collide with any constellation or a giggling Star. It was a fearful and chaotic spectacle, but only for those who were not let into Santa Claus's secrets. In fact, everything was under control, while such a ride in the sky was the most joyous activity one could experience. Those looking up into the sky from below must have noticed a fast-moving point. If you ever spot one on a particular night just before Christmas, be sure it is Santa Claus with his Helpers!

"Raspberry tea!" announced delighted Santa Claus and continued singing while waving his cup in the air. Soon all of them (including the Elves and the Reindeer) were singing: *Fa la la la la, the Northern Star is Rising!* The Milky Way led them higher and higher towards the tip of the sky. Suddenly, they almost collided with the Northern Star—the famous *Polaris!* The Northern Star looked at them with big, peaceful eyes and sent them a silver wink. For a moment, the sleigh was motionless, practically suspended in the sky. The glimmer of the Northern Star reached the sleigh and crossed its path in a sudden but comforting way. It wasn't a blinding light but the one which blesses the onlookers with brilliance and grace. In this moment, they all thought that the Northern Star was exceedingly beautiful. A few seconds later, the sledge began descending. It was the next exciting part of the journey, although one had to hold on tight. Merino, Shetland and Santa Claus took hold of their caps. The Reindeer kept running faster, faster, and faster back towards the Earth . . . towards Walmland. In less than no time they found themselves back on the ground—everyone safe and sound and the Elves still giggling in their elfish way.

"Ho, ho, ho!" cried Santa Claus in order to announce his appearance. Firstly, he reached for his travel bag and produced a big bottle of warm water.

"Here you are, my brave Reindeer!" he exclaimed. Rudolph and the rest were, indeed, very thirsty, but soon they felt invigorated again, as the water was not only warm and tasty but, obviously, magical too!

Shetland delved into the Christmas bag in order to find the gifts selected for children and adults from Walmland.

"This is Bunky Hippo's house," announced Merino ceremoniously.

They all looked around in wonder. Walmland was very quiet and peaceful tonight but, at the same time, filled with a mysterious anticipation lingering in the air. It was a pleasant type of quiet which usually offers a satisfying sense of order and bliss. The Walms' house was very calm. It was nestled next to the local road, surrounded by gentle pine trees and spruces with needles sprinkled with fresh snow. An indoor glow reaching the front yard tempted and comforted our interstellar travellers, making them think of delicious cakes, fluffy carpets and grandfather clocks.

"What a lovely house," Shetland whispered.

On leaving the sledge, Santa Claus discovered huge snowdrifts and decided that it would be necessary to jump through them in order to reach the house. The sleigh stopped nearby the front gate where uncle Bill and aunt Barbara's old car was parked and Santa took a moment to admire this old model which he remembered so well from his early youth. Oh, in his heart he kept so many memories from those olden days! Despite two thousand years of work, he also had his youth and early adulthood to dwell upon! And truly, he was always interested in cars, just as much as Mrs. Claus loved knitting and collecting patterns for advanced knitters.

"Really, this car is in a great shape!" he said to himself with a voice of an expert, nodding his head in approval. The car reminded him of eventful trips with Mrs. Claus. Back then, Mrs. Claus had two pigtails and a fringe. They still kept their old car in the North Pole garage, as it was immensely hard to part with it and all these priceless memories.

But certainly, it wasn't the right time to reflect on cars. Santa Claus sighed and directed his steps towards the magic bag. Merino and Shetland were already working very hard, selecting and ordering parcels around the nearest snowdrift.

"Ho, ho, ho!" rejoiced Santa Claus, reaching for the gifts.

And then, very, very quietly, he tiptoed towards the front gate—as quietly as Santa Claus could do—and jumped through three snowdrifts and through the Walms' fence almost as gracefully as a cat! How it was possible—no one knew! And then Santa Claus saw the Snowman standing in front of the Walms' house. He smiled at the Snowman mysteriously and reached into his pocket, producing from there a small bottle of silver-pink powder –a very special kind of stardust from the Milky Way. He opened the bottle and threw a little bit of stardust at the window located behind the Snowman. In this very moment, the window dissolved in the air for several seconds and Santa safely stepped into the Walms' living room. As soon as he found himself inside the room, the window miraculously returned to its previous place, becoming visible and tangible again. Yet, the Snowman wasn't surprised at all—he probably knew everything about Santa Claus's magic.

Santa Claus looked around in delight: he saw a cheerful fireplace, a bright Christmas tree, colourful stockings, elegant portraits of the Walms' ancestors and gingerbread cookies invitingly placed on the table—everything contributed to a homely atmosphere which he cherished so much. He quietly removed his boots, as he did not want Mrs. Walm to worry about cleaning the carpet once again. Then, he carefully distributed the gifts around the Christmas tree and retreated from the fluffy carpet, putting on his boots again. A pleasant thought crossed his mind—how special it would be to get to know Bunky Hippo and his cousin Rodney in person! However, he knew that it was against Santa Claus's general etiquette to wake up good children on Christmas Eve. They were meant to find gifts on their own, after Santa Claus's departure. If all the good children in the world wanted to greet Santa, Christmas would last until summer and gifts would not be dispatched on time!

The Walms' clock struck 11:00 p.m. and Santa Claus reached for his magic bottle and threw some powder towards the window. In this way he could noiselessly return to the sledge without opening and closing the front door. He had resigned from travelling through chimneys a long time ago, especially since the time when he found this new, magical method of visiting houses. Just before leaving the Walms' living room, he suddenly saw a letter placed on the windowsill. A letter addressed to him!

"How curious!" thought Santa Claus, "A late Christmas letter! It must be important!"

He placed the letter in the bottomless pocket of his coat and minced across the shovelled front yard towards the sledge. Merino and Shetland were sitting on the highest snowdrift, taking notes about a successful delivery of gifts. Santa Claus jumped into the sledge but, all of a sudden, he felt weary and confused, almost forgetting where they were supposed to go. It was as if he felt the weight of all the long years. However, the feeling lasted just for a moment and he felt young and happy once again.

Before the Reindeer started their run, Santa threw a glance at the Walms' house and became more than surprised: there was a silhouette of a tiny person standing in the window. "Oh!" gasped Santa Claus, "Is it Bunky?"

Merino and Shetland threw cautious looks at the house.

"It is Rodney Williams, Bunky Hippo's cousin!" announced Shetland, "Apparently, he is awake!"

"Santa Claus!!!" shouted Rodney so loudly that the entire house almost began shaking.

"Here he is, then!" smiled Santa Claus and raised his gloved hand, "Merry Christmas, dear Rodney! Ho, ho, ho!"

He waved to Rodney and sent him a friendly wink as the sledge began moving forward. Rodney opened his mouth in surprise and then smiled in the happiest way. He raised his tiny paw in order to wave to Santa Claus too. Soon, apart from the mysterious light in the sky and a silver-pink clump of powder which Rodney found on the floor next to the window, there was no trace of the sleigh. Rodney sniffed the powder and sneezed.

"What happened? I had been sleeping blissfully until I heard your screams!" grumbled Bunky who just entered the living room. And, Dear Readers, you know what happened afterwards . . .

"No," said Bunky Hippo making a wry face, "no, no, no."

"But why not? Don't tell me that you don't like these little chocolate pralines!" pleaded aunt Walm. She offered Bunky the whole box of these delicious chocolates, each in a glittering, golden wrapper. It wasn't in her nature to encourage anyone to eat at such a late hour or, especially, to encourage her family to have any sweets at night, but this night was different. Bunky was sitting on the fluffy carpet in the state of grumpiness mingled with disappointment.

"Please," begged him Mrs. Walm," Try one. It will do you good."

"No. Yes," responded Bunky Hippo in a non-obvious way, finally reaching for a praline.

It was well past midnight. They all gathered in the living room around their unwrapped gifts. Rodney and Plum looked cheerful and satisfied with the presents, but the general atmosphere in the living room was verging on confusion. Bunky was in the centre of this drama. He was stubbornly gazing at the floor while holding his gift in both hands. It was a cookbook entitled *The Bliss of Cooking: Easy and Smart Recipes for Lovers of Delicious Cuisine*. It did not look like his longed-for skating boots.

What made Bunky especially grumpy was the fact that the family of Mice received a pair of lovely snow-white skating boots, even though Bunky knew that they wished for colourful bows to decorate their tails with. He was trying with all his might to keep his word—he was trying with all his *bunky might* to feel happy for the Mice, but it was exceedingly difficult to be happy, especially when his dream faded away.

The Mice were giggling cheerfully, jumping into and out of the new skating boots, already polishing them with tiny soft cloths. The skating shoes were so big and spacious for the Mice that they could use them as a little sledge. They completely forgot that they had ever wished for colourful bows. But Bunky did not forget that he was hoping for skates and wondered how such a mistake was possible. After all, he was an example of good manners and proper behaviour—if not through the entire year, than at least through this entire month before Christmas! Bunky already imagined the Mice venturing out tomorrow with these snow-white skating boots, having a lot of fun on the frozen lake, laughing and jumping joyfully in the crisp wintry air.

"The Mice will be probably using each skating boot as a cart," he thought.

And what was he supposed to do? Stay in the kitchen with all the available frying pans and pots, trying out recipes, pretending that it is very exciting? He looked at the cookbook woefully.

Plum was carefully staring at Bunky. He was wearing his new festive blue bow which looked very similar to the one that the Mice were meant to receive this year. Plum was exceedingly happy with this elegant accessory. It was his first Christmas and he didn't even expect a gift. He was grateful at heart. Bunky gave him a hug and complimented him on the bow. Indeed, Plum was very handsome, especially in blue. The blue bow matched his deep blue eyes which looked like a reflection of a clear, peaceful sky or a calm surface of the ocean. Still, it dawned on Bunky that there must have been some mistake: aunt Walm received a set of screwdrivers and, even though she insisted on them being very useful, Bunky felt that they would be of more use to uncle Bill. At the same time, uncle Bill received a knitting set. Bunky looked at his uncle doubtfully and then glanced at aunt Barbara who was holding a charming bowler hat—an excellent hat, but definitely more suited for Sir Williams! Constantly cheerful, Sir Williams was staring gratefully at a figurine of the Egyptian cat. Only Mr. Elk and Mr. Meow received accurate gifts—silver harmonicas in satin boxes.

"Cousin Bunky, take another praline, please," said Rodney quietly. Bunky looked at his cousin doubtfully. Rodney was very cheerful and satis-fied, wearing a violet bow which looked like one of these bows designed for the Mice.

"What happened here?" asked Bunky quietly, glancing at the cookbook.

"But everything is so great and everyone is so happy!" rejoiced aunt Barbara, "These gifts came as such a great surprise! I hardly remember re-ceiving a better surprise in years!" And she put on the bowler hat.

"Sir Williams would look amazing in it," Bunky thought.

"How amazing you look, my dear!" raved uncle Bill, "Such a great style!"

"Quite unique," snapped Bunky, reaching for another praline.

"Yes, yes!" good-naturedly agreed uncle Walm who was sipping his tea, wearing one of these new, elegant mousey bows which made Bunky feel quite desperate. It suited him very well, but Bunky could not resist the thought that his uncle would enjoy the cookbook much more.

"Something is wrong," he kept telling himself. What really made him angry was the fact that everyone pretended that everything was alright. He disliked nonsense.

"It's time to sleep, everyone!" announced Mrs. Walm and patted Bunky on his head, "We are having Christmas tomorrow!"

"Christmas!" growled Bunky quietly.

"Dear cousin," said Rodney and there was a look of concern on his face, "I will be in my room. Just so you know where to find me. And Plum will be resting in your room as usual."

Bunky's face brightened up for a moment. He loved his cousin Rodney and he loved Plum. Despite his short temper, he still had a good, noble heart—I think that you wouldn't doubt it. We all have moments of anger, disappointment, and grumpiness. Now, confess, Dear Readers—isn't it so?

The Noble Hero of this story—Bunky Hippo—is also allowed to have his grumpy days. Even if he was to receive cookbooks for Christmas every year, he would dearly love Rodney and Plum without a change.

"Of course, my dear ones," Bunky answered, "Please rest a lot. Plum had a long day and you both were up for too long."

And to give Bunky credit, he got up and hugged Rodney and Plum and then returned to the carpet to sulk over the cookbook again. The living room was quiet again. The whole party was quite sleepy and tired but, actually, in contrast to Bunky, they all loved the presents from Santa Claus. They had a lot of fun unwrapping their gifts and they enjoyed all the unexpected surprises. They discovered that even though they didn't get what they hoped for, they still received something truly endearing! And now, when the excitement was over, it was time to go to sleep again. Or maybe these were the white, petite snowflakes bouncing and prancing outside that made them feel quite sleepy . . .

5

Bunky Bravely Faces an Inner Struggle

Mrs. Walm was the only person apart from Bunky who did not leave the living room. She approached her little Bunky and sat down on the fluffy carpet next to him. The living room was completely quiet now, as even the Mice went back to sleep, but it was still cosy with the fire cracking in the fireplace. Mrs. Walm looked at Bunky with all the love and under-standing she possessed and placed her hand on his shoulder.

"My little Bunky," she said, highlighting how little Bunky was still in order to cheer him up, "What came over you, dear?"

"Anger," answered Bunky sharply but honestly.

"I thought so," answered Mrs. Walm quite genuinely too, "You are not very happy with your cookbook, are you?"

"No," growled Bunky and stared at the carpet in order to throw a little tantrum.

"But look at me," said aunt Walm and Bunky looked at his aunt. He didn't want to make her sad, even though the cookbook was all over his mind.

"I dreamt about skating boots," he confessed quietly and tears almost came to his eyes. The skating boots were there, beside the Mouse Hole.

"But dear," said Mrs. Walm, hugging Bunky lovingly, "I will buy you these skating boots even just after Christmas. Just think how amazing this cookbook is! When you are *that* surprised with your gift, it is a *real surprise*! Gifts are the true, unexpected joy."

"The *Mouses* got skates," said Bunky bitterly.

"The *Mice*?" corrected him Mrs. Walm, "Yes and they seem happy. We should be happy that something good happened to them! You care about our Mice, don't you? You always did!"

"I do love the *Mouses*, I grew up with them in this house and I care about them a lot, but these skating boots were meant to be mine," answered Bunky, still not paying much attention to the grammatical aspect of the word, as in his mind these were always the *Mouses* anyway, "Everyone received a gift suited for someone else. The bows look mousey. And you got screwdrivers."

"And perhaps this is the most beautiful lesson this Christmas," continued Mrs. Walm, "Why do we expect *at all* that we will receive a gift? A gift is something offered from one's heart. It should not be rejected or criticized. It is not something to be taken for granted and expected each time. I wasn't aware how useful screwdrivers could be! And Plum, Rodney, and uncle Walm are so handsome in their new bows, don't you think so, Bunky?"

Bunky remained quiet. He realised that his aunt was right. Not only screwdrivers were useful, but also Plum, Rodney and uncle Walm looked very presentable in their new bows. And the cookbook was quite useful too. Gifts were given unexpectedly, from the heart—it must have been Santa Claus's plan. After a minute of silence, he decided that it would be fair to agree with his aunt.

"Yes, I do think so," he admitted.

Aunt Walm smiled. "Don't you want to become a cooking master?" she asked.

"No. Yes," responded Bunky ambiguously, as his heart was still conflicted on this matter. He was still hesitating but, nevertheless, he decided not to be angry with Santa Claus. Maybe there was a deeper meaning behind the cookbook.

"Wouldn't you like to become a cooking chef like your uncle Walm?" continued Mrs. Walm encouragingly.

In truth, Bunky deeply admired his uncle and his amazing cooking skills. There weren't many uncles in this universe who possessed such skills.

"Perhaps. Maybe yes. Maybe I would like to," said Bunky quietly and stared at the cookbook in a more friendly manner than before. It was a nice hardcover book in a blue wrapper—Bunky's favourite colour—with the title engraved in silver letters. The cookbook was like a volume full of magic spells. In a way, recipes are like magic spells: they can go perfectly well and they can go perfectly wrong. Bunky decided to think about his gift in a more approving way.

"You are the only one who received the cookbook," observed Mrs. Walm, "That means something."

Bunky looked at his aunt and then at the cookbook again. Was he the Chosen One to become a Cooking Master? But why? To follow into his uncle's footsteps? He opened the cookbook hesitantly. *Recipe One: Potatoes in Tomatoes*—the title in silver letters announced—*Easy and Fast, for the Whole Family!*

"Ehm," Bunky grunted.

Aunt Walm smiled. "It's time to sleep, isn't it?"

"Yes," agreed Bunky, who was already more kindly disposed towards the cookbook and Santa Claus's choices. Aunt Walm took him by the hand and, as in those times when Bunky was very, very little, went with him to his room, tucked him in and kissed him goodnight. Then, she also kissed Plum, even though he was in a deep sleep among his cosy blankets. Mrs. Walm gently closed the door and tiptoed nearby Rodney's bedroom. It was very quiet, so she decided that Rodney must be already fast asleep. Then, she went to her bedroom and thought with pleasure about the possibility of some refreshing sleep.

As soon as the door closed, Bunky felt that he was no longer sleepy. It was a strange feeling because, just a while ago, he was exhausted. When aunt Walm left, he closed his eyes and thought about his downy duvet and soft pillows surrounding him, but soon he realised that the desire to sleep gave way to restlessness. He started tossing around from one side to another and then decided that all this tossing around makes too much noise and the best option would be to quietly get up and occupy himself with something noiseless enough not to wake up Plum. Deep at heart, Bunky was very caring and he wouldn't like his four-pawed friend to suffer any inconvenience caused by his restless state.

He quietly got up—as quietly as Bunkies could do—and gazed at the nightly sky. The snow was still falling outside, while the rest of the world appeared to be motionless. There was no trace of Santa Claus's sleigh, but as soon as Bunky got used to the darkness, he spotted a very bright point on the horizon. It was the brightest start on the entire sky and Bunky knew that it was *Polaris*—the famous Northern Star. You, Dear Readers, are already well-acquainted with this famous Star. *Polaris* was shining with all her strength and might, as if informing the world that Christmas was already here. Bunky sighed. *Polaris* was so beautiful that it was both pleasant and nostalgic to glance at it. What a night, oh what a night to be at home with the cookbook instead of his skating boots! But then Bunky remembered that gifts were not to be taken for granted and that they were always offered from the heart. Thinking about it, he endeavoured to smile. He also thought about his cousin, Rodney, and about little Plum. Yes, Plum was the true Christmas gift this year!

Suddenly, a bright trail of light crossed the sky and something orange and elusive glimpsed and disappeared in the darkness. It was a Shooting Star flying fast like a fiery phoenix only to disappear somewhere on its mysterious path. Bunky closed his eyes and quickly made a wish. He was hesitating for a moment between skating boots and the Bunky Princess, but it was only a moment of hesitation and now he had no doubt—he would like to meet the Bunky Princess more than receive his skates! He sighed again and tiptoed towards his bed. Underneath the bed, there was Bunky's secret—his renowned book—so far renowned only in the circle of the Readers of this novel! Bunky reached for his carefully guarded secret and sat with his one-hundred-page blue notebook at the desk. He quietly turned on the lamp in such a way that it would not disturb his sleeping friend Plum. He took his blue pen and began writing. It was the next part of this enchanting story—*Happy Ever After*:

> *. . . from the happy day of Bunky's emergence from the bush, Bunky Hippo and the Bunky Princess would spend all the time together. Oh, those days were filled with many glorious moments: the moments of joy and light-heartedness! Bunky Hippo and the Bunky Princess were known as inseparable in the whole Bunky-land. In the mornings, they would sail in a boat on an azure lake and Bunky would row, while the Princess would sing and admire water lilies. In the afternoon, they would dine together and smell fragrant flowers growing on the meadows which encircled the castle with incredible colours and, in the evenings, the Princess would play the harp, while Bunky would sit at her feet knitting a sweater as the proof of his undying love and devotion, for the sweater was meant to be worn by the Bunky Princess herself.*
>
> *On one such night Bunky Hippo and the Bunky Princess were sitting together on a beautiful terrace and Bunky was knit-ting vigorously, while the Princess was singing her enchanting songs. They took a moment to gaze at the sky in a romantic way and there they encountered the most charming spectacle! It was the night of Shooting Stars and they could see them flaring up and disappearing on the navy blue sky. The Princess sighed in delight! Suddenly, a dazzling Shooting Star brightened up the night and glided across the sky like an orange phoenix with yel-low wings!*

As you can see, Dear Readers, Bunky was writing partly from expe-rience (he saw the Shooting Star from his bedroom), what attests to his exquisite writing skills.

> *"Oh!" exclaimed the Bunky Princess in wonder, abandoning her harp and raising her hands towards the sky. Bunky also aban-doned his knitting and became speechless for a moment, but only for a moment, as Heroes such as Bunky always know what to say and how to act on unexpected occasions.*
>
> *"That was the most agreeable Shooting Star I have ever wit-nessed," said Bunky in a very elegant manner, putting emphasis on the word "agreeable" which, in his ears, sounded like the most suitable expression for the tender ears of his beloved. And truly, he loved the Princess's fluffy ears as well as her beautiful, noble heart!*
>
> *The phoenix-like Star began descending with a fiery speed. Bunky and the Princess watched her disappear behind the castle*

and the yellow trail of light slowly dispersed too. Not hesitating even for a moment, the chivalrous Bunky jumped to his feet and rushed to the backyard. The Bunky Princess was noble and courageous, therefore a thought of abandoning her beloved Bunky in such an exciting moment never crossed her mind. She carefully gathered her dress and followed her Hero in her tiny, glittering slippers.

The backyard was strewn with the most enchanting flowers which the Princess brought here from all over the world, including Snapdragons and Spider Flowers. At present, all the yellow Snapdragons and pink Spider Flowers were wide awake, curiously tilting their stems towards the yellow Daffodils growing nearby. In the middle of the flowerbed with yellow Daffodils there was something bright and flickering. It was the amazing Shooting Star which, a while ago, flew like a phoenix across the sky, high above Bunkyland!

. . . and here, Dear Readers, Bunky apparently resorted to his imagination, which is also a strong characteristic of exquisite writers! We can be reassured that he was a true writer, although not recognised by the world yet!

Bunky directed his swift steps towards this glittering spot and the Princess bravely followed him. They both experienced infinite warmth and peace coming from the Star. It felt like being wrapped up in the softest blanket or being in the most pleasant, happy dream. Bunky leant over to reach for the Star, but he felt that his paws were shaking and his steps were unsteady! His excitement was great, as it does not happen too often that a beautiful Shooting Star lands in the middle of a flowerbed. After a while and three deep breaths, he felt bunkyful and peaceful again and, finally, reached for the Star. He was doubly careful, as the Princess hoed and raked the flowerbed last week and he didn't want to spoil the final effect or trample over the yellow Daffodils. At last, Bunky victoriously raised his hand to show the world the Shooting Star. Oh, what a Star it was! The light it emitted cannot be described by any known words. Bunky reached for his pocket and found there a golden thread. Recently, as he took up knitting, his pockets were filled with colourful threads which he would use to bind off stitches. It hardly ever happens that one loves so much that he resorts to knitting and bravely undertakes such a strenuous exercise, yet Bunky was capable of this and not only of this—he already knew how to make knitting patterns! This easily explains why there were so many beautiful threads in his pocket.

Obviously, he selected the most beautiful one, matching the Star in colour and elegance.

After a minute or two, Bunky emerged from the flowerbed with the most beautiful necklace Bunkyland had ever seen: it was the phoenix-like Star on his golden thread! The Princess blushed gracefully and tears of joy appeared in her eyes. She was already very beautiful, inside and out, but the Star highlighted her qualities even more, making her the most beautiful and noble Princess in the entire universe. Whoever saw the Bunky Princess wearing the Shooting Star on the golden thread was immediately struck by an uncommon grace and tenderness coming from her heart. Her ears became even more fluffy, her step became even lighter and her heart filled with even more beauty. Such is the story of the Shooting Star brought to the noble Princess by her devoted Hero—Bunky Hippo.

Bunky sighed, finally putting down the pen. He was satisfied with his writing. Apparently, he thought, a literary masterpiece was born during these sleepless hours! Yet, suddenly, Bunky thought that he could have added something more about the curious Snapdragons and Spider Flowers which were so eager to see the Star. Inspired by his unlimited imagination, Bunky resumed his tale:

> *The Snapdragons and Spider Flowers gave a sigh of surprise and raised their petals towards the Star. They began dancing and swaying, as the Shooting Star made them feel happier than ever before, even though it was hardly possible to imagine a more joyous place than Bunkyland. After a while, they got tired and went back to sleep.*

The passage ended rather abruptly, but Bunky acknowledged that the above-mentioned Snapdragons and Spider Flowers where in the background of the story as mere supporting characters and did not require a lot of space in the novel to do their dancing and sleeping. In truth, he planned to devote the majority of pages to the Bunky Princess and himself.

After laying down his pen again, Bunky hid his priceless notebook underneath the bed, gently patted Plum who was fast asleep all this time, removed his dressing gown, neatly placing it on a nearby chair and, finally, went back to sleep. His heart was lighter than an hour or two ago and he fell asleep with ease.

૨♥

It only remains to be said what happened in Rodney Williams' room. Rodney could not sleep as well and, while aunt Walm had an impression that he was asleep, Rodney was wide awake, but very quiet and motionless. Wrapped up in warm, comforting sheets, he kept thinking intensely about his cousin Bunky. That he loved Bunky as if he was his brother, he had no doubt and he acutely felt his cousin's disappointment with the Christmas present. He loved his new bow—it mattered to him very little that he did not receive a toy or a mascot, since he received something so beautiful and precious! Everything that Rodney had ever received was precious to him because he never expected anything. He knew how to appreciate gifts but still, he understood Bunky's disappointment. Rodney thought about his piggy bank in uncle Bill and aunt Barbara's house and tried to remind himself how many coins he had managed to collect so far. Would it be enough for Bunky's skating boots? And then he thought about his cousin as a writer and he reflected on the story of the Bunky Princess. That Santa Claus received his letter in which he described the Bunky Princess, Rodney had no doubt too. What would be the result of it—he did not know, but he kept hoping. There was a lot of hope in his noble heart and with this hope he finally went back to sleep. He dreamt about Santa Claus waving at him, flying above Walmland in his magic sleigh.

Bunky woke up refreshed and energised. It was very early, around 7:00 a.m.

"Christmas!" thought Bunky in delight and then he remained himself about the cookbook, but it was no longer a gloomy thought.

"Cookbook!" Bunky tried to create an exhilarating thought in his mind and it did work.

He immediately left his bed, combed his beautiful, blue fur and got dressed in his favourite new sweater with the squirrel and snowflakes. A sudden thought crossed his mind that Plum must be awake and hungry. The guests were still fast asleep but, indeed, Plum was already awake: the basket was empty and the blankets resembled a maze.

Bunky put on his soft slippers and tiptoed to the living room in order to look for Plum. There he was, licking his paw underneath the Christmas tree! Just in few seconds, Plum jumped into Bunky's arms. He was already wearing his elegant bow. Bunky thought that Plum looked very handsome.

"How did you sleep, my dearest Plum?" inquired Bunky, patting Plum's soft, shiny fur. It was the most beautiful Wolf he had ever seen, with the most bluish eyes underneath the sun.

"Very, very well!" responded Plum softly, wagging his tail cheerfully, "I am so happy since the morning!" Indeed, this was the happiest morning of his life.

"Me too, my dear friend!" said Bunky sincerely, because grumpiness completely abandoned him. Last night the thought struck him that Plum was his best-ever-Christmas gift.

"I am so happy to have found you!" he exclaimed.

Throughout all his early life, Bunky had been longing for a pet to love and take care of and, now, his dream came true. Indeed, his dream came true on Christmas! Why should he fall into *bunky fits* of grumpiness over such a beautiful cookbook? Only today did he realise that it was the best

Christmas ever! Sometimes we don't realise such things immediately and it was so in Bunky's case. At last, he fully realised how fortunate he was.

"My precious Plum," said Bunky and placed his paw on the little Wolf's back.

They were in the same living room, but it was so different in Bunky's eyes, since today he was in a delightful mood. They were sitting in silence next to each other, looking through the terrace glass door as the new day was slowly beginning. At first, it was a subtle glitter of blue, then some stripes of pink and then the sun gloriously emerged on the horizon, painting frosty pavements all over Walmland with silvery sparks. Bunky and Plum were sitting quite motionless in complete silence and felt that something good began in their lives and that it was here to remain forever. Plum was still very little and Bunky knew that he would grow bigger. Bunky would be with him every day: he would be playing with him, conversing with him, measuring his growth by means of a mark left on the wall next to the front door, singing to him, brushing his fur, feeding him. Feeding him . . .

"Plum, but you must be so hungry!" exclaimed Bunky, reminding himself about this important fact and putting an end to the pleasant silence between them, but also beginning the fresh hope of breakfast. In order to grow bigger, Plum needed to eat. Bunky rushed to his bedroom and quickly returned with the cookbook. He no longer made wry faces on seeing this beautiful book.

"Now, let's go to the kitchen!" he said quietly, "I will surprise everyone with a delicious breakfast!"

He giggled quietly while thinking about it, and imagined how everyone would be wondering that a positive change came over Bunky in the course of the night. Bunkies are very expressive creatures and, perhaps, a little short-tempered, but they are persistently genuine and truthful when it comes to expressing their feelings.

When in the kitchen, Bunky curiously glanced at the cookbook. Today he found it pleasing to the eye and absorbing when read thoroughly. He donned an apron, vowing to make his uncle Walm proud. Plum nestled himself in a small armchair and admired Bunky's endeavours.

"*Potatoes in Tomatoes*," read Bunky, "Does it sound like a great breakfast meal?"

Plum doubtfully shook his head.

"Alright," agreed Bunky, "What about *Cheese Cupcakes with Chocolate Pralines and Freshly Gathered Cherries*?"

Bunky loved the idea of chocolate for breakfast, even though it was against aunt Walm's healthy beliefs.

"I am not sure," said Plum, "We do not have any freshly gathered cherries, do we?"

Bunky gazed through the kitchen window and saw leafless trees with trunks covered in snow.

"Uhm, not really," he estimated and then opened the fridge in hopes of finding there fresh fruit.

"Let's be serious! There are no cherries!" he said finally, actually addressing himself, "The recipe entitled *Scrambled Eggs with Mushrooms* and *Baked Winter Toasts* sounds just like what we are looking for!"

Before proceeding, Bunky warmed up some milk and poured it carefully into a blue stoneware bowl so that Plum could enjoy it in the meantime. Like all the inhabitants of Walmland, Plum the Wolf was a magical creature who loved milk and scrambled eggs. I know that his cousins from other places in the world would rather enjoy a steak or fillet, but Plum did great with milk and eggs.

"Abracadabra!" exclaimed Bunky while juggling ten eggs. He found an enormous frying pan in one of aunt Walm's cupboards and discovered mushrooms stored in the fridge.

"This frying pan allows one to easily prepare the biggest possible family breakfast just in one step!" he observed.

Once in a studious pose with his nose in the cookbook, and once leaning over the frying pan as an experienced cook would do, cautiously checking the heat to prevent the meal from burning, Bunky was immensely enjoying his work. The final result almost resembled what was expected from the recipe or, to be honest, the final result was something much better than what was expected:

"Oh dear!" exclaimed Bunky, "I think we ended up with an *Omelette with Mushrooms* instead of the *Scrambled Eggs with Mushrooms*!"

And then Bunky found out that he missed one line from the recipe advising to "mix eggs before pouring them onto the frying pan."

"How lucky that I missed this step!" rejoiced Bunky, as he didn't want to look like someone who failed, "Now we have a huge, delicious omelette instead of the scrambled eggs! I think that the omelette is more nutritious for such a wintry morning!"

Plum raised his head from the bowl with milk and licked his own nose.

"Yes!" he exclaimed, "I'd love an omelette! It must be soooo delicious!"

Poor Plum! You must realise, Dear Readers, what a big change it was for him! How could he ever sniff at omelettes? From a homeless creature squatting underneath a bush on a cold night, he became a fully-fledged member of the Walms' family—their dearest little Wolf and Bunky's best friend! He loved omelettes, scrambled eggs and everything that was offered to him, but the most of all he loved Bunky and his family.

"My dear Plum," said Bunky, kissing him on the soft forehead, for he suspected how Plum felt inside. Bunky knew that he would always protect Plum and stand by him with all his *bunky* heart. He also felt very, very proud of Plum. And he was very, very responsible. Aunt Walm knew that quite well when she emphasised that caring for another creature is the greatest responsibility of one's life.

"My little Plum," continued Bunky, "Now I shall carve the omelette and wake up our family and guests."

He carefully climbed a little kitchen ladder and opened a cabinet where he found white plates with pink roses—Mrs. Walm's favourite ones. Soon, he climbed down, put the ladder aside and divided the omelette into even portions while counting all the guests and members of his family.

"One, two, three, four, five . . ..," counted Bunky and then, suddenly, he heard steps.

These were the steps of someone sleepy; someone wearing cosy slippers shuffling on the floor. The door opened and . . . it was no one else but uncle Walm! He stopped in the door and looked at the scene in the kitchen, wondering for a moment that he might be dreaming. Bunky, dressed in his uncle's apron, grinned from ear to ear and Plum wagged his tail.

"Oh my little ones!" smiled uncle Walm, "And yet, at last, you did follow in my footsteps!"

"Yes uncle, we prepared a huge family omelette!" grinned Bunky victoriously.

Tears of joy appeared in uncle Walm's eyes.

"I've been always hoping that you would share some of my interests," said uncle Walm and grinned as widely as Bunky, "Now, what a surprise!"

"Yes, surprise!" exclaimed Bunky, swirling around the kitchen like a snowflake, since he was very happy at heart.

Plum left the armchair and kept swirling around the kitchen with Bunky and soon uncle Walm joined them too. Dancing and prancing around, they moved from the kitchen to the living room and laid the table for breakfast. It wasn't long before the rest of the family and guests gathered in the living room, still sleepy but greatly surprised that such a delicious meal was already waiting for them! The ancestors mysteriously smiled at Bunky from their portraits.

"My little Bunky prepared today's breakfast together with our Plum!" exclaimed uncle Walm, beaming from ear to ear and proudly pointing at the omelette.

"I really knew that Bunky will eventually follow in your footsteps!" rejoiced aunt Barbara with a glitter in her eyes.

"I am so proud, so proud!" kept repeating overjoyed uncle Walm.

Indeed, this morning there was nothing taster under the sun than Bunky's omelette and his baked toasts! Bunky's misfortune—the transformation of scrambled eggs into an omelette—turned out to be an unprecedented success. Happy little Plum enjoyed his omelette in blissful silence, sitting on a stool next to Bunky's chair.

"Delicious! Exquisite!" praised the omelette Sir Williams in his sophisticated way and these were important words because he was the owner of a well-known restaurant! Rodney sat close to his cousin and pressed Bunky's paw in a friendly manner.

"Cousin Bunky," he whispered, "I am so proud of you and so happy for you today! It seems that the cookbook was a good idea after all! Merry Christmas!"

"Merry Christmas!" smiled Bunky and embraced Rodney with his left arm and Plum with the right one.

"Smile, everyone!" exclaimed Mrs. Walm, entering the living room with a camera. But everyone was already smiling. "One, two, three! What a delightful photograph!"

"We will place it next to the portraits of our ancestors," decided Mr. Walm with a sparkle in his eye. His joy was so great that he kept telling jokes to Sir Williams through all the morning.

"Merry Christmas, everyone!" shouted uncle Bill, raising his mug with tea.

"Merry Christmas!" responded a cheerful choir of voices and everyone raised their mugs.

Tea was a favourite drink of all inhabitants of Walmland. Bunky raised his mug for both himself and Plum. He felt blissful at heart. How nice it was to be good and kind. Acting quite mysteriously, he left the table and placed a piece of omelette next to the Mouse Hole.

"Merry Christmas, little *Mouses!*" he whispered.

And the entire day would pass in such a blissful, carefree manner, if not an event which slightly distracted the Hero of this story—that is, our Bunky Hippo. It is difficult to be good all year round and it is not always easy to be generous and loving, especially when there are trying moments . . .

Just after breakfast, Bunky wrapped himself up in a scarf, put on his winter boots, found his blue mittens and sneaked out of the house for a brief, solitary walk. On this special Christmas morning he intended to think about the Bunky Princess in the bliss of solitude. At first, he had to walk through the busy street of Walmland. Many inhabitants of Walmland were out and about now, giggling, walking, jumping, and exchanging Christmas wishes. There were lanterns decorated with Christmas wreaths and the sky was so blue and clear. This colour reminded Bunky of his precious Plum and his deep blue eyes. Plum and Rodney stayed at home in order to pre-pare a Christmas play and they were patiently awaiting Bunky's return.

Bunky directed his steps towards the Walmlane. He passed Sir Wil-liams' famous restaurant and turned right. After a few further steps, he entered a park where nightly frost decorated trees with white garlands and diamond-like icicles. Although it was a cold morning, the landscape was heart-warming. Bunky giggled and looked around. The pond was nearby and Bunky could hear the laugher of skaters. He turned in that direction and soon the pond appeared in front of his eyes. There, among sprightly skaters, Bunky saw his neighbours from the living room: Mrs. Mouse and Mr. Mouse were pulling the snow-white skating boots, while the little Mice were sitting inside them, enjoying their ride on the frozen surface of the pond, waving their tiny hands in the air and loudly cheering "whohoo!".

It was a charming and exhilarating scene, but not for Bunky's eyes. He grunted and headed back home. All the romantic thoughts abandoned his mind, giving way to those less generous thoughts concerning the skating boots.

"Unfair!" growled Bunky while mincing through the snow. But was it really so or only in his mind?

While Bunky was gloomily walking back towards home, aunt Walm was having a secret conversation with uncle Walm. They went outside and hid behind the Snowman in order to discuss a "very important issue," as aunt Walm called it.

"I think," began aunt Walm with concern in her voice, "that we need to buy our Bunky skating boots."

"I am of the same opinion," agreed uncle Walm, "He was very upset on the night before Christmas and I know that he had been dreaming about skating boots all year long! However, the cookbook was an excellent idea as well!"

"Of course, it was an ingenious idea!" instantly agreed aunt Walm, "But I will go to the city tomorrow and try to find skates for Bunky. It will be our secret."

"Yes, yes," chimed in uncle Walm, "But then, shall we get some gifts for everyone too? Something small, so that no one will feel left out?"

"Absolutely," agreed aunt Walm, "And I will buy you those beautiful cotton gloves for the kitchen! The ones with Christmas patterns!"

"Please find something nice for yourself too!" insisted uncle Walm and felt that, indeed, he would love to have those new kitchen gloves with Christmas patterns.

And this is how the conversation continued behind the Snowman who, once again, became an involuntary witness of mysterious events.

In this moment the front gate opened and Bunky appeared.

"Hello!" said uncle Walm on seeing Bunky, "How was the walk?"

"It was . . .," Bunky kept searching for the right word in order not to reveal his rather gloomy mood.

"It was good!" he said finally, keeping a brave face, "Many skaters are there around the pond!"

"Our Mice also went out to skate!" observed the unsuspecting uncle Walm. Aunt Walm gave him a strange look.

"That is the reason why I returned," answered Bunky quite honestly.

He noiselessly opened the front door and went straight towards his room, hoping not to meet anyone on the way. In a gloomy fit, Bunky threw himself on bed and remained there angry and motionless for half a minute. After that, he decided that throwing tantrums was pointless and that there should be a different way of dealing with such feelings. After this sensible reasoning, Bunky bravely got up and decided to do some outdoor exercises in order to let go of his frustration. He still remembered about his

Christmas promise to remain as good and kind as possible. Bunky's efforts and his heroic inner struggles should be admired by us, the Readers, who are quite often less than perfect in our own resolutions (the Authoress of this book including).

In short, Bunky got up and opened the door of his bedroom. He immediately encountered Rodney and Plum who, not knowing anything about Bunky's inner struggles, were just planning to knock on his bedroom door. They were both wearing the new bows. Bunky also noticed that Rodney held a basket filled with colourful fabrics.

"Oh cousin Bunky, we are preparing costumes for our Christmas play!" squealed Rodney excitedly. Plum immediately began wagging his tail and looked at Bunky with his big, loving eyes. He was always so happy on seeing Bunky.

"That is so amazing!" said Bunky, who had no heart to throw tantrums in front of his precious Rodney and Plum. He already decided that throwing himself on bed just because the Mice were skating on ice was entirely stupid.

"Yes, it is all *so* exciting!" admitted Plum, for whom it was the first true Christmas of his life.

Bunky's heart melted on seeing his happiness. As it was already indicated in this story, Bunkies are very expressive creatures who completely follow their hearts and emotions. Whatever is there, in Bunky's heart, will definitely influence his mood. On seeing Plum's joy, Bunky forgot all about his gloomy thoughts and grinned with genuine pleasure.

"Cousin Bunky," continued Rodney ardently, "would you like to appear in our Christmas play as one of the actors?"

"By all means!" responded Bunky courteously. How could he ever make these two unhappy even on such a bleak day as the one on which the Mice were riding in his skating boots?

"Cousin Bunky, would you like to be the Christmas Star? It is the most important role in the play!" squealed Rodney.

Bunky was stunned, but only for a short moment.

"Absolutely!" he answered, "I would be so happy! What am I supposed to do?"

"Oh!" rejoiced Rodney, "You will be a very, very happy Star which shines joyfully on Christmas night! Plum and I will prepare your costume!"

Bunky wondered for a moment what it could actually mean to perform as a *very, very happy* Star and also, most possibly, in front of the Mice, but decided that he could bravely deal with it. Of one thing he was sure: he loved the Mice. They were his neighbours for so many years, since his early bunkyhood when he was a toddler. Back then the Mice were toddlers too and they were all playing together in the living room, all of them wearing nappies and not having a care in the world. Yes, he loved the Mice, cared for them and wished them well. But it wasn't about them—it was about Bunky's dream and this dream was out of reach. Anyway, what was the importance of skating boots if the Bunky Princess wasn't here? Well, he could have practised in the meantime—until the glorious day of her arrival! Then, he could show her his skating skills! She would be impressed and, perhaps, she would fall in love with him. Bunky thought about this possible future day and decided to be brave.

"Dear cousin, do you agree?" asked Rodney.

"Please, dear Bunky, please agree!" howled Plum and it was a very pleasant, friendly howl.

"I'm in," said Bunky without a shadow of hesitation, imaging himself as a *very, very happy* Christmas star and the Mice clapping their hands after his *very happy* performance.

"What are your roles?" he asked.

"Well," said Rodney with a mysterious smile, "the play is entitled *The Christmas Star meets a Snowflake and an Angel*, so I am this Snowflake and Plum is the Angel."

Bunky thought that it was a curious idea, but he could not disagree: indeed, Plum was his little angel. His true Christmas gift.

"Do you have the script?" he inquired.

"We are working on it," said Rodney, "Will you join us, Cousin?"

"Yes, absolutely! I will be back just in a while!" agreed Bunky.

"Oh, you are here, children!" said aunt Walm, who was just passing by with a huge soup tureen with reindeer patterns, "Sir Williams, Mr. Elk, and Mr. Meow will be back here in the afternoon and we will have a very special Christmas dinner with carols and Christmas stories. But your Christmas play will be the highlight of the day!"

"Hooray!" squealed Rodney, waving the script in the air, "Bunky will play our happy Christmas Star!"

"Oh, that is so lovely!" smiled aunt Walm, "Merry Christmas, children!"

"Merry Christmas!" cheerfully responded Bunky, Rodney, and Plum.

"I will join you in a while," Bunky repeated his promise.

Rodney and Plum ran to the living room, while he remained in his bedroom. Only now did he realise that he was still wearing boots. The snow from the boots turned into two small paddles. Bunky looked at the paddles with disapproval and cleaned the floor with a piece of cloth. After that, he went outside, instinctively feeling that being outside would help him to feel better, so that he could return to Rodney and Plum with all the Christmas cheer he had in his bunky soul. After all, Christmas was always his favourite time of the year. He began rolling a snowball, running in circles around the house. Mrs. Walm looked curiously through the kitchen window.

"What is our little Bunky doing?" she asked Mr. Walm.

Mr. Walm joined her in the window, following Bunky with his eyes.

"I think that he is rolling a snowball," he aptly concluded.

"Why is he running so fast?" wondered aunt Walm.

"Perhaps," said uncle Walm, "it has to do with the skating boots. If you are frustrated or sad about something, it is the best way to fight off such a feeling."

"Oh," said aunt Walm, "Our mature Bunky!"

Bunky finally got tired. In fact, he rolled two big snowballs and, eventually, built another Snowman. In a while, the two Snowmen were standing next to each other in front of the living room window.

"Now you will have company," said Bunky, patting the first Snowman on his arm. He felt exhausted but also peaceful at heart. He whistled a well-known Christmas tune from Walmland, *The Snow is Dancing*, while his mind was preoccupied once again with beautiful, noble thoughts concerning the Bunky Princess.

This time Bunky entered the house triumphantly, without any grumpiness or frustration, and triumphantly took off his boots without creating paddles.

"My little Bunky!" started aunt Walm who, miraculously, was passing by again, this time in the vicinity of the hall, "How was it outside? Did you build another Snowman?"

Aunt Walm was also similar to other aunts, mums and grandmothers in this respect that she would always mysteriously appear in those places where she was needed the most. In truth, aunt Walm hoped to learn whether Bunky felt better.

"Yes, dear aunt," said Bunky cheerfully, "It is very nice outside and I thought that our Snowman needs some company!"

Aunt Walm estimated that Bunky finally sounded like himself.

"How thoughtful of you! You managed to build such a huge Snowman on your own!" she continued, "You must be very tired!"

"Oh, aunt!" said Bunky, "I am not tired! I mean, it is not that I experience any tiredness which would exhaust me. I feel much better inside!"

"It is always a good idea to resort to outdoor activities in order to feel better," observed aunt Walm and winked at Bunky.

"Yes, aunt."

"What is your plan for the rest of the day, my dear?"

"I will be helping Rodney and Plum to prepare our Christmas play!"

"Oh yes, my little Christmas Star!" smiled aunt and kissed Bunky on his forehead, "In the meantime, uncle Walm, uncle Bill, aunt Barbara, and I will finish our dinner preparations, so that we will be ready for the arrival of our guests!"

"And the *Mouses*?" asked Bunky meekly, "Did they return from the pond?"

"Yes, I do think so," replied his aunt, adopting a seemingly indifferent tone of voice, "I think they are back in their Mouse Hole, probably warming themselves up!"

"Did they get cold?" worried Bunky, as his better feelings entirely took hold of him.

"No, my dear, surely they will be alright," promised aunt Walm, "I gave them a couple of little towels. The towels were pleasantly warm from ironing and the Mice will be alright! If only you saw their happy faces after skating!"

"Oh, I saw them skating!" admitted Bunky, blushing secretly under his blue fur, "And . . ."

"And . . .?"

" . . . and I am very happy for them," said Bunky courageously. Indeed, he was. At present, he was only a little upset about the skating boots. But, as Bunky discovered in his heart, his disappointment had nothing to do with the Mice themsleves.

"Please join Rodney and Plum. They must be waiting for you!" smiled aunt Walm and then she leant over and whispered in Bunky's ear, "Uncle Walm and I are so proud of you. We realise that feelings are often quite complex."

Bunky looked at his aunt and offered her a loving, bunkyful hug.

6

The Northern Star Asks to be Followed and Bunky Becomes a Hero

"*I'm dancing around, swirling up high, so high in the sky that I've met an An-gel!*" sang Rodney the Snowflake with his tiny voice and began swirling across the living room towards Plum the Angel, who howled melodically:

"*I'm dancing in heavens on Christmas Day, encountered the Snowflake so tiny and white! We went together for a morning flight! Hey ho! We went together for a morning flight!*"

And then Plum the Angel shook himself off in order to move his paper wings designed by Rodney. This way Plum the Angel looked as if he was really flying, just like the song professed. Bunky was a proud co-author of the script. At present, he appeared in the middle of the living room, mysteriously emerging from behind the curtain, dressed in a costume created from a yellow cardboard box. He unexpectedly performed a pirouette and kept spinning gracefully around the room, finally jumping on the table to perform his part (this time aunt Walm allowed him to do so, but only this time). The audience, including aunt and uncle Walm, aunt Barbara, uncle Bill, Sir Williams, and the Mice, followed Bunky's moves with excitement. Everybody loved annual Christmas plays and even aunt Walm could make allowances for such frightful activities as jumping on the table.

"*Falala!*" began Bunky, "*I am the happy Christmas Star! Whom do I see coming my way? These are the Angel and the Snowflake—how lucky they are, for I have some cake for them up here on Christmas night! How lucky for them to meet me tonight, the very happy Christmas Star!*"

"*Look!*" squealed Rodney the Snowflake, assuming a look of surprise and addressing his winged companion, Plum the Angel, "*The happy Christmas Star! Oh joy, we reached our destination and now it is Christmas!*"

Plum jumped happily in response to Rodney's speech and his wings rustled.

"*Welcome, weary travellers!*" announced Bunky the Christmas Star looking at them from the table, "*Now we shall feast together, dance, and sing joyfully, for it is Christmas and Christmas is only once a year! We have a chocolate cake, warm buns with honey, and raspberry tea! All this is here ready for thee!*"

Thus saying, Bunky hopped off the table (to aunt Walm's great relief) and approached the piano.

"Bravo!" cheered the audience and they began clapping hands.

Bunky was glad that the play was turning into a success. While gracefully dancing through the room towards the piano, he saw the Mice jumping up and down, clapping their tiny hands too. Apparently, the Mice were greatly enjoying the play. At present, they were rooting for Bunky's piano performance. Bunky felt warm sparks of joy rushing through his heart and yet, at the same time, the skating boots came back to his mind so very, very strongly. . . .. This persistent thought overwhelmed Bunky for a moment and frustration gathered somewhere around his paws and feet. Bunkies are very emotional creatures and no one can help it. Bunky immediately recognised this dangerous feeling and decided to fight it off in a truly heroic way.

"No, no, no to being angry!" he thought, "The *Mouses* are dear, dear creatures!"

He sat at the piano in his star-like cardboard attire and hit the keys with a double force. It was definitely much stronger than necessary and rather unexpected. The audience got startled for a moment, but everyone attributed this untypical beginning to Bunky's artisitic manner of self-expression.

"*Falalalala, lala, lala!*" yelled Bunky and then, feeling that frustration abandoned him as soon as he hit the keys, he decided to improve his performance and repeated the whole scene as if nothing had happened, this time more gently and cheerfully: "*Falalalala, lala, lala!*" After that, Bunky performed another graceful pirouette, finally joined by Rodney the Snowflake and Plum the Angel who were meant to perform a special Christmas dance. Mr. Elk and Mr. Meow, so far hiding behind the piano, emerged from behind the instrument. In the play they were meant to perform the part of the Choir and began singing *"ding dong, ding dong,"* while the remaining actors were swirling around the piano. Finally, Mr. Elk played a carol, accompanied by Mr. Meow's exquisite voice.

"Bravo!" cheered the audience.

Rodney, Plum, and Bunky bowed and smiled. Bunky felt happy again, with not a single bad feeling in his bunky heart. He hugged Rodney and Plum and shook hands with Mr. Elk and Mr. Meow. He also looked around the room in order to spot the Mice and realised that they placed a miniature bench next to their hole under the Christmas tree. At present, they were all jumping on the bench, cheering with their tiny voices. Bunky carefully crept underneath the Christmas tree. In order to do it, he had to release himself from his cardboard costume.

"Hello *Mouses*," he said, "I wanted to thank you for rooting for us and watching the play. Will you have Christmas dinner with us?"

On saying this, Bunky felt light as a feather—light at heart and free of any troubling thoughts. He returned to the table, gently caring the Mice and their bench in his paws. Aunt Walm immediately offered them a very special dinnerware which she received together with a doll house many years ago when she was as little as Bunky in this story. The elegant Mice donned their bows and feasted in the middle of the table, while all the other guests dined in a circle around them.

It was the most pleasant evening ever, Bunky thought. Finally, he was fully reconciled with the Mice. "I will look for some nice shoelaces to decorate their skating boots," thought Bunky generously.

There was plenty of laughter and joy at the table, just as it should be during Christmas dinners. Sir Williams, the most talkative this evening, shared a story about his uncle, Sir Laurent, whom he was planning to call with Christmas wishes just after the dinner. Sir Laurent, Sir Williams explained, could never visit him for Christmas for the two important reasons: firstly, he lived in the remotest part of Walmland in the Snowy Chocolate Hill County and, secondly, it would be quite impossible for him to travel, as he owned a farm full of Alpacas. He and his wife, Lady Octavia, had one hundred beautiful, fluffy Alpacas with pointed ears who needed constant care and attention. Sir Williams imagined Lady Octavia and Sir Laurent having a special dinner with their Alpacas, since they treated the Alpacas as the closest family. On Christmas morning, there would be a long table placed in front of the house—as long as a diameter of the entire farm—and Lady Octavia would lay the table, placing on it the most exquisite cutlery and the most charming mistletoe. All the Alpacas would be wearing red Christmas scarves, having tea and singing a Christmas song in a harmonious choir.

Sir Laurent and Lady Octavia made the Snowy Chocolate Hill County famous for their Alpacas and Christmas sweaters. Once a year, on the first day of summer, Sir Laurent and Lady Octavia would gently trim their Alpacas' fur. Not only did it allow the Alpacas to feel refreshed and beautiful, but also allowed Sir Laurent and Lady Octavia to gather wool for their famous sweaters. The earnings from the sale of the sweaters were dedicated to the Alpacas. Oh, what a cheerful company they were, the Alpacas, Sir Laurent and Lady Octavia!, Sir Williams remarked. Sir Williams' imagination would often get the better of him. However, Dear Readers, we have some strong basis to believe him this time. They all listened to Sir Williams most attentively, musing over the cheerful Alpacas and Lady Octavia's silverware.

Bunky listened while supporting his chin with both paws. He was already dreaming about singing in a choir with the Alpacas and knitting these special Christmas sweaters in a warm, cosy barn, but then he thought about Plum the Wolf and the soft Christmas sweater with the squirrel which he had received from his aunt. It donned on him that his life was exactly the best one for him and that he should never compare it with other persons' lives.

"Every Bunky in the world has the best personal story," thought Bunky, quite truthfully.

"Since he cannot come here to pay you a visit, why don't you visit your uncle next Christmas?" uncle Walm inquired.

"Well," answered Sir Williams, "I would be dearly missing all of you here."

In truth, it was impossible to be in the Snowy Chocolate Hill County and in the Walmland Village at the same time. The distance between these two places amounted to one day of travel by car or twelve days of travel on camel's back, whichever option you prefer. It would be probably a little faster to reach the County in a hot-air-balloon, but Sir Williams did not possess one.

"Is it possible for your uncle to visit us in the company of his Alpacas?" inquired tiny Miss Mouse in a faintly voice. She was very curious about the Alpacas too.

The family of Mice was currently feasting on the delicious grapes which aunt Walm bought for this special occasion in a local grocery store.

"Well," wondered Sir Williams, "Where would the Alpacas stay?"

"We would have to build a barn!" Bunky interjected.

"A barn, a barn!" squealed little Rodney and Plum wagged his tail.

"I could try!" offered uncle Walm for whom nothing was impossible and, conversely, anything was possible.

"Well, one hundred Alpacas need a lot of space," observed aunt Walm, slightly worrying about the possible final effect of this project.

Finally, it was agreed that the barn project would be postponed. Sir Williams was offered a telephone and he quickly dialled the number. He knew his uncle's telephone number by heart. He also remembered all his cousins' and distant relatives' telephone numbers. Sir Williams memorised all the important phone numbers in such an easy way as you and I memorise multiplication table. He would often practise his memory, untiringly memorising recipes, designing sophisticated shopping lists and solving most complicated crosswords whenever he had some free time. Similarly to our Bunky, he also held a precious secret—Sir Williams was a budding author of the yet unknown book which he entitled: *A Full and Detailed Guide to The Perfect Life of An Old Bachelor.* He had spent at his desk many sleepless nights—too many, in truth. Sitting comfortably among his shopping lists and *Walmland Cooks* magazines, Sir Williams had been writing and writing, describing the perfect routine of his daily life and offering invaluable advice to other bachelors whose life routine wasn't that perfect and needed correction. He was aware that self-improvement books grew in popularity and hoped to find a publisher who would appreciate his work—with some luck, it could hopefully happen after Christmas, he thought while reaching for the telephone kindly handed over to him by aunt Walm.

"Children, Sir Williams will be talking with his uncle, so please try not to disturb him for a while," aunt Walm announced.

The Mice, Plum, and Rodney were giggling quite loudly, laughing at Bunky's joke. At this point Bunky completely abandoned any resentful thoughts towards the Mice. On hearing aunt Walm's request, they became quiet.

"We will be drawing," offered Rodney, "Plum, would you like to draw with me?"

"Let's draw ourselves!" Plum rejoiced.

"That's an amazing thought!"

"We will be skating!" giggled the Mice quietly and left the table on aunt Walm's shoulder.

"I will be writing," said Bunky Hippo cautiously and quietly withdrew to his room. There, he reached for the secret blue notebook and made himself comfortable at the desk. Bunky and Sir Williams shared a similar secret.

However, Bunky didn't write for fame or fortune. He didn't care about offering others his advice. All he ever wanted was to keep daydreaming about the Bunky Princess. It was *his* story written on the pages of *his* notebook. *His* secret shared only with his important cousin Rodney.

Rodney followed Bunky out of the room with his soft, friendly eyes. "Oh, I hope that Santa Claus answers my letter!" he thought.

> *The noble Hero, Bunky Hippo, was sitting on the terrace at the Princess's feet, diligently knitting a wondrous sweater when, out of the blue, he felt a light gust of the western wind. It surprised him, as usually the wind in Bunkyland was coming from the south. The gentle Bunky Princess raised her eyes and looked up into the sky. She had been preparing a fragrant garland for her beloved Hero, having daises and herbs gathered all around her. On her neck glittered the most glorious Shooting Star of Bunkyland heavens—the most precious gem attesting to Bunky's love and deepest devotion.*

Here Bunky Hippo raised his pen and thought for a moment. When the moment passed, he continued in the following manner:

> *She raised her eyes towards the sky and exclaimed: "Oh! Can it be true?"*
> *Bunky Hippo the Hero sprang to his agile feet and bravely faced the sky with eyes as sharp as those of a hawk.*

"Lo and behold![1]" said Bunky in a romantic way.

(It appeared to Bunky that such an expression would be considered romantic. Then he decided to make a slight correction and continued:)

> *"Lo and behold!" ~~said~~ exclaimed Bunky in a~ THE MOST romantic way, "Isn't it the Dragon of Bunkyland himself? He is the one who brought the western wind!"*
> *"Indeed," answered the Princess, ready to faint, but Bunky caught her just in the right moment. He placed her comfortably in a rocking chair standing nearby on the terrace and reassured her that the Dragon was no cause for alarm. It was, Bunky said, just another flying creature, just like a butterfly. The Bunky Princess began fanning herself frantically with an elegant, lacy*

1. It is a very old and sophisticated phrase which introduces a new major event; for example, the appearance of the Dragon of Bunkyland.

fan, while Bunky the Hero ventured out into the front yard with a frown on his noble forehead.

"Mr. Dragon!" he addressed the Dragon, "Come down here and let's talk!"

The Dragon heard Bunky's thundering voice and obeyed his order.

"Oh noble Hero, why are you raging?" he meekly inquired.

"We shall fight," said Bunky and his voice made the treetops shake.

The Dragon looked flabbergasted[2].

"Oh Bunky the Hero, don't you see that I am perfectly culti-vated? Is there anything uncouth about me?"

Now it was Bunky's turn to look a little gobsmacked[3], but his noble heart told him to admit the truth.

"No," he confessed, "You are a perfectly cultivated Dragon. Please accept my apologies, oh Mr. Dragon!"

On saying this, Bunky stopped frowning and his face as-sumed a friendly expression.

"I came here," continued the noble Dragon, "to search for the protection of the Hero and the Bunky Princess. I came to Bunky-land from Dragonland where life wasn't easy and I hoped to find peace and safety here."

"I am the Hero of Bunkyland!" said Bunky, "You may al-ready feel safe and protected."

Here Bunky stopped writing and, after a moment of reflec-tion, added an adjective:

"I am the Hero of Bunkyland!" said Bunky MODESTLY, "You may already feel safe and protected."

"Thank you, oh generous Hero of Bunkyland!" said Mr. Dragon gratefully.

"How do they call you and why was your life in Dragonland uneasy?" Bunky the Hero inquired, completely putting aside his grim looks in exchange for his warmest smile.

"My name is Maurice," explained Mr. Dragon, "I am a book-worm and nothing offers me more joy than reading. Meanwhile, in Dragonland, my cousins are all interested in flying competi-tions and dragonlike-type of activities, such as collecting golden necklaces in caves or roaring in the evenings in order to practise

2. Very, very astonished!

3. Stunned and amazed!

> *their voices. They made fun of my reading habit, but I can't help being sentimental!⁴"*
>
> *"I am also very sentimental!" reassured him Bunky the Hero, "We are very sentimental here and you will be one of us. Here you will be able to read daily as much as you please, as long as you will allow the Bunky Princess to pet you!"*
>
> *"I would be the happiest of Dragons!" admitted Maurice, wagging his dragon tail like a dog, "I especially enjoy reading sentimental stories with good endings."*
>
> *Meanwhile, the Bunky Princess got up from the rocking chair and bravely approached them, as she never hesitated to accompany her Hero in the most turbulent moments. She heard the entire conversation. She placed her delicate hands on Maurice's green head and patted him gently.*

Here Bunky stopped writing again and bit the pen. Mrs. Walm would disapprove of biting pens. Bunky crossed out the word "green" and began thinking about a word more suitable for a grand literary text.

She placed her delicate hands on Maurice's ~~green~~ emerald head and patted him gently.—wrote Bunky and felt that he managed to sustain in this way the poetic flow of his thoughts.

> *"Welcome to Bunkyland, dear Maurice," she said melodically, her words forming a soothing song. Maurice bowed his head and roared happily. In fact, he purred happily like a cat but, because he was a dragon, it sounded like a roar. Then the Bunky Princess addressed Bunky in the following words: "My Hero." Bunky the Hero felt dizzy from joy. These were, apparently, the best days of his life. Maurice offered to take them for a flight and, in a moment, they were admiring the whole Bunkyland from above! The castle looked like a gleaming pearl on a green meadow . . .*

. . . on an OLIVE ~~green~~ meadow . . .—corrected himself Bunky the writer, in order to avoid repetitions . . .

4. A "sentimental" person is someone guided by feelings; someone who loves thinking about the past and enjoys watching romantic sunsets!

. . . and they felt gentle gusts of wind running through their fur. Only from above one could see the true majesty and excellence of Bunkyland, with its abundant forests and rosebushes scattered in clumps among sandy roads leading to such beautiful places as Bunkyland golden beaches and Bunkyland dreamy hills. They were so close to the sun that Bunky the Hero suddenly thought to break off two of its rays and offer them to the Princess in the form of earrings, but he abandoned this thought, realising how ugly the sun would be without its two missing rays. He also understood that the sun was dangerously hot. He closed his eyes and thought how happy he was. It all began on the day when he ventured out from behind the bush to reveal himself to the Bunky Princess as Bunky the Hero . . .

From that day, the Bunky Princess and Bunky the Hero were taking care of Maurice as if he was their dearest pet. They looked after him in the same way one looks after a beloved cat, dog, or guinea pig. The Bunky Princess would pet him and comb him lovingly every morning, and Bunky the Hero would pace the endless meadows and forests of Bunkyland in his company, teaching him the game of throw and fetch, playing football together and preparing for him delightful bubble baths. Maurice would eat delicious blueberries, bananas, and waffles with cream—his favourite desserts. The rest of the day he would spend while sitting on a local tree, invariably holding in his paws a new book which he would find in the Princess's vast library.

"What are you reading today, Maurice?" they would ask him while passing nearby the tree and Maurice would always tell them that it was a sentimental story with a very happy ending.

While he was reading, the Bunky Princess and Bunky the Hero would stroll around the garden and talk about all the important and fascinating matters, predominantly including dinosaurs. Snapdragons, Daffodils, and pink Spider Flowers would gaze at them in a mysterious silence and then they would stretch their petals towards the warm sun. Bunky the Hero felt that the Bunky Princess was his soulmate.

ॐ

Bunky yawned and put a full stop at the end of the last sentence. He closed his notebook and safely stored it underneath his bed. Bunky yawned not because he was bored of writing—not at all, he was delighted just thinking about this literary masterpiece!—but rather because he put a lot of mental effort into this work. Yawning is not always a sign of boredom but often a sign of a great mental effort.

"Sir Williams must have finished his phone conversation by now," Bunky thought and returned to the living room.

Indeed, the phone conversation was over, as Sir Williams, Mr. Elk, and Mr. Meow were sitting on the floor in a circle, deeply engaged in a game of pick-up sticks. Aunt Barbara lit a fire in the fireplace and the room immediately filled with warmth. She had left the house with uncle Bill a few minutes ago in order to take a walk to the pond and back and visit the festive-looking centre of the Walmland Village. Bunky looked at his aunt and uncle. They were reading the local newspaper, *Echoes of Walmland*.

"Look, cousin Bunky!" squealed Rodney, waving in his paw a piece of paper filled with colourful drawings.

Plum's ears perked up on hearing Bunky's name. Bunky curiously glanced at the drawing. It presented his likeness in a sledge rushing down a white slope with two figures by his side who looked like Rodney and Plum.

"It's delightful!" said Bunky, offering a hug to Rodney and Plum.

"Let's do it!" squealed Rodney, looking at Bunky pleadingly, "Let's go on a sleigh ride just like the one in the picture!"

What would be a better day for a sleigh ride! The sledge was located in uncle Walm's shed where he kept and collected gardening tools, drills, screws, spades, shovels, rakes, ladders, and everything else uncles keep in such places. Thanks to collecting All the Possible Useful Objects, uncle Walm could easily repair Anything in the World that would ever need repairing or simply use a ladder to decorate the highest spruce in the neighbourhood with a merry Christmas star.

"Oh!" exclaimed little Plum on seeing all the tools collected in the shed and immediately took a liking to gardening. He would like to plant some herbs and primroses in the spring, he thought. He was wrapped up in a brown poncho with the reindeer pattern. It was aunt Walm's idea, who wanted Plum to stay warm.

"Here is the sledge!" exclaimed Bunky triumphantly, spotting the very object in the corner of the shed next to a wheelbarrow. Bunky's attire consisted of his beloved sweater with the squirrel among cotton snowflakes, a warm, woollen scarf, his favourite pair of blue mittens and warm winter boots.

"Hooray!" squealed Rodney, dressed in a thick, woollen sweater with brown and yellow stripes. He was stepping from one foot to another in the highest excitement of somebody preparing for a sleigh ride on Christmas day.

Bunky stepped into the shed and moved the wheelbarrow aside in order to reach the sledge. It was dusted and covered with cobwebs, so they had to use a piece of cloth to bring the sledge to its former glory. It had a wooden seat and silvery skids. The rope attached to the sledge was of a faded red colour. The sledge had been in the Walms family for many years, since the day Bunky was born. Or, perhaps, not for so many years, if we assume that Bunky was still *very* little. Today, the sledge looked somewhat smaller in his eyes. He took a step back and glanced at it suspiciously. The same strange feeling crossed Rodney's mind. They looked at each other questioningly.

"What is it?" asked Plum, energetically wagging his tail, as he could hardly wait for his first sleigh ride. He had never had a sledge, not to mention a single Christmas before this one.

"What happened with the sledge?" asked Rodney, "It looks smaller than last year."

"It shrank," explained Bunky in a voice of an expert, "It shrank because it's cold."

"But last Christmas it was bigger!" Rodney insisted.

"Well, perhaps it wasn't that cold last Christmas?" Bunky scratched his head with a blue mitten, hoping that this action would help him to come up with a new idea.

"It was colder," Rodney reminded him, "So cold that we couldn't open the front gate and uncle Walm had to repair it."

"Perhaps you are both taller this year," observed Plum, "It seems that the sledge is smaller, but perhaps you've been growing up through all this time!"

"What a misfortune!" groaned Bunky, who greatly disliked all talks about growing up or growing taller.

"What a joy!" said Rodney and jumped from joy very, very high. His boots sank into the snow as soon as he found himself back on the ground. Rodney was dreaming about becoming grown up enough to use uncle Walm's drills and screws. He had a vision of himself as the future constructor of a tree house which would be placed on an apple tree in the backyard.

"We are not *that* grown up, as we still fit into the sledge," observed Bunky, trying to cheer himself up.

"Yes, and even the three of us will fit perfectly well into the sledge!" rejoiced Rodney.

"Hooray!" howled Plum joyfully.

"Yes!" admitted Bunky and he was complaining no more, at least not aloud.

They decided to take a path to the hill leading next to the pond. Bunky was pulling the sledge, while Plum was sitting in it. Rodney took Bunky's free hand in his and gave it a gentle squeeze. He loved spending time with his cousin. Bunky kept muttering and grumbling quietly about growing up too fast, but soon his melancholy mood was over and he began admiring the landscape. Glistening, silvery spruces were greeting them on their way, while the snow was creaking pleasantly beneath their boots. Plum contemplated the landscape from the sledge and could not believe in his own happiness.

Soon they approached the pond—the very pond which we had already visited with Bunky this morning. How different it was from this morning, though! This time Bunky experienced inner peace and, somehow, it allowed him to see the pond in a new light. Everything seemed happier and more beautiful now as he made peace in his heart with the Mice, Santa Claus, and himself. He finally noticed that the pond had an inviting, crystal-clear surface covered with a sparkling layer of freeze in which he saw sunbeams and his face. The pond was also surrounded by spruces and pine trees. Their branches were hanging low around the pond, moving gently with every fresh gust of wind and sifting snow on the merry skaters below. Bunky could hear their cheerful voices and laughter, and this time it didn't make him feel grumpy. On the contrary—he was happy with their happiness. The usually verdant hills looming on the horizon were all dressed in white today, providing a captivating background for this light-hearted scene. Bunky sighed and crinkled his eyes, shifting his face towards the sun. He immediately felt its warmth on his face. It was very comforting, just as the sun on a frosty winter day should be.

Rodney squeezed Bunky's hand again and patted Plum. While looking at the pond, he realised that nothing was as soothing and peaceful as nature. It was a perfect day: this beautiful scenery and the company of Bunky and Plum.

"It is so beautiful here," he whispered.

"It is exceptional," agreed Plum.

"This is so *bunky*ful," stated Bunky in his own way, with a special emphasis on "bunky" part.

In the meantime, at home, aunt and uncle Walm put aside *Echoes of Walmland* and began a quiet conversation, hoping not to disturb the three players engaged in the game of pick-up sticks. Currently the house was filled with a pleasant smell of coffee. Sir Williams, Mr. Elk, and Mr. Meow were still sitting in a circle, this time with their coffee cups. Mr. Elk was winning because he was very patient. Sir Williams, on the contrary, had no patience with pick-up sticks, but he was immensely enjoying the game and good company. He was also enjoying his coffee.

"I'm going to the city centre tomorrow in order to find Bunky's skating boots," aunt Walm whispered, holding in her hand a coffee cup and pretending that she is very preoccupied with it, "I will also purchase small gifts for everyone."

"I will go with you," offered uncle Walm, "You will have plenty to carry and I will be of help."

"If you go too, everyone will notice and start wondering. There will be no surprise," aunt Walm insisted, "Otherwise, if I go alone, they will think that I do my usual morning shopping."

"I can't think of you doing your morning shopping without my help," protested uncle Walm, who was a truly chivalrous and well-mannered husband, just like husbands should be.

Aunt Walm smiled. "What a great husband I have," she thought.

"Perhaps then we should go together," she said, looking with admiration at Mr. Walm.

"Bunky, Rodney, and Plum went to the hill for a sleigh ride," she continued.

"I am so glad they are spending time outdoors together," observed Mr. Walm.

"Absolutely," agreed Mrs. Walm, "They have such an interesting childhood and do so many wonderful things instead of sitting in front of the TV and entertaining nonsense."

And she poured more coffee into Mr. Walm's cup, as it was his usual afternoon coffee time.

Bunky, Rodney, and Plum reached the top of the hill. Bunky, who was pulling the sledge all the way up the hill, thought that more daily exercise would be beneficial to him. He allowed Rodney to sit in the sledge next to

Plum and pulled them both to the very top of the slope. It was a brave deed, but now he needed to rest for a while in order to catch his breath.

"Now, I'm fine," he concluded after five minutes of resting. Rodney was fanning Bunky with the sleeves of his sweater, while Plum vigorously wagged his tail.

"I'm fine," repeated Bunky, "Now we can ride down the slope, but don't expect me to pull the sledge up here again."

"We don't!" promised Rodney and Plum.

"Let's go!" announced Bunky and hopped into the sledge.

The hill was quite steep and the sleigh ride was very pleasant. Bunky knew the hill very well—he used to ride down this slope every year.

"Whohoooooo!!" shouted Bunky, Rodney, and Plum, as they all hurried down the slope. Rodney held onto Bunky, and Bunky held onto Plum, which offered them an illusion that they were fully secure in the sledge. It was such a special feeling to rush through the soft, skiddy snow, while the landscape was moving fast in front of their eyes. In the end of the ride, the sledge obtained unexpected speed and triumphantly bumped into a clump of bushes, stopping there in an abrupt silence. Happily, the tiny leaves of the evergreen boxwood protected the riders from any injuries.

"That was fantastic!" squealed Rodney.

Bunky shared his opinion despite a dizzy feeling in his head. The landscape was still moving around him for a while and then it suddenly stopped. The trees returned to their proper places and the hill was no longer upside down.

"Aunt Walm wouldn't be *that* happy with our ride," he thought.

Plum was exhilarated, wagging his tail from side to side, constantly perking up his grey ears.

"We lead a dangerous lifestyle!" squealed Rodney, jumping around joyfully.

"I hope we don't," said Bunky, removing the sledge from the bushes.

"Let's roll in the snow!" Rodney suggested.

"Aunt Walm would be worried about us drenching our clothes," said Bunky with a grave expression on his face, hoping to be regarded as an authority and aunt Walm's main representative.

"Let's have a snow fight then!" kept squealing Rodney and soon he and Plum ran through the snowy field towards the slope.

They were two happy, carefree figures on the background of the bright sun. Bunky smiled and decided to let them be. He looked carefully at the sledge to estimate whether it needed any repairing and he was glad to find that it didn't.

"Thank you for growing here!" he addressed the clump of boxwood. He didn't talk with plants every day, but today was a special occasion to be grateful for their presence.

"Our sledge is intact, and all thanks to you, dear Boxwood!" continued Bunky with gratitude in his voice.

But then, there was a sudden rustle in the bushes and something brownish yet sprightly and bright jumped out and hid again, leaving behind a silvery trail of stardust. Bunky anxiously stepped back, rubbing his eyes and winking in disbelief.

"It must be another consequence of this sleigh ride," he muttered, "I must be going insane."

"Mr. Bunky, I am here!" said a soft, silky voice that didn't sound like Rodney's or Plum's. Bunky thought that the boxwood would probably sound differently, but, still, he wasn't sure about that.

"I'm getting worse," he groaned, "Bushes are talking to me."

He glanced at Rodney and Plum to make sure that they were safe and then turned towards the boxwood again, rubbing his eyes and ears in disbelief. Rodney and Plum were safely bouncing around in a distance, apparently not engaged in any conversations with local bushes.

"Perhaps I didn't clean my ears well enough after the last bath and now I hear voices that do not exist," Bunky thought.

"Mr. Bunky!" pleaded the soft, silky voice.

"I'm here!" moaned Bunky with audible resentment, "I'm here, Mr. Boxwood!"

"I'm not a plant!" answered the voice, this time filled with a pearly laughter, as if the owner of the voice was smiling. Bunky had to admit that it was a very soothing voice. However, he decided to be tough.

"Me neither!" he responded wryly and winked again.

Today he didn't feel like becoming the Hero of his novel. He just wished for a happy Christmas day. Bunky reminded himself that aunt and uncle Walm asked him not to engage in conversations with strangers. Strangers, they said, could be misleadingly pleasant, offering sweets and candies which may be poisonous or, even worse, such strangers might be kidnapping heedless, unsuspecting individuals. Bunky was far from being heedless.

"I don't want any sweets!" he groaned.

"I don't have any here. They are all left in the magic bag," explained the voice.

"Aha, magic bag!" thought Bunky, "Someone thinks that I might be naive."

"I have plenty of sweets at home and I don't talk to strangers!" muttered Bunky and turned around in order to leave, pulling the sledge behind him.

"No, Mr. Bunky, please, do not leave!" pleaded the voice.

A sudden thought struck Bunky. He turned around and asked:

"How do you know my name?"

The bushes rustled again and Bunky saw the owner of the soft, silky voice. It was no one else but the Glorious Deer. Bunky dropped his arms and felt dizzy once again, this time from excitement. He *knew* that it was the Glorious Deer! His soft, brown fur was glistening so beautifully, making the day even brighter than it really was. There was an aura of magic and good cheer around the Deer as he gazed at Bunky from beneath his long, dark eyelashes. His bright, red nose revealed his name.

"I am Rudolph the Reindeer," he said.

"I am Bunky the Hero," introduced himself Bunky, instantly changing his mind about not becoming the Hero today. He felt as if he entered a fairy tale.

"Bunky the Hero, I was looking for you everywhere!" said Rudolph, approaching Bunky with a soft smile.

Everything was soft about Rudolph the Reindeer: not only his fur and voice, but also his manners and his kind, gentle behaviour had a certain touch of soothing softness. When Rudolph looked into his eyes, Bunky experienced a carefree feeling surrounding him from all around. It felt like being back home after a long journey. It was the feeling of Christmas. Bunky felt proud that Rudolph addressed him as the "Hero." He thought that the day was going to be very special.

"The world needs you," announced Rudolph quite unexpectedly.

On hearing this, Bunky fell to the ground, but soon he put himself together and got up.

The entire world needed him! It was too much for someone even as heroic as Bunky. "Your friends need you," "the city needs you," even "Walm-land needs you" sounded better than the entire world needing him! Bunky decided to be brave though.

"That's rather . . . unexpected," he mumbled, looking attentively at his blue mittens. In fact, he didn't want the Reindeer to realise how dizzy he was. Heroes shouldn't be dizzy at all events, but still, the entire world needing him was slightly too much. The Bunky Princess would be proud of him, he thought. Bunky pinched himself in order to make sure that it was all a dream, but it turned out that he was facing a complex reality.

"The world needs you," repeated Rudolph the Reindeer, looking at Bunky with his soft, peaceful eyes. Yet, Bunky experienced some inner hesitation.

"Today?" he groaned, "I wanted to have Christmas! I'm having winter holidays! I don't attend school this week and I was hoping for peace and quiet!"

Rudolph stared at Bunky thoughtfully. Santa Claus told him that Bunky was the Chosen Hero. Was it true? Santa Claus used to be right, as he could read others' hearts.

"Perhaps this complex heart hides a true, noble flame that could save this year's Christmas?" the Reindeer thought.

"Yes," he said peacefully, still carefully looking at Bunky, "And it *is* about Christmas. I'm glad there is no school this week."

"Blah," said Bunky inaudibly, as he didn't want to offend Rudolph the Reindeer.

In fact, he was extremely impressed by the Deer's appearance. As it is with Bunkies, he felt everything in his heart much stronger than others. Bunkies are always guided by emotions and now, in Bunky's heart, there was a tiny flicker of the true Hero coming back to life. Something began sparkling there and he felt that the world needing him wasn't so bad. It would be worse if the entire galaxy required his help. The world was still much smaller than the galaxy and much more manageable.

"It could have been worse," thought Bunky comfortingly. He also realised that he didn't want the Reindeer to get offended and leave. There was such an excitement in this new adventure! Bunky began thinking that, actually, he *could* do something about the world needing him—perhaps, somehow, the Bunky Princess would learn about his courage and come to Walmland in order to see this brave Hero?

"Are you really Rudolph the Reindeer?" asked Bunky, more out of amazement than out of suspicion, "Can I pet you?"

The Glorious Deer lowered his head so that Bunky could scratch him behind the ear. Bunky removed one of his blue mittens and patted Rudolph on his head. The Reindeer's fur was as soft and silky as his ethereal voice. After petting the Deer and scratching him behind the ear, Bunky noticed a glistening stardust on his paws. It had a lovely scent of gingerbread cookies and milky cupcakes; the scent of home, Christmas, joy, and safety.

"I believe you," said Bunky, "You are Rudolph the Reindeer and it is all truly magical!" In his amazement, he forgot about uncertainty and fear.

Rudolph calmly nodded his head.

"Why does the world need me today?" asked Bunky with curiosity and decisiveness in his voice, as if saving the world was a daily, casual affair. Rudolph acknowledged Bunky's answer with contentment and became hopeful that Bunky was indeed the Chosen Hero.

"Dear Bunky," he began, "It is a matter of utmost importance! I had been running to you through all the Milky Way with such a speed! Santa Claus, my Reindeer colleagues, and our helpers—two Elves, are left in the Faroe Islands and cannot proceed any further until the sledge is repaired!"

"Impossible!" cried Bunky, "And what about Christmas?! What happened with the sledge?!"

"A bolt detached from one of the skids and we didn't have a proper screwdriver," explained Rudolph.

"Ugh!" exclaimed Bunky.

"Then," continued Rudolph with a grave face, "We suppose that Santa Claus is having a slight memory problem and there was a minor confusion with some gifts . . ."

Bunky was almost ready with a tirade concerning the misplaced gifts, but he reminded himself that he was meant to be kind, generous, and forgiving and, immediately, his heart filled with a loving glow again. He also truly began enjoying the cookbook and didn't want to complain anymore. Instead, he gazed at Rudolph with a mixture of awe and understanding. He still couldn't believe that the Deer was here with him and that it wasn't a dream.

"It happens sometimes," he said generously, "But it's fine."

"Santa Claus suspects that your gift was also misplaced," continued Rudolph.

"Not a big deal," offered Bunky, "I just adore the cookbook."

Rudolph smiled and became convinced that Bunky must be the Chosen Hero since he was so selfless and forgiving.

"Santa Claus knows that you had been dreaming about skating boots all year long," reassured him Rudolph, "We received your letter."

"Ah!" said Bunky, blushing and waving his hand, 'skating boots or no skating boots, it doesn't matter!"

And, actually, he felt that it really didn't matter anymore—there was nothing as fascinating as meeting the real Rudolph the Reindeer and being asked to save the world. Bunky was no longer scared or upset, but truly proud that the world needed him. He only hoped that the world would not give him too much trouble.

"Santa Claus knows a lot about you," continued Rudolph, "and about your heart. He recommended you as the Hero. We would like to ask you to come with us and help us, if it is not too much to ask . . . there is still a chance to save this Christmas—there is still Christmas Eve in some places around the world . . ."

"No problem," stopped him Bunky, "I will find a screwdriver and I'm coming!"

"But," continued Rudolph, "before all that, I would like to tell you that Santa Claus offers you the title of the Official Helper and Hero of this Year's Christmas. We humbly ask you to accept it—would you agree?"

Bunky had to admit that the title was exceptional, but also it was clear that many duties were hiding behind it. He wondered what kind of duties these might be. He had many duties at home: he would vacuum the carpets and wash the dishes, water aunt Walm's flowers and take out the trash, but this time and with *such* a title—anything was possible!

"What does the Hero of this Year's Christmas do?" he asked cautiously.

"He helps Santa Claus and distributes gifts all over the world!" explained Rudolph with a joyful spark in his soft eye.

"What?!" groaned Bunky, "The entire world?! This will take the whole year! Aunt Walm won't be happy with my long absence, and I will not graduate from school! I will end up being illiterate[5]!"

Naturally, as it often happens with Bunkies, our Bunky slightly exaggerated everything: not only was he very far away from becoming illiterate, but also he had been writing his secret novel. Rudolph didn't know about the novel, but he knew that Bunky could write very well, as he had read his Christmas letter.

"Ah," he protested, "Our trip will take only one night. It's all about magic!"

---

5. An illiterate person is someone who cannot read and write. Bunky can. He reads and writes in an excellent way.

Bunky started thinking about Rudolph's offer. He had never been abroad and it was an outstanding occasion to travel around the world in just one night! Perhaps he would even encounter the Bunky Princess!

"Bunky the Hero," Rudolph addressed him, this time quite officially, "would you like to become the Official Helper and Hero of this Year's Christmas and save the world?"

"With pleasure," answered Bunky and there was no hesitation in his voice. Despite all the grunting and muttering on his side, how could he ever say "no" to such an adventure? A round trip around the world, meeting Santa Claus and Rudolph the Reindeer, becoming the Hero of this Year's Christmas and, perhaps, even meeting the Bunky Princess—these were all the advantages of such a generous proposal.

Rudolph looked at Bunky and smiled with relief.

"What about my cousin Rodney and my friend Plum?" inquired Bunky, "Actually, I would like to make them my confidants."

It was no longer necessary to dwell upon it, as Rodney and Plum came back running: Rodney—squealing with excitement and Plum—wagging his tail in circles. They stopped in front of the Glorious Deer, Rodney pressing both paws to his cheeks and Plum looking into Rudolph's soft eyes.

"It is the Glorious Deer!" said Rodney with a trembling voice, "It is Rudolph the Reindeer!"

Bunky felt a little jealous that Rodney recognised Rudolph faster than he did, but this bad feeling quickly disappeared.

Plum and Rodney bowed in front of the Deer and looked questioningly at Bunky. Bunky also bowed, even though he realised that he should have done it much earlier. Rudolph nodded his head in an elegant, royal-like manner.

"Dear Rudolph," said Bunky, "please meet my cousin Rodney and my Plum—they are both my best friends and I hope that we can share with them the Mysterious Plan."

"The Mysterious Plan?" squealed Rodney and pressed both paws to his cheeks again.

"Dear Rodney, Dear Plum," Rudolph addressed them, "I came to ask for Bunky's help and offer him the title of the Hero of this Year's Christmas."

Bunky blushed on hearing the word "Hero" in connection with his name.

"You are, as Bunky tells me, his best friends," continued the Deer, "Would like to help your cousin and become the Official Helpers of this Year's Christmas?"

Bunky blushed doubly, but no one noticed it underneath his blue fur.

"Hooray!" squealed and howled Rodney and Plum.

"From this moment on you are the Official Helpers of this Year's Christmas!" continued Rudolph, "Rodney, there is also a private matter that Santa Claus would like to discuss with you."

Rodney also blushed, immediately thinking about his letter.

"Yes," he answered quietly, his heart full of hope. He thought about his cousin Bunky and the Bunky Princess—was she already in Walmland?

Bunky looked at Rodney and then looked at Rudolph, feeling a pang of jealousy again, but then this feeling also passed away in the same way that snowstorms pass when winters end, and he felt proud of his cousin Rodney, whatever it was that Santa Claus wanted to discuss with him in private. He had no doubt that Rodney was very good this year.

"Please, tell us what happened!" inquired Rodney.

And Rudolph shared his story again.

"Don't forget about the screwdriver part," Bunky reminded him, "This is the main task of the Hero."

Rodney jumped from joy. Anything to do with screwdrivers, bolts, and drills was dear to him. He loved all sorts of do-it-yourself activities. At last, when Plum and Rodney learnt what happened with Santa Claus's sledge, they all began discussing the details of their travel around the world. Finally, they came up with the following plan:

1. Bunky, Rodney, and Plum were meant to return home and behave as if nothing significant happened.

2. Rudolph was hungry and tired, so Bunky promised to cook him an omelette and bring it to the bush in the backyard where Rudolph was meant to hide.

3. At 10:00 pm Rudolph was meant to knock with his hoof on Bunky's bedroom window and they were meant to be ready with supplies of sandwiches, thermos bottles, water, and a screwdriver.

4. They would travel on Rudolph's back to the Faroe Islands (towards the east) and repair Santa Claus's sledge.

5. They would distribute presents all over the world and Santa Claus would bring them back home at 10:00 am. This is the time when aunt Walm would be checking if everyone slept well and she would discover Bunky, Rodney, and Plum in their bedrooms, as if nothing happened.

"Good," agreed Rodney, "but why can't we tell aunt Walm the truth?"

"You can and you should," suggested Rudolph, "My only worry is that she may not let you go, thinking that such a travel—with strangers and all around the world—might be dangerous."

"And isn't it dangerous?" grunted Bunky, but quickly corrected himself, "Of course, it's not *so* dangerous."

"Of course not," offered Rudolph, "But telling the truth is the spirit of Christmas."

Bunky muttered something inaudibly and waved his hand in the air.

"Therefore," continued the Deer, "I suggest to tell aunt Walm the truth."

"What if aunt Walm is too worried to let us go?" said Bunky, "Who will be the Hero then?"

He got worried that someone else would become the Christmas Hero. The thought that the Princess might meet some other Hero was terrifying.

"You can leave your aunt a letter," offered Rudolph.

"We can leave it in Bunky's bedroom!" said Rodney, jumping up and down from joy and excitement. Such adventures did not happen every day.

"Bunky will write it," continued Rodney, "My cousin has an excellent handwriting!"

He almost wanted to say that "Bunky is even writing a novel," but stopped abruptly, reminding himself that it was meant to be a secret. Everything written in his letter to Santa Claus was also a secret, Rodney assumed.

"I'm still literate[6] and I can do it," agreed Bunky.

"Very, very literate," smiled Rodney mysteriously.

Rudolph smiled too. He was very relieved that he met Bunky and that this little Bunky agreed to save Christmas.

They all returned home and Rudolph found a hiding place in the backyard. Bunky, Rodney, and Plum were trying to behave as if nothing had happened, but aunt Walm immediately noticed their mysterious faces.

"You are so mysterious today, my little Bunky," she said, pouring some hot soup into his bowl. It was the usual dinner time and the entire merry company, the Mice including, gathered in the living room, accompanied by the friendly ancestors smiling from their portraits. Bunky could almost swear that the ancestors knew everything. He almost jumped on hearing his aunt's words.

"Mysterious?" he asked with what he hoped was an indifferent voice, "Why mysterious?"

"You appear to be very thoughtful," aunt Walm observed, "and so are Rodney and Plum. Did you have any adventures today? I hope that no one bothered you. Did you encounter any strangers?"

"Strangers? Why strangers?" echoed Bunky, as he didn't want to tell a straightforward lie and yet, he tried to keep the secret.

"Well," said aunt Walm patting him, Rodney, and Plum on their heads, "I hope you had a truly great time!"

"Yes!" squealed Rodney, waving his spoon high in the air, "We were riding down the slope almost with the speed of light and Bunky pulled us in the sledge all the way up the hill!"

"Oh, my dear Bunky, that is why you are so tired!" rejoiced aunt Walm, feeling much more peaceful at heart.

And the dinner continued in this peaceful way, although Bunky still felt that the ancestors were gazing at him. After the dinner, he mysteriously went to the kitchen and reached for the cookbook, searching for an omelette recipe.

"I didn't suppose that the cookbook would become so important in my life!" he thought.

---

6. A person who can read and write. Bunky is the perfect example here.

"My little Bunky, are you cooking?" asked aunt Walm, who just entered the kitchen and smiled at Bunky in her usual loving way. Bunky almost jumped again.

"I'm so glad you like the cookbook!" continued aunt Walm, "Uncle Walm will be so delighted on hearing that you are cooking again! What are you planning to prepare, my dear?"

"An omelette," mumbled Bunky.

"An omelette!" rejoiced aunt Walm, "My dear, I will leave now and check on the guests in the living room. Mr. Meow, Mr. Elk, and Sir Williams find our living room quite delightful on Christmas! So do the Mice! I am so glad! And where are Rodney and Plum?"

Rodney and Plum were in Bunky's bedroom, secretly packing their rucksacks.

"Mmm," said Bunky, "I think they are somewhere . . . in the house."

Aunt Walm sent Bunky a kiss in the air and gently closed the kitchen door.

Bunky began furiously mixing all the ingredients. He was thinking how he would love to tell his aunt about everything—not in the letter which he was meant to write, but in person. Still, he wasn't sure what would be the result of it. He didn't like keeping his aunt away from the truth, even though he didn't tell a single lie. Bunkies are very straightforward and honest creatures.

Such thoughts accompanied him in the kitchen and he felt very, very uneasy about the new secret. Finally, the omelette was ready. Bunky closed the cookbook, placed the omelette and a bowl of water on an ornate tray, and left the kitchen in order to find his scarf and boots. At last, warmly dressed, he went with the tray towards the front door. He had to pass through the living room and met there with many curious looks but, happily, aunt Walm was engaged in a deep conversation with aunt Barbara and did not notice Bunky creeping with the omelette towards the front door. Bunky sighed heavily and thought that it was very difficult to keep this new secret. Telling the truth was so easy and difficult at the same time!

"Hey, hey!" whispered Bunky.

The backyard appeared quiet and desolate, but he immediately heard rustling in the bush. Rudolph the Reindeer emerged from the boxwood among flickering specks of stardust which were always swirling around him. He began drinking water.

"Thank you from my heart, dear Bunky," he said, "The omelette looks delicious."

Bunky felt very happy on hearing Rudolph's words and gently patted his nose.

"I also brought you a warm blanket," he said, placing the blanket on Rudolph's back, "Are you sure you don't want to come inside the house? Everyone would be delighted to meet Rudolph the Reindeer!"

"I would love to, but I am slightly worried whether they would allow you to go on a trip around the world," wondered Rudolph.

Bunky gazed at the sky and felt a little nostalgic. He had never been abroad before but now he began worrying too.

Rudolph understood Bunky's silence. "You will be back tomorrow morning," he smiled, "It's Santa Claus's word."

"Then it must be true," decided Bunky, "because Santa Claus and Rudolph the Reindeer are those whom we can fully trust. Otherwise, nothing would be true . . ."

Bunky used ten eggs to prepare the omelette because he saw that Rudolph was very hungry and weary. He was so glad to see the Deer's strength quickly returning. Even Rudolph's fur began shining brightly; so brightly, that the nearby lanterns appeared to give off less light than usual. Being a magical creature, Rudolph the Reindeer could enjoy omelettes for supper in the same way that Plum the Wolf could have his bowl of milk for breakfast. In our world, Dear Readers, Deer would probably prefer some grass or leaves, but we are here, in Walmland, and this magical place is so different from our world.

"The stars!" said Bunky dreamily, admiring the tiny, flickering objects high above in the sky.

"It's time to get ready," said Rudolph.

The Northern Star was just above them, glimmering like a pearl on the dark blue background. It was twinkling and twinkling in a mysterious way and Bunky thought that it filled the entire sky with its glow. Or was it Rudolph the Reindeer's fur that was shining so brightly?

"The Northern Star is asking us to follow her," exclaimed Rudolph. He loved the nights on which he and Santa Claus would travel around the world, following the Northern Star and bringing everyone joy. This year, they would have an adventure like never before—of that he was sure.

Bunky picked up the tray and directed his steps towards the house. He felt excited about the adventure but still quite uneasy in his heart. "We will be waiting at 10:00 pm!" he confirmed before leaving and then, he suddenly turned back again and embraced Rudolph's neck with both of his arms. He felt the Deer's soft fur filled with the scent of gingerbread cookies and milky cupcakes. Hugging the Christmas Deer is one of the best things one can do in one's life. It is something never to be forgotten and something to be always remembered. How lucky are those who have this opportunity! Bunky had been planning to give Rudolph a hug through the entire day, but he was too shy to do so and worried that the Deer may consider it childish. Now, as he gathered all his courage, he felt immensely happy inside. No, it wasn't *childish* but very, very *childlike* instead. He felt a great warmth reaching his heart—he had never experienced more inner peace before. This is, indeed, what hugging the Christmas Deer makes one feel. If you encounter the Christmas Deer, Readers, you will be very lucky to give him a hug and you will remember it even when you are more than a hundred years old.

Bunky instantly felt braver and stronger. "Thank you, dear Rudolph. We will be waiting at 10:00 pm," he repeated and went back towards the front door, this time with more courage and confidence.

"Merry Christmas!" smiled Rudolph and Bunky saw the Northern Star reflected in his shining eyes.

7

Rodney and Plum Become the Christmas Heroes too, and Bunky Emerges as an Even More Heroic Christmas Hero than in the Previous Chapter

The clock in the living room was ready to strike 10:00 pm and the Mice began yawning very loudly. They had been skating all afternoon, gliding through the pond with other exhilarated skaters. Everyone was already sleeping or was meant to be asleep. Plum, Rodney, and Bunky belonged to the group who "was meant to be asleep" but, in truth, did not go to sleep. Currently they were all sitting on Bunky's bed. Bunky was writing a letter to aunt Walm—the letter which he didn't like too much and which, at the same time, appeared to be quite essential. Bunky felt that the content of the letter was rather unexpected and slightly ridiculous.

> *Dear Aunt*, the letter began, *Rodney, Plum, and I are safe and well. If you read this letter, you will see that we are not here, but please rest reassured that we will be back very soon. We went to the Faroe Islands with Rudolph the Reindeer where we are going to repair Santa Claus's broken sledge (we borrowed uncle Walm's screwdriver in order to succeed), and then we will help Santa Claus to distribute Christmas gifts all over the world. Christmas is at stake and we have to save it! Santa Claus will bring us back home at 10:00 am. Please do not worry because we took warm*

clothes, sandwiches, and hot tea, as you always advise us to do.
Dear aunt, we love you and will be back soon!

Bunky, Rodney, and Plum

Bunky read the letter aloud to Rodney and Plum. Somehow the letter made him feel very nostalgic and guilty. It also made him almost tearful, but he knew that he had to remain brave in front of Rodney and Plum. They also looked uneasy, staring at the letter in silence.

"The letter is stupid," thought Bunky.

"I will be right back," he said and tiptoed to the living room in order to spend there a nostalgic moment of solitude. He didn't want to appear weak in front of his friends. The living room was the same old, friendly place, with the cheerful fireplace, magnificent Christmas tree, fluffy carpet, and teacups scattered all over the table as Mr. Meow, Mr. Elk, and Sir Williams were great lovers of tea. Yet, the ancestors glanced at Bunky from their portraits with these very unusual, mysterious smiles. Bunky could swear that their faces were slightly altered. Great Grandma Walm looked even a little mischievious and Bunky was sure that he had just seen her winking at him.

A sudden thought struck Bunky—once, in the past, Great Grandma Walm could have been personally acquainted with Rudolph the Reindeer! Maybe he, Rodney, and Plum weren't the first to repair Santa Claus's sledge and save the world? Perhaps it was a secret family tradition? Maybe more than a hundred years ago, when Great Grandma Walm was a girl, she was secretly packing her sandwiches, waiting for Rudolph to tap on her window?

"Somehow they know," thought Bunky and blushed, "Ancestors are those individuals who know everything and one can tell so only by looking at their portraits."

Followed by his ancestors' gaze, Bunky tiptoed towards the Christmas tree.

"*Mouses!*" he whispered and, in a moment, he heard quiet giggles coming from the hole. He kneeled underneath the Christmas tree and leant over, stretching his hand towards the Mouse Hole.

"I brought you a gift," he said gently, "These are the colourful shoe-laces from my previous shoes which are too small for me now. I always loved these shoelaces and thought that you might use them to decorate your new skating boots."

The Mice giggled and stretched their little paws towards Bunky. Bunky shook each tiny paw very gently and smiled with his most generous smile.

"I am so glad you are happy," he said truthfully and felt light and peaceful inside, "Goodnight dear *Mouses*, have ice-skating dreams!"

He left the living room in a hurry, as it was already a minute after 10:00 pm, and quietly returned to his bedroom. As soon as they dressed in warm clothes, they heard a quiet tap on the window.

"Let's go," announced Bunky, looking determined. He glanced at the letter they placed on his bed and felt anxious again. He quickly thought of Great Grandma and decided to be brave. This is how thinking about ancestors often helps. The world needed him, Bunky thought, and the world needed Rodney and Plum. And he, Bunky Hippo, promised not to leave Plum alone. Plum would go with him everywhere. And Rodney too.

"Let's go," repeated Bunky and opened the window. The air was cold but refreshing and a few snowflakes flew inside the room, quietly settling down on the floor. Finally, they ventured out into the darkness, dressed in their warm sweaters, boots, scarves, mittens, and a poncho—in Plum's case.

Winter is this special season when being outside feels like being surrounded by a soft kind of silence. In this silence, every single step feels like stepping on a cushion, while talking resembles a loud whisper. The whole world was converted into a big snowy pillow comfortably wrapped up in a pleasant stillness. Rudolph the Reindeer was standing in the middle of the backyard with his fur glimmering even brighter than in the late afternoon hours. There was the usual scent of gingerbread cookies and milky cupcakes around him and a sense of welcoming peace. Bunky no longer had any doubts that it was the *real* Rudolph the Reindeer and that it was the *real* Christmas adventure.

Dear Readers, you will always recognise Rudolph the Reindeer after his brownish, glimmering fur and stardust swirling around him; you will sense the feeling of peace and bliss surrounding him and you will hear his soft, peaceful voice. Other than that, do not follow strangers anywhere and please remember, not everyone is Rudolph the Reindeer and not everyone has good intentions. If you don't live in Walmland, it is always better to tell your mum or dad, aunt or uncle, grandma or grandpa or anyone whom you trust about everything.

But here we are in Walmland, the safest and most magical place one could imagine, and it is a true Christmas story therefore, Dear Readers, rest reassured that our Rudolph the Reindeer is as real as you and I.

Bunky, Rodney and Plum jumped on Rudolph's back. The magical aura surrounding the Deer was to them like every warm thought, every good event, every smile from a loving person, and every good thing that had ever happened to them. The Deer's presence was very comforting, making them feel like on a happy Christmas day from their early childhood. They decided to be *extremely* brave and ready to save the world and, for a moment, Bunky even considered saving the entire galaxy if it was necessary.

"Do you have the screwdriver?" he asked Rodney.

"Absolutely! It's in my rucksack," answered Rodney and reassuringly squeezed his cousin's paw. Plum was sitting between them, for safety reasons, as Bunky remembered his promise to look after him for eternity.

"Cousin!" squealed Rodney quietly, "Do you really believe that this is happening?"

Bunky thought for a moment before answering.

"Honestly," he began, "it is very difficult for me to believe that it is not a dream! But this is what magic is all about: we need to have faith to enjoy this miraculous dream!"

On hearing Bunky's words, Rudolph shook his brownish fringe and smiled. "It is not the first time I hear such words," he rejoiced.

Bunky instinctively thought about Great Grandma Walm. Why was she constantly appearing in his thoughts in connection with the Deer, he couldn't understand.

"Ready to travel and save the world this Christmas?" asked Rudolph.

"Yes!" exclaimed the three travellers.

And then, something unexpected happened! Naturally, unusual events are usually intermingling with unexpected happenings . . .

"Who is it?" asked Bunky fearfully.

Indeed, they saw a mysterious silhouette treading through the snow— treading with a heavy step of someone who had too much Christmas cake for supper. The silhouette came closer and, in a dim light of the Christmas tree reaching them from the front yard, they saw uncle Bill.

"Shhh . . ..," said uncle Bill reassuringly, making signs with both of his hands.

"Oh no!" groaned Bunky.

"Shhh . . .," said Rudolph.

"Uncle!" squealed Rodney.

"It's me," admitted uncle Bill, "I couldn't sleep and thought to go out and refresh myself."

He was dressed in pyjamas and wrapped up in a cosy blanket which, most probably, he took from the sofa in the living room. It was one of aunt Walm's decorative blankets, definitely not intended for a winter garment.

Obviously, uncle Bill was also young in the past. He also felt younger and younger inside with each new year, therefore he easily understood that there was some kind of an exciting secret between Bunky, Rodney, Plum, and the Deer.

"Your secret is safe with me," promised uncle Bill, smiling good-naturedly at the whole company, "And isn't it you, Rudolph?"

"Do you know Rudolph, uncle?!" asked Bunky, immediately forgetting all about groaning and grunting.

"Of course I do!" smiled Bill and gently patted Rudolph's nose, "The last time I saw you was when you were a very tiny Reindeer!"

"And you were a very tiny Walm, too!" rejoiced Rudolph, "I do remember!"

"What do you mean?" inquired Bunky. He was completely taken by surprise.

"It all happened when I was very young," continued uncle Bill, "I was hiding in a living room on one Christmas night."

"Wow!" squealed Rodney and Plum excitedly wagged his tail.

"Do you really know each other?" Bunky was more than curious. He realised that he didn't know everything about his uncle and, actually, he didn't know the best stories from uncle Bill's life. It happens quite often: younger generations do not realise that the older ones also keep Very Mysterious Secrets from their youth or, sometimes, even More Mysterious Secrets than the younger ones would ever have!

"Yes, yes, we do!" smiled uncle Bill somewhat mischievously, reminding Bunky of Great Grandma Walm, "We had a cup of tea with Santa Claus and a long conversation about Christmas, and the Reindeer were also there, Rudolph the Reindeer among them. It was in my old house in Chocolate Grove."

"And I remember Bill bringing us some warm water and many delicious twigs," Rudolph remarked.

"Ohhhh!" sighed Rodney, "What a story! So Rudolph is your *old* friend!"

"We are not so old," said uncle Bill, "But tell me please, what are you up to tonight?"

"Bunky is saving the world and Christmas, and we are his Helpers!" explained Rodney, as he couldn't wait to share the news.

"That sounds very serious. Is there anything I can help you with?" asked uncle Bill.

Initially, Bunky worried that their travel was over as soon as uncle Bill appeared outside in aunt Walm's decorative blanket, but uncle neither protested, nor lectured them on dangers of travelling with strangers. Apparently, uncle Bill was well acquainted with Rudolph the Reindeer and fully trusted him.

"And it means," thought Bunky, "that we should share with uncle Bill the entire secret."

And so they did. When Rudolph finished explaining everything, uncle Bill was serious but also visibly happy and calm.

"That's a very demanding task, a very demanding one!" he said, his face brightening up, "I will keep your secret but please, return safely on time! Bunky, Rodney, Plum, Rudolph—I am so proud of you!"

And then uncle Bill thought about something else.

"Just a moment!" he exclaimed, "Please, wait just for a moment!"

He ran back home and quickly returned with a small jar filled with capsules.

"It is a gift from me for Santa Claus, with best wishes and greetings from Bill—for the sake of our happy meeting in the past!"

"What is it, uncle?" asked Bunky.

"Memory-improving capsules!" announced uncle Bill, "Only natural, herbal ingredients from Walmland! I take them myself from time to time and I remember every single thing from my entire life!"

"Oh!" said Rudolph, who was visibly moved, "It is impossible to forget you and your noble heart, Bill!"

"Indeed, I always remember you too and I remember all my happy memories!" rejoiced uncle Bill, "Bunky, Rodney, Plum, keep our family tradition of meeting Rudolph the Reindeer alive! I know that you will make our family proud! I will be waiting for your return!"

"We will meet soon again!" said Rudolph softly, touching uncle Bill's cheek with his warm nose.

And then, he started running, his hooves slowly detaching from the ground until they were so high in the sky that uncle Bill was a small figure waving to them from a distance.

Bunky thought about his uncle with a new sense of admiration. He thought about his bright personality and wondered whether it was the meeting with Santa Claus that helped him to preserve this positive attitude towards life.

"Now," thought Bunky, "it must be much nicer to be like uncle Bill than to be groaning and grunting all the time!"

Suddenly, he realised that they were very high in the sky, but he wasn't afraid at all and attributed his new sense of courage to Rudolph's presence. Nothing bad could happen when they were here with Rudolph the Reindeer. Bunky, Rodney, and Plum were mesmerized by the enchanting travel on his back. Indeed, they had never been so high above Walmland, not to mention that they had never been abroad.

"Are we abroad now?" inquired Bunky.

"Not yet," answered Rudolph while smoothly running through a glittering path in the sky, "but we will be leaving Walmland just in a minute!"

"But we have been travelling only for two minutes!" squealed Rodney, "We must be travelling so fast!"

"Faster than light!" observed Plum.

"Time is not important up here on the Milky Way! You can be everywhere in five minutes!" Rudolph explained.

Bunky thought that it would be so nice if the path to school was leading through the Milky Way. "It would be possible to get up five minutes before the classes and still, I would be on time!" he reflected.

They were rushing through the Milky Way and their path was strewn with white trails of milky flowers and silver stars. Plum bashfully licked one milky flower and found out that it tasted like chocolate cereal with milk.

"Delicious!" he thought.

"I have never supposed that flowers might be growing even here!" wondered Bunky. He was fidgety from excitement and completely amazed by the view. Apart from being amazed, he became thoughtful too. He imagined little uncle Bill waiting behind a curtain in order to meet Santa Claus on one snowy Christmas night.

"Dear Rudolph," said Bunky, "please tell me why does Santa Claus bring gifts secretly when everyone is fast asleep? Why wouldn't he meet everyone in person?"

"There's an easy explanation," responded Rudolph, still running faster than light, although Bunky had a feeling that they were moving with an average speed because he could easily admire the landscape, "First of all, if

Santa Claus stopped in each house to greet everyone, distributing presents would last at least one year! And then, believing that Santa Claus exists is the most important part. Believing in someone or something is very important. Everything you hope for will come true in your life if only you fully believe. You cannot see Santa Claus, but you have to have faith that he is there."

"That makes a lot of sense," agreed Bunky after a long moment of silence, "It is the same with dinosaurs—everyone believes in them, although no one encountered a single one. We have to believe and have faith—only then every dream will come true . . ."

Rudolph kept pacing through the Milky Way, while the Northern Star kept rising in front of their eyes until she filled the entire horizon with a bright, pearly light. It wasn't a kind of blinding or bewildering light but, instead, it was a warm and inviting glow one would like to reach for or be surrounded with. The closer they were to the Northern Star, the more comfortable they felt: it was the feeling of order and peace, as if all the troubles that had ever taken place were gone for good, becoming an insiginificant memory. They felt an amazing clarity of mind too, with a premonition that it was only here, close to the Northern Star, that they could make sense of everything—of every single event in life and every single thought. It was, on the whole, the feeling of bliss.

"I love this *place*, if I may call it a *place*!" Bunky declared and thought about the Bunky Princess and how beautiful she would be while surrounded by the glow of the Northern Star.

"Her beauty is always unmatched," thought Bunky dreamily.

"We are almost there!" exclaimed Rudolph and this remark immediately met with sounds of disappointment from the three travellers who were enjoying the ride too much to think of its end.

Bunky was so absorbed by the beauty of the Milky Way and the Northern Star that he didn't think even once about sandwiches or food in general. It was very rare in his case. At present, he began thinking about meeting Santa Claus and offering him uncle Bill's gift—the herbal treatment for memory loss. They began descending with the light speed, but they didn't feel any discomfort. It rather felt like gliding down on a sparkling wave of stardust. Bunky, Rodney, and Plum were watching the changing view in a ceremonious silence. They knew that they would never forget the ride on Rudolph the Reindeer's back. Apparently, it was a privilege. The more time they were spending with Rudolph on this magical Christmas adventure, the better and kinder they were feeling, as if all the negative thoughts left them for good. They hardly noticed that the travel came to an end and that the Deer stopped.

"We are here," announced Rudolph, but Bunky, Rodney, and Plum were reluctant to leave his back. After a while, they agreed that it was necessary to spring into action and save Santa Claus, Christmas, and the world in general.

"Now," said Bunky, doing gymnastics on a nearby snowdrift, "It is very cold here, in the Faroe Islands!"

Plum and Rodney were doing gymnastics nearby too. Rudolph felt very warm after the ride. He was quietly standing close by, observing his friends with joy and curiosity. After several push ups and stretches, the three Walmland travellers looked around only to discover the beauty of this new landscape unwinding in front of their eyes.

"We are abroad!" whispered Bunky.

Even though it was the middle of the night and slightly cold, he thought that he had never seen a place so beautiful. It was the novelty of travelling that took hold of his soul—when travellers visit new places, they are usually struck by something entirely novel and unique which they have never encountered before.

"It is a dreamland!" admitted Bunky still in a whisper, looking with admiration at the snowy hills, distant emerald bays, and waterfalls frozen in artistic motions. It was their first time abroad. The sky above them adopted a dark blue hue, filling itself with merrily dancing northern lights reminding one of fireflies. Rodney could finally fully express his excitement by pressing both paws to his cheeks and squealing, while Plum was wagging his tail, continuously jumping around. In the brown poncho, he looked like a night butterfly flying around in this enchanted landscape, although I doubt whether butterflies could fly around in winter in the Faroe Islands.

"Ho, ho, ho! Merry Christmas!" they heard in the darkness and turned around.

"Santa Claus!" squealed Rodney so loudly that Bunky thought they must have heard him in Walmland, if not all over the world. Rodney always reacted in this way whenever Santa Claus appeared.

"Welcome, my dear ones!" said the voice merrily and Santa Claus appeared in front of their eyes.

Bunky wasn't sure how to behave—whether to jump from joy or faint from fear, as suddenly he found himself overwhelmed by conflicting memories. On the one hand, he remembered all the times when he was kind and generous—the last time was when he offered the Mice his old, colorful shoelaces—but then, his memory was filled with pictures from the past of him groaning and muttering for a variety of trivial reasons.

"Ah!" said Bunky with a faint, uneasy voice, "Santa Claus!"

Rodney was probably more at ease with his past memories, as he ran towards Santa Claus without any hesitation and gave him a hug. Bunky closed his eyes nervously, trying to figure out whether he was more naughty then nice or otherwise, but soon he also found himself in Santa Claus's embrace.

"Merry Christmas!" repeated Santa Claus in a cheerful voice and Bunky saw no anger on his face.

Even though his sleigh needed repairing and Christmas was at stake, he was visibly happy because of their arrival. Bunky was still anxious though. He knew that Santa Claus was looking at him and felt even more worried. He also realised that Santa Claus was very old. There were numerous wrinkles around his eyes and mouth which, surprisingly, shaped his face in such a way that it actually made him look cheerful and youthful. And then Bunky realised that all Santa's wrinkles originated from laughter. It was his secret of ageing in a handsome way. He was wearing a long, woollen coat, enormous woollen cap, huge mittens, and fluffy earmuffs. All of his clothes were designed by Mrs. Claus. He was a portly man with kind, blue eyes, and very red cheeks—the last one being the result of spending too much time in the cold.

"It's cold in the Faroe Islands, isn't it?" he addressed Bunky in a pleasant voice which sounded like Christmas bells.

"Yes, it is," admitted Bunky, shaking all over not from the cold but at the thought that he had been naughty in the past.

However, Santa Claus continued merrily: "I am so pleased to meet you, Bunky the Hero of this Year's Christmas! Thank you for arriving so promptly!"

Bunky arrived to the Faroe Islands in a heroic mood, ready to save the universe if necessary, but now he felt small and insignificant.

"I am so grateful that you thought about me," he mumbled, "and about my cousin Rodney and my friend Plum. But I feel that I . . ."

The rest of Bunky's speech became inaudible.

"I am sorry, my dear, I often experience hearing problems," said Santa Claus, leaning forward in order to hear better.

"But I'm afraid that I've been . . . I've been . . .," mumbled Bunky, blushing all over his face, although it was impossible to see the blush underneath his fluffy, blue fur.

Santa Claus understood what Bunky wanted to say, but he also knew that Bunky had to explain everything himself. It was Bunky who needed to acknowledge his mistakes—only then would the Christmas magic truly work. Santa Claus knew every corner of each person's heart. He saw Bunky with the eyes of his soul and saw honesty in his heart. Bunky, too, reminded himself that he was meant to be the Hero and that Heroes are supposed to be courageous, even if they have to acknowledge their own mistakes.

"I've been . . . a little grumpy this year! At least sometimes!" admitted Bunky with desperation in his voice, "How do I deserve to be the Christmas Hero?"

And he felt bunky tears running down his eyes. But Santa Claus knew that these were healthy tears which fully healed Bunky's heart.

"My dear," he said seriously, offering Bunky a cotton handkerchief which he found in one of his pockets, "During my whole life I have not encountered a single person who wouldn't be grumpy at times. The fact that you recognise your behaviour makes you the true Christmas Hero. Heroes are those who struggle with themselves inwardly and emerge victorious from these fights."

Bunky looked at Santa Claus gratefully and loudly blew his nose.

"Thank you, dear Santa Claus," he said quietly, "Thank you for having a good opinion about me still. I just wanted to add—I really love the cookbook from you. I tried an omelette recipe."

And in this moment Bunky became the true Christmas Hero. All the doubts were gone. Santa Claus smiled at him and offered Bunky a reassuring hug.

"Everything will be alright," he promised.

Bunky smiled and felt stronger and braver than in the beginning of his travel. He also felt light as a feather.

"I have something for you, Santa!" he reminded himself and found the jar with capsules, "Here you are! These are natural, herbal capsules for memory problems from uncle Bill who greets you and sends you his best wishes, hoping that you remember the past!"

"Do I remember your uncle Bill?" rejoiced Santa Claus, "Naturally, even with all kinds of memory problems I do remember your dear uncle Bill! I am so glad that you are his nephew, Bunky! I missed your uncle! How is he doing?"

"Thank you, Santa Claus! He is well and he is a very good person who knows that there is no point in growing up too fast and who also knows how to keep secrets!" answered Bunky truthfully, and then added: "I feel that he really wanted to see you again."

"Then he is on the right track," remarked Santa Claus, "I also hope that we will be able to meet again. Such wishes often come true! Sooner than he might think! This gift is so thoughtful of him! Let's hope that the capsules will solve my memory problem—it is mostly connected with confusing gifts and their recipients! But, somehow, I still remember my childhood years! I will always remember solving this difficult equation on the blackboard when I was at school. Oh, how nervous I was!"

"I'm sure that these were decimal equations," offered Bunky and they both began laughing.

After a while, Santa Claus invited everyone for a meal. Dear Readers, please do not think that it was a waste of time—how would our Christmas Helpers work all night without a nutritious meal and a cup of hot tea? Bunky, Rodney, and Plum were officially introduced to Shetland, Merino, and the Reindeer. For the first time in their lives they encountered Elves and discovered how agile and energetic they were. The Elves were taller than the Mice and smaller than Rodney. They were staring at the newcomers with both kindness and curiosity, as finally they were able to meet them in person too. Bunky, Rodney, and Plum were also curiously gazing at the Elves. The Reindeer were quite similar to Rudolph—all of them had soft, glistening, brownish fur and pleasant, deep eyes—but only Rudolph had the red nose. Apart from his distinctive nose, he had a great sense of direction and could easily guide the sleigh through the Milky Way.

Even though it was very cold, they were all rejoicing in the beautiful, northern landscape, leading friendly conversations in the sleigh parked underneath the dark blue sky filled with pink and green auroras. No one felt really cold anymore. Wrapped up in warm blankets, they feasted on Mrs. Claus's pancakes. Everything tasted better in this enchanting place. Usually everything tastes better when there is a sense of adventure in the air.

At last, the Important Moment arrived—their Christmas work or, if you prefer, Dear Readers—the Christmas adventure officially began! Bunky got to his feet and thanked Santa Claus for the pancakes. Then he stretched several times in order to be ready for all the heroic deeds.

"I should be in good shape tonight," thought Bunky, "It doesn't happen every day that one delivers gifts all over the world!"

Rodney and Plum followed him, looking expectantly at Santa Claus. Yet, deep inside they knew that it was the Christmas Hero's moment.

Rodney reached for his rucksack and found uncle Walm's screwdriver. It glistened on the background of the sky as Rodney held it high above his head. Bunky thought that the screwdriver became slightly magical too—it happened, most probably, thanks to the presence of Santa Claus and his Helpers.

"Let's save Christmas!" squealed Rodney, accompanied by other cheerful voices.

"Hooray!" rejoiced the Reindeer, gracefully jumping around with the Elves. Everything the Reindeer did was graceful and elegant, while everything that the Elves did was swift and energetic.

"Who would think that a screwdriver might become such an important thing to have!" wondered Bunky.

"Ho, ho, ho!" good-naturedly exclaimed Santa Claus.

And then, they all looked at Bunky. "Now," thought Bunky, "I think that I am supposed to make a lofty[1] speech."

"Dear All!" he began, "As my cousin Rodney said, it is time to save Christmas and we will start by saving Santa Claus's sledge! There is no time to spare and we have already had pancakes, therefore I will not dwell upon my joy on becoming the Christmas Hero, but we will immediately spring into action! I have been thinking about everything and I would like to ask Rodney and Plum to repair the sledge. I offer them this important task because they are my most important friends."

Here Bunky looked at his cousin and Plum, hoping that they would say something too. Indeed, he had been thinking about it for some time—actually since the moment they had pancakes in Santa Claus's sledge. While eating pancakes, Bunky reasoned with himself that this would be a perfect way to honour Rodney and Plum. He, Bunky, was willing to resign from a part of his glory for the sake of those whom he loved the most. When they were having a delicious dessert—Mrs. Claus's warm apple pie—he was completely reassured that this would be the right decision. Not only Plum and Rodney deserved to be the Christmas Heroes too, but also Rodney was always so fond of uncle Walm's shed and all the interesting screwdrivers, drills and bolts. Yes, this would be perfect, thought Bunky, emptying the last cup of tea. It wasn't about repairing *any* sledge—it was *Santa Claus's sledge*!

1. A "lofty" speech is an important kind of speech with many sophisticated words. Speeches of this type can be found in Bunky's novel, especially when the Hero is addressing the Bunky Princess. A "lofty speech" is a speech for an important occasion, such as saving the world or Christmas, or graduating from school!

Rodney and Plum looked at Bunky with surprise, searching for the Right Words. However, the Right Words did not come. This is usually the case with the Right Words when they are needed. Also, not everything can be expressed by means of words.

"For Christmas!" Rodney whispered, "Thank you, dear cousin!"

Plum licked Bunky's ear. In an instant, Bunky understood that he was the happiest, richest, most carefree Bunky in the world.

Santa Claus reached into his pocket in order to find the unlucky bolt. He offered it to Bunky and Bunky gave the bolt to his cousin. Rodney placed the bolt between the sledge and the skid. In the meantime, Plum held the skid with both paws, so that Rodney could properly lock the bolt in place with the screwdriver. In a minute, the bolt was locked in its previous place and the sledge was ready for a new travel! Rodney victoriously looked at uncle Walm's screwdriver—the most famous screwdriver in the galaxy, between the world and the Milky Way!

"Hooray!" he squealed.

"Hooray!" howled Plum, jumping into the sledge.

"Hooray!!!" shouted Bunky the loudest he could, since he believed that being Rodney's cousin and Plum's best friend obliged him to express his joy in the most clamorous manner.

"Full speed ahead[2]! Ho, ho, ho!" announced Santa Claus.

The Reindeer lined up in front of the sledge and the Elves began counting them just to make sure that not a single Reindeer would be left behind in the Faroe Islands. Soon they all followed Plum, hopping onto the sledge one by one. Finally, the Reindeer were all ready in a line, waiting to carry them through the Milky Way and all over the world! The adventure would begin! Bunky was rubbing his eyes for a moment just to make sure that he wasn't dreaming or sleepwalking. Even if he was sleepwalking, he thought, it was the most beautiful dream for sleepwalking one could wish for. But no—it was real! Soon the sledge was rushing through the sky again, moving past the giggling Stars. Apparently, the Stars celebrated Santa Claus's return. The Reindeer were running very fast again and Bunky managed to throw the last glance at the shimmering frozen waterfalls and emerald bays of the Faroe Islands—all bathed in the first sunrays of the approaching dawn. He thought that he would never forget this view.

2. "Full speed ahead" means moving forward in the fastest possible way!

"I will return here one day," he promised himself, "Such a scenery deserves a good painting and, perhaps, I will become a painter. Apart from being the author of my novel, of course."

Travelling in the sleigh was different from travelling on Rudolph's back: the sleigh was shaky and, at times, almost out of control, but any danger was only an illusion as all the nine Reindeer were fully in charge of the passengers' safety. Being used to this mode of travel, the Elves did not pay attention to the bouncing sledge—at the moment, they were carefully scrolling through the nice list. Santa Claus was listening to their remarks but, at the same time, he was also glancing at the snowy cliffs below. Soon the Faroe Islands disappeared out of sight but, after a while, the Milky Way reappeared with its enchanting milky flowers.

"Ah, cousin Bunky," sighed Rodney, "If we didn't have such important Christmas duties, I would gladly stay there a little longer."

"Me too," agreed Plum.

Bunky also sighed and thought about the heroic night ahead.

Aunt Walm woke up very early in the morning. It was 6:00 am and she was already busy in the kitchen, neatly dressed in her festive attire, with the usual white cotton rose in the collar of her woollen dress. Uncle Walm was almost ready to venture out into the snow. He was a very loving and devoted husband. He and aunt Walm met at school and fell in love with each other when aunt Walm shared her pencil with uncle. Uncle Walm always kept that pencil in his desk.

Everyone else in the house was still fast asleep and aunt and uncle Walm decided to return home as fast as possible so that no one would notice their absence. After all, it was meant to be a surprise! They also wanted to have breakfast with their family and guests.

Before leaving, Aunt Walm stopped in front of Bunky's and Rodney's bedrooms and listened carefully, but it was very quiet and she imagined that they were fast asleep. She thought about Bunky and Rodney sleeping quietly under the warm blankets and about little, grey Plum resting comfortably in the wicker basket. She wondered that today she might buy those enchanting Christmas mugs whom everyone loved so much. Yes, Christmas mugs for everyone—the family of Mice including, and a big Christmas bowl for Plum! Aunt Walm gently clapped her hands while thinking about the surprise. She loved preparing gifts for others. It made her feel even happier than receiving them. She also thought about her little Bunky's face on seeing his longed-for skating boots.

"How nice it is to make others happy!" she thought and wrapped herself up in a warm shawl. Uncle Walm was ready to go. He took aunt Walm by the hand and they went outside. Winter mornings are so mysterious, peaceful and quiet—especially in Walmland! Aunt Walm felt that there was something magical in the air; or, perhaps, she felt intuitively that something magical was happening, even without her full knowledge. Aunts have this kind of intuition. She felt that perhaps it had to do with Bunky, but she could not explain why.

"But," she thought, "he is sleeping in his bedroom and everything is alright."

They passed near the Snowmen who both looked very impressive in the morning sun. Indeed, the sun was already rising, hoping to wake up all the inhabitants of Walmland. The three of them were still far away. However, there were three more hours left until 10:00 am—the promised hour of their return. Aunt Walm held in her hand a cotton shopping bag for skating boots and all the Christmas mugs she was hoping to buy—and she smiled lovingly at uncle Walm. He was always by her side.

Bunky jumped through a snowdrift and reached the front door. It was a place *Somewhere in the World*—or, at least, this is how he called it. They had no time to consult maps and, instead, they put all their trust in the Reindeer. Their hope was that all the gifts would reach good children and adults on time. Thanks to Santa Claus's goodness, even those who were naughty could expect gifts this year but, in such cases, a slight delay was possible. Bunky prided himself on receiving his gift—the cookbook—so early, since it signified that he belonged to the nice list.

As soon as the sleigh stopped, Rodney, Plum, Santa Claus, and the Elves split up into two groups in order to distribute the proper gifts around the neighbourhood. Bunky, the Christmas Hero, had to make sure that gifts and their recipients were not confused. He was drawing circles on the nice list around the recipients' names in order to verify that no one was left without a gift. He had to deliver the gifts on his own. They had been following this procedure through the entire night and it was anything but boring! Bunky truly enjoyed his new tasks. Many of us wonder for years what would be our perfect job—and what a joy it is when we can at last call this job a "hobby"! Bunky made such a discovery on Christmas night—not only did he find his perfect job, but also he discovered that this job was a perfect hobby! He was no longer groaning and complaining but, instead, truly enjoyed being the one who offered or withheld the gifts and yet, he had not denied a single gift to anybody during the whole night. He had no heart to do so. After all, everyone deserved some additional chances to improve. "Perhaps two," Bunky thought. During this Christmas night, he was honest and generous in every situation. He was also trying his best to be kind and understanding—these two, he found out, were more difficult.

Carrying the magic bag filled with gifts on his back, Bunky looked around cautiously and realised that soon it would be a new day dawning. While tiptoeing around the house, he looked quite suspicious but, from close, everyone could easily tell that he was the Christmas Hero—who else would be carrying Santa Claus's magic bag?

Bunky stopped and wiped his brow.

"We will manage to do everything on time!" he said quietly, trying to convince himself that it was really possible.

Then, he crept towards the window and swiftly opened the magic bag. The magic bag had a magic pocket and from there he took a small portion of the stardust powder and threw it at the window. The window disappeared, revealing a cosy living room with a huge Christmas tree—so huge that it was almost necessary to remove the ceiling and the second floor to make space for it. Bunky courageously stepped into the living room and the window reappeared in its previous place. The living room was warm and inviting, but Bunky had no time to delight in the scenery. He worked as hard as Santa Claus would. He only threw a glance at the table situated in the centre of the room and there he found a plate of delightful cookies with a note: *For Santa Claus*. He was already reaching for a cookie, but then he carefully studied the note and decided that it wasn't addressed to him. Still, he could pretend that he was incapable of reading, but this thought quickly disappeared as Bunky desired to be only good, generous and honest. He honestly admitted that he understood both words: *for* and *Santa Claus*, as well as the overall context. He placed one cookie in his mitten, resolving to offer it to the proper addressee. Being the Christmas Hero is a serious business and requires a lot of fairness, even if not everything is fair in the Christmas Hero's life. Have you ever seen a plate full of Christmas cookies with a note: *For the Christmas Hero*? Well, no? That's why it is so difficult to be the Christmas Hero!

Our hard-working Bunky knelt in the centre of the room and leant over the magic bag. A teddy bear, a new umbrella, some cotton tennis shoes and a book entitled *A Thousand Most Curious Flowers* were on the list dedicated to this house. Bunky was searching untiringly for all these gifts and, finally, he had all of them ready on the floor apart from the book *A Thousand Most Curious Flowers*. Bunkies are slightly impatient creatures, so he flipped the bag over and shook it anxiously. *A Thousand Most Curious Flowers* left the bag with a loud bang and Bunky, with a sigh of relief, placed the bag on the floor again. The magic bag always contained what was necessary at the moment.

Bunky adjusted his scarf in a way which would make him look more dignified as the Hero. Through all the night he was wearing his beloved sweater from aunt Walm. It reminded him of home and he kept thinking about his bedroom and their cosy living room. What kind of looks would the ancestors give him on his return? During this night he had visited many different houses from all over the world, but none of them was as homely and precious to Bunky's heart as his own. He thought about the mysteriously smiling Snowmen standing in front of the window and about uncle Walm adjusting the Christmas star on the spruce, and then about every moment in his house which was so dear to him. Even though he didn't want the adventure to end, he was concerned about aunt and uncle and didn't want them to worry. Will they return on time? . . .

Bunky shook off these troubling thoughts and arranged the gifts underneath the Christmas tree in such an elegant way as Santa Claus would do himself—or, at least, it was Bunky's hope. His creativity was endless, therefore he placed the medium-sized gifts on the biggest parcels, and the smallest gifts on the medium-sized ones, what resulted in an elaborate tower of gifts.

"Ho, ho, ho!" whispered Bunky, getting ready to leave the room. He wanted to tiptoe unnoticed out of the house but then, all of a sudden, he heard a noise coming from the adjoining room. Perhaps, he thought, it wasn't a noise, but someone crying and whining. Bunky felt concerned and immediately changed his mind, directing his steps towards the mysterious room. He gently opened the door and bravely looked inside, at the same time hoping to remain unnoticed. Being noticed would mean a delay in their travel. He saw a very little Bunky—perhaps a four-year-old one, throwing a perfect tantrum on the floor. His mum was leaning over him, speaking quietly and patiently with a very soothing voice. She acted like a person who would enjoy reading *A Thousand Most Curious Flowers*, Bunky thought. He imagined that reading *A Thousand Most Curious Flowers* required a lot of patience.

"My dear," she addressed the unruly little Bunky, "you know very well that you cannot have *everything* for Christmas! No one can!"

"I can, I can!!" yelled the little Bunky, hitting the floor with both of his fists.

Bunky the Hero got terrified on seeing this spectacle. Personally, apart from some little grumpiness, he had never acted in *such* an outrageous way. The floor, innocent as a lamb, obviously didn't deserve it. The little Bunky's mum sighed heavily and got to her feet. She left the room in order to prepare some herbal tea for her rowdy son.

"Blah," thought Bunky, "What an awful behaviour!"

He managed to hide behind the door in the last safe moment, but the little Bunky still kept on yelling. Bunky the Hero could not stand it anymore. He decided to emerge from behind the door and reveal himself to this little Bunky as the Christmas Hero who would offer him a lesson of good behaviour.

"What do you mean by this?" said Bunky the Hero, unceremoniously emerging from behind the door. The little Bunky was so surprised that he stopped hitting the floor. He opened his mouth and stared at Bunky the Christmas Hero in disbelief.

"What is this fuss about?" continued Bunky, taking a seat on the edge of the little Bunky's bed. The little Bunky remained quiet and still.

"Look," continued Bunky, "I was meant to leave unnoticed, but you greatly annoy me. I heard you whining that you would like to receive *everything* for Christmas. How can I possibly provide it? My Christmas bag is heavy enough."

Thus saying, Bunky the Hero shook the magic bag to show the little Bunky how heavy it was. The little Bunky didn't respond, but opened his mouth even wider. He sat on the floor and stared at Bunky the Hero with surprised eyes.

"Let's see," Bunky the Christmas Hero continued his speech, "are you on the naughty or nice list?"

He reached for the list and studied it carefully, selecting the number of the house.

"Unbelievable!" he declared, "Well, you are so lucky still being on the nice list! I brought you some beautiful gifts!"

The little Bunky's blue ears perked up when he heard the word "gifts."

"It seems that you have been good for the major part of the year," continued Bunky the Hero, "I think that you will be delighted to discover some gifts in the living room, but I advise you to stop entertaining nonsense."

The little Bunky winked in disbelief. "Who are you?" he whispered, "Are you Santa Claus?"

"No," announced Bunky the Hero, "but you were quite close, for I am Santa Claus's Helper and the official Christmas Hero. I bet that Santa Claus would be greatly disappointed to see you in such a disgraceful state. Who gave you this idea that one can get *everything* for Christmas?"

"My friends said," whispered the little Bunky, "that they can get for Christmas *everything* they want to receive."

"Ah, that's naughty," answered Bunky the Hero, "so naughty that I even do not have to reach for the naughty list to know that they are on it. Do you also want to receive *everything*?"

"I thought that if they can, I can too," explained the little Bunky.

Bunky the Hero wondered for a moment. "That makes sense," he thought.

"That's fair," he admitted after a while of silence, "but have you ever thought *where* you might keep *everything*? Storing *everything* takes a lot of space. It can be quite overwhelming."

"In my room," said the plucky little Bunky.

"I assure you it's too big to fit into *any* house!" professed Bunky, "What are you going to do with *everything*? You would not even have time to look at each thing thoroughly. And the most important of all, my dear: you would be the most miserable Bunky in the universe."

"How is that possible if I would have *everything*?" inquired the curious little Bunky.

"What a stubborn Bunky, more stubborn than I am!" thought Bunky the Hero quite angrily but, being the Christmas Hero, he knew that he had to remain patient and loving.

Sometimes, Dear Readers, it is difficult to be patient and loving, but Bunky the Hero was capable of it in the most daring circumstances! He gathered all his strength an thought generously that the little Bunky was too little to understand everything properly and that he, the Christmas Hero, was sent to enlighten him. He decided to immediately come up with a reasonable and proper explanation.

"My dear friend," said Bunky the Hero, trying to be confidential and friendly, "if you receive *everything* in one day, what are you going to *dream about* for the rest of your life? There will be nothing left to dream about under the sun and you will feel so unhappy!"

The little Bunky opened his mouth even wider and then got up and nodded his head.

"That's so true and scary!" he said in a serious voice, "I have to warn my friends!"

"The silly ones who want to get *everything* for Christmas?" asked Bunky the Hero.

The little Bunky nodded his head again.

"I assure you that they will be alright," continued the Christmas Hero, who also got up from bed, slowly preparing to leave, "No one, including myself, is able to receive *everything* during one Christmas night, there is no such danger. And now, my little Bunky, it's time for me to visit other children. Be good and kind to your mum, because she has to endure your tantrums."

The little Bunky blushed but, just like in the case of the big Bunky, his blue fur prevented the blush from appearing on his face.

"I'm so sorry," he whispered. The Christmas Hero's heart melted.

"You know," he said, "I also had some grumpy moments on Christmas. But one day I changed. Do you know why?"

The little Bunky shook his head.

"Because," continued the big Bunky philosophically, "I realised that we should be grateful for each and every gift and we should never expect gifts, reject them or take them for granted. And it also proves that *everything* is not a good gift."

The little Bunky smiled at the Christmas Hero.

"Ok," said the Hero," before I go, come here, I will give you a hug. Now, you are fully on the nice list."

"Ho, ho, ho! And Merry Christmas!" he said and hugged the little Bunky. Afterwards, he waved to him in a Santa Claus-like manner, spinned around and left the room. But the unruly little Bunky followed him.

"Can I wave you goodbye from here too, dear Christmas Hero?" he quietly inquired.

Bunky the Hero remembered his own surprise on seeing Rudolph the Reindeer and he thought that he understood the little Bunky.

"Well," he grunted, "I will be doing some magic, but . . . ok, come with me, but let's hurry before your mum returns!"

"I LOVE magic!" exclaimed the little Bunky, quite louder than he should, and began jumping up and down on the floor, "I always wanted to become a magician! Are you a magician, Christmas Hero?"

"No," said the big Bunky, "That is, usually not, but today I know a trick or two."

And he also blushed.

"Wow!" shouted the little Bunky.

"Shhhh!" whispered the Christmas Hero as patiently and lovingly as he could. He wasn't sure if it would be a good idea to encounter the little Bunky's mum. It would involve too many explanations—of that he was sure. How would he explain his presence in the house, not to mention all the matters connected with the Christmas Heroes, Elves or Fairies? As if the Christmas Heroes, Elves and Fairies weren't the simplest truths! That's why, Bunky thought, he would never ever grow up inside. He would be mature and responsible, but also childlike at heart, just like uncle Bill.

"Don't grow up too fast," he advised the little Bunky, "It's boring. You may even stop believing in magic. And there is plenty of good magic. It is the one coming from your heart."

"I will never stop believing in *you!*" said the little Bunky eagerly, gazing at the Christmas Hero with admiration.

On hearing it, the big Bunky felt like the actual Christmas Hero—a character from novels and movies, someone very powerful and amazingly courageous.

"I will always believe in you too," he said modestly, "You know better than getting *everything* in one day. You have the whole life for such things."

He hugged the little Bunky again and opened the magic bag. From there he took a little bit of the magic stardust and threw it at the window. In that instant the window enchantingly dissolved in the air and the Christmas Hero hopped onto the front yard.

"Woooooow!" exclaimed the little Bunky.

It all happened just in one moment and, after a short while, the window and the wall were in their right places again. The little Bunky stood in the middle of the living room quite speechless, gazing at the Christmas Hero treading through big snowdrifts towards the gate. And then the Christmas Hero was out of sight.

The little Bunky felt that from now on nothing would be the same. Nothing at all! It was a feeling similar to that experienced by Rodney on seeing Santa Claus in his sleigh.

"From now on," thought the little Bunky, "everything will be much better, because *I* will be much better and nicer!"

He turned around, just like Rodney did, and saw the gifts underneath the Christmas tree. He thought lovingly about the Christmas Hero and decided that he would never ever throw a single tantrum again.

"I will be like him when I am a little older!" he thought.

"Clap, clap"—he heard his mum's slippers. He saw her concerned face and a cup of herbal tea in her hand.

"My little Bunky," she said on seeing her son in the living room, "what are you doing here?"

"Mum!!" shouted the little Bunky—but this time happily and not with anger, "The Christmas Hero was here and left us Christmas presents!"

"Oh, really!" said mum in a tired voice. She wasn't sure if it was true, but then she saw the gifts underneath the Christmas tree and said: "oh, really!" once again—this time with full conviction that something truly magical had taken place and someone had been here not only to deliver the gifts but also to change her little Bunky's heart.

"Indeed!" she said, half frightened and half surprised, "Who was here, my Bunky?"

"Another Bunky, the Christmas Hero!" explained the little Bunky.

"And you weren't scared?" asked Bunky's mum, feeling slightly frightened herself.

"Scared? How could I be scared of someone *so* amazing!" exclaimed the little Bunky, jumping up and down from joy, "I don't want to receive *everything* for Christmas anymore! He explained to me what a mistake it would be!"

"And you really don't want to receive *everything*?" hesitated Bunky's mum. She was very tired but began feeling happier with every word.

The little Bunky stopped jumping and looked at his Mum seriously. "*That* would be *so scary!*" he said, "And I am very sorry for being so ridiculous."

Mum's face instantly lit up. "My little Bunky," she said and they both exchanged a hug, feeling that the true Christmas had just begun for both of them.

પ

Bunky reached the secret hiding spot just on time. They were all there, waiting for him. On seeing Bunky, Plum instantly began wagging his tail. Bunky patted Plum and smiled. It was so good to see them all again. Santa Claus and the Elves were brushing the Reindeer next to the sleigh but, on seeing Bunky, they came closer to hear his report.

"How did it go this time, cousin Bunky?" anxiously asked Rodney.

Even though Rodney was his very little cousin, he radiated with peace and offered everyone so much comfort, Bunky thought.

"It was really nice and interesting," he said truthfully, "I had an adventure with a little Bunky and I will always remember this meeting. How did it go for all of you?"

Rodney smiled. "All gifts delivered, Christmas Hero!" he announced, "Merino and Shetland helped me to carry a washing machine to the house on the corner of the street. It seems that this washing machine was somebody's Christmas dream!"

"A very nice and practical dream!" observed Bunky.

He gradually began to understand what gifts were all about: some received cookbooks, others—washing machines. Apparently, as Bunky found out, not everyone dreamt about luxuries or fancy clothes. There were those who hoped for a washing machine and those who hoped for a vacuum cleaner; those who couldn't afford to buy a new set of bedclothes or waited eagerly to find a new set of pyjamas or a new sweater underneath their Christmas trees. There were also such individuals as Bunky who dreamt about skating boots but received something else—something actually very much needed because, Bunky realised, it was very important for him to learn how to cook. If he didn't know how to prepare an omelette, how would he feed Rudolph the Reindeer when it was necessary? Now he saw everything much clearer and felt grateful for every gift he had ever received and for every gift he had left in others' houses on this long Christmas night.

The Reindeer were already standing in a line, ready to continue their trip.

"My brave Christmas Team," said Santa Claus and his voice reminded them of Christmas bells once again, "What would I do without you!"

"What would we do without *you*, Santa!" answered Rodney and Bunky thought that it was so true.

"Where are we now, Santa?" he asked curiously. After all, the world was such a big place and he had already seen so many different places and houses: houses with pitched roofs, houses with flat roofs, houses located in the hills, houses next to the rivers, houses in busy cities and those located on the prairies.

The world was such a curious place! Bunky could not even enumerate all the places which he had seen! There were cities covered in snow, cities where it was very warm—as warm as in the summer time, towns full of beautiful buildings, places full of skyscrapers and little, cosy villages next to the sea or in the mountains—places where Bunky felt the most comfortable. All these places had something in common: in each place, everyone eagerly awaited the arrival of Santa Claus. Yet, none of these places was like Walmland, Bunky realised. The more he was travelling, the more he was learning to appreciate his home.

"Ho, ho, ho!" rejoiced Santa Claus, "We are already back in Walmland! And now it's almost time to drive you back home!"

Bunky appeared surprised. "So the little Bunky is living in Walmland," he thought.

It donned on him that he had just met another Bunky—an undeniable sign that they were already back in Walmland. Bunkies live only in Walmland and inhabit this land in quite a large number.

"What time is it?" he inquired, feeling surprised that he forgot all his tiredness, but also a little disappointed that the night had already passed so quickly. Santa Claus checked his watch.

"It is twenty to ten in the morning!" he announced.

Bunky looked around and saw the first tiny sunbeams appearing on the horizon. The sun was waking up to a new day. He gazed at the snow underneath his feet—the snow of Walmland—and realised that they were truly back home. He recognised now this familiar, inviting scent of pine trees. He always associated it with home. He thought about their amazing adventure and then about his aunt and uncle. They had twenty minutes left. The sky was changing its colour and a little thrush started his morning song. They were back home!

"Let's hurry!" said Bunky and quickly jumped into the sledge, followed by Rodney, Plum, the two Elves and, obviously, Santa Claus himself.

The Reindeer began their usual run and soon they were swiftly moving in the air. Merino reached for his notebook to study its content in silence. These were the Most Important Moments of their travel: Merino wanted to make sure that everyone—good and bad—had already received a gift. He was frowning while studying diagrams, numbers, and figures. His pencil stopped next to a small dot almost in the end of the nice list.

"Hey, hey everyone!" Merino shouted, "We have one more person on the nice list! Also, it is the last person in the world without a gift!"

Bunky felt dizzy.

"Really? We forgot about this one person?!" he asked in disbelief.

"Yes," said Merino, "There is this one last person from Walmland. Quite close from here!"

"What shall we do?" thought Bunky. "Will we manage to reach home on time? Is there enough time to deliver this last gift?"

All these questions were spinning restlessly around his head like glittering silver stars.

"Will we manage to deliver this last gift and be back home on time?" inquired Rodney, repeating Bunky's thoughts, and Bunky recognised the look of concern on his face. Everyone looked at Bunky and Santa Claus.

"Why are you looking at me . . .," began Bunky, but then he reminded himself that *he* was the Christmas Hero and the one who should know the answer. He was Santa Claus's right hand. He was here because the world needed him—yes, Bunky reminded himself that too. But now, in the moment of distress, Bunky felt that he would gladly take a nap in his room and think about the world afterwards. Suddenly he felt really tired; so tired like Santa Claus in the beginning of this story. Believe me, Dear Readers, it was only natural—Bunky had been delivering gifts worldwide for almost twelve hours! He saw an inquiring expression on Santa Claus's face.

"Yes!" he answered decisively, "We will quickly deliver the gift and we will be home on time."

Bunky had never been so decisive in his whole life. His answer came out quite unexpectedly and even he was surprised how reassuringly it sounded. This is how Heroes often feel: on the surface, they appear unmoved and intrepid[3]. Inside, they are shaking from uncertainties. No one is fully free from uncertainties or fear; not even the bravest Hero, like our Bunky, but the point is to stay strong throughout all the difficulties. There is no true heroism in foolish fearlessness.

"I will stay strong and we will be home on time," Bunky declared, "I will deliver this last gift very fast."

He thought about his aunt and uncle again and how he didn't want to let them down; he thought about Plum and Rodney and how he wanted to make them proud and, finally, he reflected on the Bunky Princess and how he promised her once, while writing in his dear blue notebook, that

---

3. Fearless!

he would never give up, no matter what came his way, even if it was the last forgotten Christmas gift. Finally, he thought about chocolate cookies and promised himself to have one or two on their return back home.

"When all this will end well, I will have some cookies with Rodney and Plum!" he decided.

"We are descending!" exclaimed Santa Claus and winked at Bunky to help him feel more confident. He recognised everything that Bunky felt inside. After all, Santa Claus had been delivering gifts for over two thousand years!

At present, the Reindeer were running towards the Earth through a steep, invisible slope, as if the sleigh was sliding down a pitched roof. Bunky was patting Plum in order to make him feel comfortable and Rodney placed his paw on Bunky's arm. They didn't exchange a single word but they were very close to each other with their thoughts.

The Reindeer stopped quite abruptly behind a rosebush next to a nice-looking, spacious house with a green, pitched roof. The house resembled a small mansion or a petite palace. The rosebush still had some withered leaves and waited patiently for the arrival of spring in order to look fresh and enchanting again.

"I am invincible," whispered Bunky in order to fully convince himself that it was so. Words have a tremendous power allowing one to transform the reality—after a moment, Bunky felt truly invincible.

"Here we have to deliver a book entitled *Cross-stitch Embroidery for the Advanced* and a bedding set for a pet," read Merino from his notebook.

Shetland nodded his head and offered Bunky the magic bag. It was the Christmas Hero's last task.

"Everything will be alright," Shetland whispered, "There's still some time left."

"My dear Bunky, hurry!" exclaimed Santa Claus.

"Hurry, cousin!" squealed Rodney, "Everything will be alright and we will be waiting here!"

He felt that he would like to run after Bunky and, at least, keep him company, but Santa Claus gently laid a hand on his shoulder. Bunky had to do it all alone—Rodney also knew. His mission as the Christmas Hero was written in the stars and the universe always knew the right way—Bunky was meant to be the Hero of this Years' Christmas from the beginning until the end of their travel.

But Bunky felt that too much depended on him and he began shaking like a jelly. Yet, he regained his strength and, overcoming the strange weakness, he rushed towards the house. Poor Bunky—too much depended on his person—the entire secret of this year's Christmas depended on him! And only twenty minutes left! Oh, he hated being placed in any situation with only twenty minutes left! If someone told him a day ago, while he was groaning over the cookbook, that the future of Christmas would entirely depend on his abilities, he would groan and mutter even more and probably abandon the whole project. But today he was the true Christmas Hero!

"If I don't manage to deliver the gift and return to the sledge on time, this year's Christmas will be incomplete!" thought Bunky with dismay.

Incomplete!—what an awful word it was. *Incomplete* sounds the most awful when it is about a sweet bun without a chocolate cream or, as in our Hero's case, when it is about the last person in the world without a Christmas gift! What an uncomfortable situation for our Bunky—the price of being called the "Hero"!

But Bunky ran untiringly, only wishing that the Bunky Princess could admire him now, and even while running he managed to make a quick observation that the house was especially nice-looking and clean. Bunky had no idea who was living here but he knew very well that houses could tell a lot about their inhabitants. After all, we put our hearts into our homes.

Bunky was hurrying so much that he almost forgot that instead of traditionally knocking on the door he should use the magic stardust. He was just going to knock when he reminded himself about the stardust powder and hastily opened the magic bag. He threw some powder at the wall and saw the interior of the house. There was a living room again. At the first glance, this living room was like a thousand other living rooms he had seen throughout this night but, in fact, this one appeared nicer and cosier, with each and every single object meticulously arranged. It reminded Bunky of the living room in his house.

The room was in the style which we, the modern Readers, would call "vintage"—that is, full of interesting objects and beautiful decorations from the past. At the same time, everything looked new and very clean and Bunky could smell that the floor was freshly mopped. He wondered whether someone went to all the trouble for the sake of Santa Claus, or whether it was a usual habit of this mysterious person—the future reader of *Cross-stitch Embroidery for the Advanced.*

Bunky cautiously stepped into the living room through the invisible wall and, apart from recognising the scent of the freshly mopped floor, he instantly discovered that the entire room was pleasantly smelling with tea and roses too. And then he had a moment of fear because something on a pink armchair moved and jumped in his direction. It took Bunky a second to recognise that it was a brown Cat with beautiful, grey stripes. The Cat approached Bunky without a shadow of fear and began purring. Bunky realised that the Cat was the future owner of the bedding set.

"Dear Mr. Cat," he said, "Merry Christmas! I have only twenty minutes left. Actually, less than twenty now!"

But the Cat was so delightful and fluffy that Bunky could not resist petting him. He also scratched the Cat him behind his ears. The Cat looked into Bunky's eyes and kept purring quietly, as if telling Bunky a very, very long story. His company was so pleasant and Bunky thought that it would be very nice to sit here in the pink armchair and listen to the Cat.

"Oh dear Mr. Cat!" he stated, "Now I really have to start working!"

He found in the magic bag the last Christmas gifts of this year and quietly placed them underneath the Christmas tree. He noticed that the Christmas tree was decorated with a great taste: some of the decorations were made out of wool and the rest—out of paper. Someone must have been working very hard to prepare all these amazing woollen robins and stars, paper snowflakes and reindeer, Bunky thought. There were also several woollen cats resembling the particular Mr. Cat who persistently accompanied Bunky.

And then, he was frightened again, as something unexpectedly moved—actually, he thought that the pink sofa moved from its place! But pink sofas do not move, even during the magical Christmas time. Bunky realised that all this time someone tiny and dressed in pink was gazing at him from the sofa and only now got up and approached him. It was an elderly lady in a pink dress which, unmistakably, was made from the same material as the blanket covering the sofa.

"Aww!" thought Bunky in despair, "The world needs me and the future of this year's Christmas depends entirely on me and here we go again! . . ."

But his fear quickly subsided as the lady smiled peacefully. She must have been very old, but her face was noble and young when she smiled. Bunky immediately recognised that the lady belonged to the lineage of Bunkies inhabiting Walmland. They all had these fluffy blue ears.

"And very friendly smiles!" Bunky thought (thinking about himself too).

"I hope I did not frighten you, young man," said the lady, "I am Amalia the Bunky and this is my dearest Cat. I am so pleased that you like him. He also seems to like you a lot. He's been waiting for his Christmas gift all the morning!"

Mr. Cat purred approvingly.

"I am very pleased to meet you, Mrs. Amalia and Mr. Cat," responded Bunky the Hero, "although I sense that I caused you some discomfort and trouble while entering your house through the wall."

"Not in the least," the kind lady reassured him, "I am one hundred and five years old and I have seen a lot of magic in my life. Are you Santa Claus's Helper, my dear?"

The question was so simple and direct that Bunky grinned. "Yes," he simply responded.

"Then I won't be troubling you," responded Amalia, as if Bunky's appearance in the living room was an ordinary event, "I know that you are in a hurry and the Reindeer are waiting somewhere behind the rosebush. They used to park there every year."

"How do you know?" asked Bunky quite rashly, not realising that through this question he fully confirmed Lady Amalia's words. But Mrs. Amalia was a good-natured and honest person.

"I know, my dear," she said, winking at Bunky, "As I told you, I am one hundred and five years old. After so many years in this world, one knows much more than one realizes. I believe that you arrived in the company of Santa Claus, the Elves and some other Helpers. Wait, my dear, I will give you some cookies so that you can share them with everyone!"

Thus saying, Mrs. Amalia moved swiftly towards the table and filled a paper bag with several dozens of delicious chocolate cookies.

"Finally cookies for me too!" thought Bunky in delight.

"I baked them for you," Mrs. Amalia said, "and I wanted to thank you for the amazing gift, my dear. I was hoping that I could do some embroidery before the arrival of spring. I am so glad that I am still on the nice list, despite being a hundred and five years old. Such a long time offers one many opportunities to drop out of the nice list."

"Oh, you are so kind!" mumbled Bunky, who was quite speechless seeing Lady Amalia's kindness. He could not imagine Mrs. Amalia being on the naughty list.

"I only wish you could stay more and talk with me," continued Mrs. Amalia, "It is very lonely here for me and Mr. Cat. We are waiting for my Granddaughter to come and join us, but she hasn't arrived yet because of the snowfall."

"I am so sorry," said Bunky, who was sorry indeed. He wished that such a good, kind and brave person like Mrs. Amalia could have some company in this beautiful and inviting house, where all the woollen robins and paper reindeer only waited for some visitors who could admire them. The whole house was a masterpiece and, indeed, it felt very lonely without conversations and laughter. Bunky complimented Mrs. Amalia on her Christmas decorations.

"I truly love these woollen robins," he admitted, "and paper reindeer too; and, of course, the woollen cats are exquisite[4]!"

"Perhaps I can visit you after Christmas to keep you company?" he said quite out of the blue, surprised by his own words. However, it wasn't "thoughtlessness" but, rather, "spontaneity." He felt drawn to this place and to Mrs. Amalia and Mr. Cat. He imagined that it would be so nice to pay them a visit or two and drink a cup of tea in their company in this rose-scented living room, while admiring all the work Mrs. Amalia performed to turn the entire house into such a welcoming place. This house needed the presence of guests. Mrs. Amalia smiled with gratitude.

"You are more then welcome, young man!" she said.

Bunky usually didn't like being called a "young man" or someone who "grew up a bit," but this time he felt like the true Christmas Hero when titled in this way. He returned the smile and patted Mr. Cat on his fluffy head.

"You need to run now, I know," said Lady Amalia, "Don't forget the cookies. Most probably, you have no more than ten minutes left. This is always the case with Christmas Helpers. Until soon, my dear!"

"Until soon!" rejoiced Bunky.

This time he wasn't surprised by Mrs. Amalia's words—after all, being one hundred and five years old, she knew everything. He hurriedly ran out of the house, this time in a traditional manner, that is—through the front door. Mrs. Amalia waved him goodbye and returned to the sofa with Mr. Cat.

"I told you that he would come!" she said to the Cat.

---

4. "Exquisite" means astonishingly beautiful—for instance, as beautiful as the Bunky Princess! "Exquisite" is the word often used by Sir Williams too!

"Purr, purr," agreed Mr. Cat.

ॐ

"Something strange but amazing happened again!" exclaimed Bunky on his return to the sledge. He placed the magic bag in the sledge and greeted everyone.

"Ten minutes left!" announced Santa Claus, confirming Mrs. Amalia's prediction, and continued: "My dear friends, I believe that Christmas is saved!! Saved by all of us and by our Chrismas Hero, Bunky of Walmland! Hooray!!"

"Hoooray, hooray, hooray!!!" they all shouted cheerfully and celebrated this happy news with several jumps in the snow.

Rudolph and the other eight Reindeer were quite impatient to start running as soon as possible in order to safely drive Bunky, Rodney, and Plum back to their house, but they were also happy and relieved.

"I cannot imagine not saving Christmas," squealed Rodney.

"Me neither. It would be unthinkable," assured him Bunky. In this moment he was feeling so brave that he could almost save the entire galaxy. He also completely forgot about his tiredness.

"It was unbelievable!" offered Plum, "Unbelieveable, and yet it really happened!"

"And we even saw skyscrapers!" squealed Rodney.

Bunky waved his hand.

"Skyscrapers are nothing!" he remarked, "I would like to see the Faroe Islands again!"

"Ahhh . . .," agreed Rodney and Plum.

"Someday, someday . . .," said Santa Claus dreamily.

The Elves were looking at them with big smiles on their faces.

"Everything is possible and everything can happen if only we keep trying and believing," observed Santa Claus. He was very proud of all his friends.

Comfortably sitting in the sledge, surrounded by such a marvellous company, Bunky finally experienced an immense sense of relief. Apart from the joy of travelling, saving the world required a great physical effort and an outstanding strength of character. Even though Bunky had the greatest time of his life, there was still a lot of pressure on him and there was a huge responsibility placed on his bunky shoulders. At last, he felt relieved. He gazed gratefully at Rodney and Plum and then at Santa Claus, Merino,

Shetland, and the Reindeer and thought that so much had changed in his life through this single night—and everything had changed for the better. This is, after all, what Christmas should be about—becoming better while recognising how much goodness might be hidden in life if only one dares to find it.

"I am so grateful for every single minute I have spent with you on this wild adventure!" said Bunky dreamily, for it was almost like a dream to him. And then he added: "But I want to say that if not for my brave cousin Rodney and my courageous friend Plum, I wouldn't find enough heroism in me to be here. If not for Rudolph the Reindeer and other Reindeer, and if not for Santa Claus and the Elves, I wouldn't even think that it might ever be possible. I just wanted to say that we are the greatest Christmas Team!"

Everyone cheered loudly. Rodney felt very proud of Bunky and so did Plum, but Plum also wondered about his life—how greatly it was altered and how magical this change was. Plum began to believe in magic too, finally understanding that magic signified goodness coming from others' hearts. Bunky slightly leant over the sledge and saw the chocolate brown rooftop of the Walms' house glistening in the first morning lights.

"Home on the horizon!" he announced.

8

What Happened in the Meantime behind the Rosebush and in the Walms' House

However, Dear Readers, before we proceed further with our Christmas story, I will use my power of the Narrator to reveal to you what actually took place in the Walms' house and near Santa Claus's sledge, next to Lady Amalia's rosebush, while Bunky was bravely delivering the last Christmas gifts.

Let's begin from the rosebush. As soon as Bunky stepped into Mrs. Amalia's living room, Rodney felt that everything would be alright. He felt Santa Claus's hand reassuringly placed on his shoulder and turned around in order to smile at him. It does not happen every day that one can smile at Santa Claus or even have a conversation with him.

"Dear All," said Santa Claus, addressing Plum, the Reindeer and the Elves, "I need to talk with Rodney. We will take a walk around the rosebush."

Rodney wasn't surprised. He suspected that Santa Claus wanted to talk with him about the Christmas letter.

"My little Plum," said Rodney kindly, "Santa Claus and I will be back soon. I think that we need to discuss something concerning our best friend Bunky. It is something very important, but nothing connected with the naughty list. He is a noble person."

Plum nodded his head and his wise, blue eyes followed Rodney and Santa Claus as they began walking in circles around the rosebush. In this way, Mrs. Amalia's rosebush became the witness of perhaps the Most Important Conversation in this story.

"Dear Rodney," said Santa Claus seriously, "you probably know that I want to discuss with you the Christmas letter which you had left on the windowsill on Christmas Eve."

"Absolutely," said Rodney truthfully.

Tiny snowflakes began dancing in the first feeble sunrays and he tried to catch them and hold them in his paws—even for a while before they would melt away. Santa Claus smiled.

"You love winter, don't you?" he remarked, "It is my favourite season too!"

"Yes!" rejoiced Rodney, "There is so much beauty in winter!"

A little snowflake landed on his nose. They stopped walking around the rosebush and Santa Claus looked at Rodney with usual warmth and kindness sparkling in his eyes.

"My dear little friend, I was very impressed by your letter," he said, "It struck me as written in a very selfless and disinterested manner and it fully matches your noble character. Our Hero Bunky is surrounded by Heroes such as you and Plum."

Rodney blushed. It was all true. I don't think that anyone would have a doubt that Rodney was gentle, noble and caring, but hearing such words as a compliment left him speechless. It was the compliment coming from Santa Claus and it left Rodney even more self-conscious. Sometimes the hardest thing to do is simply to acknowledge that we deserve a compliment.

"Plum is the true Hero," said Rodney shyly, "He had endured so much before meeting my cousin and I am grateful that he is with us now."

"Yes," smiled Santa Claus, "Plum is the true Hero and so you are, my little friend. You think so kindly of your cousin Bunky and I would love to help him too."

"Oh!" squealed Rodney, "Would it be possible?!"

"The Bunky Princess is the main heroine in the book your cousin is writing, isn't she?" whispered Santa Claus confidentially. Rodney nodded his head.

"I do not know if it is within my power to bring literary characters from novels to Walmland or send them back to novels," confessed Santa Claus, "but I promise you this, my dear friend: all the good deeds are always rewarded and all dreams are eventually coming true—it just takes patience, time, and a lot of faith. And there are obstacles, of course, too. I do not know how it will happen, but be sure of that—your cousin Bunky will be rewarded with his dream turning into reality. Just tell me, Rodney, do you believe me? Do you have faith that it will come true?"

Rodney thought for a moment. It was very, very difficult to believe that the Bunky Princess would *really* appear in Walmland. It was much easier to believe in Santa Claus and his words.

"It *just* takes time, patience and a lot of faith," repeated Santa Claus, "Even though I say *just*, I know that it is not easy."

"Oh, it is not easy," admitted Rodney, "It is very difficult. Please, tell me Santa, if I am convinced that the Bunky Princess is in Walmland, will Bunky's dream come true?"

"Yes, with time and patience, it is guaranteed," offered Santa Claus, "but your faith has to be very strong. You should be fully convinced that it *will* happen. It is a general principle of life."

"Oh, it is so difficult!" whispered Rodney, "It is so hard to be convinced that the Bunky Princess will step into our world! I will try harder!"

"Faith, faith, faith . . .," whispered Rodney. He closed his eyes and then opened them again. A new idea crossed his mind.

"Dear Santa, perhaps there is a magic spell that we can use?" he asked.

But Santa Claus shook his head. "The true magic comes only from one's heart, not from magic spells," he explained.

On hearing this, Rodney closed his eyes again. His task was almost impossible. To imagine the Bunky Princess was the one thing, but to become fully convinced that she was *real*—it was verging on impossible!

"She is almost here . . .," whispered Rodney and he thought about his cousin.

He knew that he was trying to believe in something almost impossible. But if he kept thinking that it was impossible, how would it become *possible*? It was so simple and so difficult at the same time—just like telling the truth.

Santa Claus was looking at Rodney with sympathy and kindness. "Please, remember Rodney," he remarked, "Christmas is the time when all that is impossible may easily come true if only one *believes* so."

"I *believe* so . . .," whispered Rodney and tried to imagine Bunky Hippo taking a walk with the Bunky Princess. He imagined them strolling around the pond, his cousin Bunky dressed in his Christmas sweater with the squirrel, and the Princess clad in a pink dress with a glamorous veil falling down her back.

"They are talking about dinosaurs," he thought.

And then something amazing happened: the scene disappeared and Rodney saw another place. There was a Bunky girl, perhaps his cousin's age, walking through the snowy pavements of Walmland in her pink boots and whistling a Christmas song. She was whistling so melodically, but Rodney wondered whether princesses could and should whistle at all. Perhaps this one was an exception. Anyway, whistling or not, she was very elegant and princess-like. Rodney opened his eyes.

"I saw her!" he exclaimed," She is walking through Walmland in her pink boots and she is whistling a Christmas song!"

"Ho, ho, ho!" rejoiced Santa Claus in his usual way, "The Christmas magic is working!"

"Can it be the Bunky Princess?" wondered Rodney excitedly, "I am not sure if princesses should whistle."

"Why not?" asked Santa Claus, "She might be whistling very gracefully."

"Then it must be her!" decided Rodney and looked at Santa Claus. They began laughing, until everyone in the sledge wondered what made them so cheerful.

"My little friend, you accomplished the *impossible*," said Santa Claus, "and you are the proof that nothing is impossible."

"Nothing is impossible!" repeated Rodney and felt warmth in his heart. It was even nicer to accomplish the *impossible* for a person who was so important to him.

They returned to the sledge and the rest of the company looked from Santa Claus to Rodney and from Rodney to Santa Claus.

"Ah," said Santa Claus, "You must be curious what we've been discussing with Rodney, but we cannot tell you just yet. It is related to Bunky's secret, and because it is a secret, we have to keep it to ourselves for a while more."

"And it is something very good," smiled Rodney, "very, very good."

The sun appeared in its full glory on the eastern horizon. For a while, it admired its own reflection in the pond next to which only yesterday Bunky, Rodney and Plum were passing by with their sledge. And to think that today they were travelling in Santa Claus's sledge led by Rudolph the Reindeer!

While Bunky the Christmas Hero was delivering the last gifts and Santa Claus was having a very special conversation with Rodney, Mr. and Mrs. Walm were already returning home with a bag full of wonderful Christmas mugs and with a beautiful bowl for Plum. Mrs. Walm was carrying the parcel with Bunky's skating boots, while Mr. Walm was carrying the bag containing Christmas mugs and the bowl—just like a helpful husband would do. The skating boots were of a light blue colour with red shoelaces and silvery, shiny plates. Mrs. Walm could hardly wait to give them to her little Bunky.

Back at home, she placed the parcel underneath the Christmas tree and smiled while thinking how happy Bunky would be on discovering the gift. It was ten to ten in the morning and she imagined that soon Bunky, Rodney, and Plum would be geting up.

"They had already overslept," she thought.

Mr. Meow and Mr. Elk stayed overnight and, currently, they were taking their showers. You may think, Dear Readers, that ten to ten in the morning is the time when everyone should be wide awake—but please remember that it was Christmas—the perfect time to sleep a little longer. Bill and Barbara were already in the living room, Barbara reading a book and Bill studying a newspaper. Sir Williams was also there, already showered and thinking about breakfast, yet at the same time mysteriously immersed in his writing. The book *A Full and Detailed Guide to the Perfect Life of An Old Bachelor* was absorbing a lot of his free time.

Every bachelor should dust his house at least once in two weeks—and I would like to emphasize: "at least"—Sir Williams wrote ardently with a quiet hope that other bachelors inhabiting the world would profit from his beneficial instructions and clear-sighted observations.

"Good morning!" said aunt Walm cheerfully and directed her steps towards the kitchen. There uncle Walm was already preparing warm rice with stewed apples and cacao—his speciality on winter mornings. Aunt Walm wanted to help her hard-working husband but, being so excited about the skating boots, she couldn't wait any longer and gently knocked on Bunky's bedroom door.

"Good morning," she said softly.

But there was silence on the other side—not even a yawn or a sound indicating that Bunky would be stretching after his night sleep. Aunt Walm quietly opened the door and saw an empty room. She just said "oh" and, for a while, she was standing motionless in the door. There was no Bunky in bed and there was no Plum in the basket.

Dear Readers, you cannot imagine what were aunt Walm's feelings in that moment—it was an indescribable mixture of astonishment and fear. After a short while, she thought about Rodney. She ran to his room and knocked on the door. After a while, she opened the door and also discovered that Rodney's bedroom was empty. Mrs. Walm felt faintly. But then she thought that they might be playing outside. She hurriedly went back to the living room. Uncle Walm was already there, waiting for aunt Walm to serve his special breakfast.

"Have you seen Bunky, Rodney and Plum?" asked aunt Walm nervously, "They are not in their bedrooms!"

Mr. Elk, Mr. Meow, Sir Williams, aunt Barbara, uncle Bill, and uncle Walm all stared at aunt Walm in silence. The Mice ran out of their hole. They were still wearing pyjamas and, currently, they were holding cups with their morning coffee. There was a visible concern on their faces.

"Aren't they outside?" asked Sir Williams with a lot of hope in his voice and looked through the window. Unfortunately, he didn't see much because of the Snowmen standing in the way.

"We woke up very early, but we haven't seen them so far," said aunt Barbara with a faintly voice, "What could have happened?"

"Why and where did they go?" despaired aunt Walm.

Dear Readers, you cannot imagine what a trying moment it was for her. Uncle Walm offered aunt Walm his arm and they all rushed again to Bunky's bedroom. They were greatly disturbed by the sudden disappearance of Bunky, Rodney and Plum, but it was especially uncle Bill who had the strangest expression on his face. He looked like a person who was on the verge of saying something, but who was continuously stopping himself from doing so. Indeed, he was in the middle of an inner struggle.

"What is it?" asked Mr. Meow, pointing at the letter on Bunky's bed.

"A letter!" exclaimed aunt Barbara, wringing her hands.

Seeing that aunt Walm was at her wits' end, uncle Walm picked up the letter and read the following:

> Dear Aunt,
>
> Rodney, Plum, and I are safe and well. If you read this letter, you will see that we are not here, but please rest reassured that we will be back very soon. We went to the Faroe Islands with Rudolph the Reindeer where we are going to repair Santa Claus's broken

sledge (we borrowed uncle Walm's screwdriver in order to succeed), and then we will help Santa Claus to distribute Christmas gifts all over the world. Christmas is at stake and we have to save it! Santa Claus will bring us back home at 10:00 am. Please do not worry because we took warm clothes, sandwiches, and hot tea, as you always advise us to do. Dear aunt, we love you and will be back soon!

Bunky, Rodney, and Plum

"It's four minutes to ten," observed uncle Walm, looking at his watch, "According to the letter, they should be back at ten."

"What does all this mean?" said aunt Walm with desperation in her voice, "My little children!"

"At least they are warmly dressed," offered Sir Williams, not knowing what to say in order to sound comforting. In truth, he was greatly worried too.

"Do you think that this is all true?" asked aunt Barbara, "Perhaps they encountered a stranger who told them lies?"

"Oh, that would be terrible!" groaned aunt Walm and felt tears gathering in her eyes.

It was a very sad moment. I don't think that anyone of us, Dear Readers, would like to see anyone crying in this novel and, especially, such a good person as aunt Walm, therefore let us send uncle Bill to the rescue! He was sitting quietly on Bunky's chair all this time, wondering what to do.

"Ehm ehm," began uncle Bill and he immediately received everyone's attention, "I want to say that I saw them and talked with them and they are safe."

"Oh, why didn't you tell us immediately?!" groaned aunt Barbara with a look of dismay on her face.

Everyone gave a sigh of relief and aunt Walm felt that she is becoming brave and strong again.

"When was it?" asked uncle Walm.

"It was at night," explained uncle Bill, almost turning red, "but I couldn't tell you anything—I promised to keep a secret. Now that you found the letter, I can explain."

Aunt Walm gave uncle Bill a questioning look.

"Yes, I can explain and confirm," continued uncle Bill, feeling that he sounds like a foolish person, "that Bunky, Rodney and Plum embarked on the quest to save Santa Claus's sleigh and this year's Christmas. I encountered them at night while taking a walk around the house and they were in the backyard with Rudolph the Reindeer, ready to travel to the Faroe Islands. All warmly dressed as they promised in the letter."

Here uncle Bill stopped explaining and looked at everyone's faces. It was two to ten. There was no enthusiasm in the room and uncle Bill felt that his words did not change a lot.

"Dear Bill, as much as I really like you, you must be kidding," said Sir Williams.

"Are you seriously telling us that they went on a trip with Rudolph the Reindeer?" asked Mr. Elk.

Uncle Bill felt uneasy. He saw that Sir Williams, Mr. Elk, and Mr. Meow began acting like many grown-ups would do. Their disbelief in Santa Claus was apparent—at least in this moment. How difficult it is to convince others that something seemingly impossible might be true! He gazed at aunt Barbara, hoping to find in her the support he needed. After all, she was the love of his life and always trusted him.

"I believe Bill," offered aunt Barbara, "I always believe Bill and I know that he is always telling the truth."

Now you see, Dear Readers, how important it is to always tell the truth—then others won't question your words when the moment like this arrives. Bill smiled at her lovingly and looked inquiringly at aunt and uncle Walm.

"Hmm," said uncle Walm with an undecided voice, "was it Rudolph the Reindeer himself?"

"Yes," answered uncle Bill, "I recognised him immediately! He also visited me with Santa Claus when I was just Bunky's age. Perhaps it is our family's tradition to meet Rudolph the Reindeer on Christmas!"

"And save Christmas!" smiled uncle Walm. He felt that he could trust uncle Bill.

Aunt Walm looked at uncle Bill curiously. She was trying to believe him. She liked him a lot and knew that he was a trustworthy person.

"I believe you too," she said finally and felt relieved.

"And then I do too," added uncle Walm, just to confirm it.

The tiny Mice which gathered under Bunky's desk began cheering in approval.

"What about you?" asked uncle Bill, looking at Sir Williams, Mr. Elk, and Mr. Meow. They did not look fully convinced.

"Well," continued uncle Bill, "if you don't believe in my words, how could you ever tell us that you believe in Santa Claus or Christmas? If you don't believe in Rudolph the Reindeer, why do you call Christmas a magical season?"

Sir Williams thought that the questions were also directed at him, so he decided to speak as a voice representing all the worldly bachelors.

"I thought that it was a *metaphor*," he explained, "That is, an expression that shouldn't be understood in a literal sense."

"No," said uncle Bill, "it is not a metaphor. It is the simplest truth."

"I'm really sorry, I do believe you," said Sir Williams, suddenly feeling that, perhaps, there was much more to life than logic and metaphors. He also felt slightly embarrassed. After all, uncle Bill must have been telling the truth.

"I wonder that there is nothing wrong in supposing that you are right," said Mr. Meow apologetically and Mr. Elk nodded his head. Uncle Bill's face lit up.

"It is alright," he said, "You will become fully convinced *sometimes*. Perhaps even in a while."

He didn't even realise how close this moment of revelation was for Sir Williams, Mr. Elk and Mr. Meow. The clock in the living room struck ten.

"It's ten," said uncle Walm, checking his watch again. Sir Williams, Mr. Elk and Mr. Meow looked at each other in hope and wonder. Aunt Walm and aunt Barbara looked at each other too and smiled reassuringly.

"They should be coming back *right now*," said aunt Walm quietly.

"Yes," responded Barbara in a whisper, feeling that something important was going to happen.

And then, the Christmas magic gradually filled Mr. Meow's, Mr. Elk's, and Sir Willams' hearts with a childlike hope, as suddenly they heard sleigh bells ringing outside. At first, it was a distant, almost inaudible sound of a subtle "ding, ding, ding," as if someone was shaking a tiny bell. Then, the sound grew stronger and more resonant, turning into a cheerful melody of "ding, dong, ding, ding, ding, dong, ding, ding ding dong." It was very soothing and heart-warming, as if everything was filling with joy, and even the snow outside appeared to be whiter and brighter. The sounds were coming, undoubtedly, from the bells in Santa Claus's sledge! Uncle Bill grinned from ear to ear.

"Let's go outside, let's greet them!" cried aunt Walm and, fully restored to her previous courageous spirits, she ran towards the front door. Uncle Walm followed her immediately.

"I always wanted to meet Santa Claus!" rejoiced aunt Barbara and followed them.

The Mice ran out of the room in order to celebrate their friends' arrival on the terrace.

"But they wanted to *return in secret*!" observed uncle Bill, but since no one was listening to him anymore, he just waved his hand and followed everyone to greet Santa Claus and his Helpers.

"I was trying my best and, since they found the letter, it's ok!" he said to himself and smiled. It was a huge relief to him that everything was going to end well, as he also loved Bunky, Rodney, and Plum very much.

9

The Christmas Heroes Return and Dreams Turn into Reality

We left our Christmas Heroes in the very moment when they were approaching the Walms' house in Santa Claus's sledge. As you remember, Bunky slightly leant over the sledge and saw the characteristic chocolate brown rooftop of the Walms' house.

"Home on the horizon!" he announced.

He leant over a bit more in order to see better. Bunkies are very enthusiastic, but not always careful. Bunky leant out of the sledge to the point when he could hardly keep his balance and began waving his arms in the air. Santa Claus turned around and instantly saw what was happening.

"Bunky!!" he shouted, quickly reaching into his pocket in order to find some magic stardust that would prevent Bunky from an impending fall.

Rodney and Plum, very tired after the nightly travel, were just drowsing off in warm blankets when they heard Santa Claus's alarming cry. And then, something incredible happened: Plum immediately jumped forward and caught hold of Bunky's Christmas sweater. The sweater stretched dangerously but, just in few moments, Bunky was safely back in the sledge. It all took place in the blink of an eye. Merino and Shetland gave a sigh of relief. Santa Claus wiped sweat from his forehead and immediately felt better on seeing that Bunky was back in the sledge.

"It is for the future, although I hope that it won't happen again," he said, offering Bunky the bottle of stardust.

"Oh!" groaned Bunky, looking at his sweater which instantly returned to its previous shape, what obviously attested to the high quality of the wool, "Oh, oh, oh!"

"My dear friend Bunky!" cried Santa Claus, "We all got so scared!"

"Oh cousin!" squealed Rodney, pressing both paws to his cheeks. He was fully awake.

"If not for Plum, I don't want to imagine what would happen!"

"I am so sorry!" kept groaning Bunky, "Bunkies are usually really good at keeping their balance, but this time it wasn't so!"

Bunky imagined the Bunky Princess's reaction on seeing his misfortune and it was the first time ever when he felt glad that she wasn't here to see his unintended acrobatics.

Plum was quietly sitting at Bunky's side, staring at him with his big, understanding blue eyes. Bunky embraced him, pressing his face to the Wolf's back. It was such a soft and fluffy back.

"Oh Plum," cried Bunky, "I am so grateful that you have saved me!"

"Yes, yes, I am so grateful for both of you!" cried Rodney, embracing both Plum and his cousin in order to make sure that they won't be leaning over again. It was too much for the brave, little Rodney who just woke up from his short nap.

But Plum only smiled confidently and wagged his tail. He knew that he would always help his best friends.

"I am so grateful that you saved me on Christmas Eve," he quietly responded, "You are my best friends and my true family."

"Best friends forever!" squealed Rodney and felt too moved to continue squealing. Tears were gathering in his eyes, but these were the tears of joy which usually appear together with a happy ending. Suddenly, he started missing home and felt that he needed some rest from this uncommon adventure.

With a hint of nostalgia in his heart, Santa Claus thought that the old, good Christmas spirit truly returned this year. Christmas became again what it had been in the past: not only a short-lived happiness from the received gifts but, mainly, the grand celebration of courage, friendship, empathy, and love.

"Good deeds always return to a good person," said Santa Claus knowingly, "One day you might be in trouble and someone with a kind heart might save you and then, on another day, you might become a saviour. What Plum did was truly exceptional and it will not escape my notice."

"I've already added a footnote on the nice list about Plum and his courage," confirmed Merino.

"A footnote sounds great but please, without a diagram or statistics," remarked Santa Claus, "But now, it's time to hold on tight! We are landing! Ho, ho, ho!"

Bunky was still dizzy from his unexpected adventure, but he was also aware that these were the last minutes or, maybe seconds, of this enchanting ride high in the morning skies. Will he ever be able to travel in Santa Claus's sledge again? Will he ever spend time abroad again? And where was the Bunky Princess? He had not encountered her through the entire night, and he had been travelling through the entire world! Perhaps she was fast asleep or, perhaps, Bunkyland was beyond this world. But, if so, Bunky wondered, how was he meant to find this place?

A tiny, hopeful thought passed through his mind: from now on, he will be very, very good—through the entire year! Perhaps Santa Claus will take it into account and invite him as his Helper next year too! He, Rodney, and Plum gained a lot of experience as Santa Claus's Christmas Helpers. Who would be able to take their place? Hopefully no one!

"I might still find the Bunky Princess," thought Bunky.

They were descending at unprecedented speed but, after the whole night of riding in Santa Claus's sledge, this type of commuting turned out to be far from scary and became rather exhilarating. Bunky shouted "whohoooo!" and felt a refreshing morning breeze on his forehead. At present, they were just above the Walms' house and he could see the entire neighbourhood.

"Our house is the most beautiful of all the houses in Walmland!" thought Bunky with unconcealed pride.

Obviously, he decided that the Walms' house was the most beautiful because his whole heart belonged to it. He realised how much he missed home. But then, he reminded himself about another cosy and inviting place—Mrs. Amalia's house.

"I will visit Mrs. Amalia and Mr. Cat the soonest possible," decided Bunky and thought that it would be a very kind deed.

The inhabitants of the Walmland Village looked from above like tiny ants walking back and forth through an equally tiny main road—a white, glistening stripe among miniature trees, hills, and buildings. Most probably, they were taking refreshing Christmas walks.

"There are no skyscrapers here," observed Rodney.

"I'm glad," remarked Bunky.

The whole Walmland Village was covered with fresh snow, remind-ing Bunky of his favourite breakfast—white rice with stewed apples—uncle Walm's speciality. Bunky suddenly realised how much he loved everything about the Walmland Village: not only uncle Walms' breakfast, but every road and every tree, every pond, every lake, and every star shining above this place. He had been travelling all over the world and yet, Walmland was still his favourite place. He couldn't imagine living anywhere else. Who would suppose, wondered Bunky, that he would miss every slope, every road, every lake so much! Now that he became a *worldly* and *sophisticated* indidivual thanks to his travel, he felt very homesick and could not wait to return back home. Still, he hoped to visit the Faroe Islands one day again. And then, it surprised him that that there were several onlookers in the front yard of the Walms' house.

"What is this gathering?" he asked.

As the sledge was drifting down, he was astonished to discover that it was his whole family gathered around the terrace, looking up and waving to them. Even Mr. Elk and Mr. Meow were there, still in their pyjamas! Bunky was flabbergasted[1].

"We are no longer mysterious!" he observed, "We are *discovered*! The whole family is in the front yard waving to us!"

Rodney and Plum looked down with curiosity. Merino and Shetland gave Santa Claus a questioning look.

"They must have read the letter!" squealed Rodney.

"Aunt Walm must have been in our room before 10:00 am!" realised Bunky.

Now, when all the family saw the enchanted sledge and the magic Reindeer running through the invisible road up in the air, it was quite im-possible to continue being mysterious. To their surprise, Santa Claus was very relaxed.

"It is all fine," he reassured them with a broad smile, "We have already saved Christmas and delivered all the presents on time! You left the letter with explanation and your family has the right to know the truth."

"And what will happen when they see *you*, Santa?" wondered Bunky nervously.

"What will happen? Well, they will meet me in person and they will fully believe in Santa Claus!" he smiled, "I sense that some adults believe

1. Very surprised.

in me only partially, so it is a good opportunity to convince them that I am real!"

"How is it possible to believe in something only partially?" squealed Rodney.

"I think they call it *to some extent*," offered Bunky, "This is how adults call it when they feel too grown up to believe in something which doesn't seem grown-up enough for them."

"Well, let's think about it. Nothing can exist only *partially*," observed Rodney, "This is against logic."

"Ah, logic!" groaned Bunky.

"Also, you cannot partially believe and partially not believe in something," continued Rodney.

The Reindeer made a graceful circle in the air and continued descending towards the front yard. They could already hear all the family but, surprisingly, the Mice were the loudest.

"Apparently, they are not mad at us," observed Bunky.

"Ho, ho, ho!" rejoiced Santa Claus, "I feel that they are very proud of all the three of you!"

"Hopefully, hopefully!" exclaimed Bunky.

The sledge parked in the middle of the front yard, just in front of the terrace where the Mice were dancing a very complicated dance, some of them still holding miniature coffee cups.

"The *Mouses* are dancing on the terrace! They are happy that we are back!" said astonished Bunky and felt very moved.

"I would like to share with them all my favourite shoelaces," he thought.

Aunt and uncle Walm ran towards them with open arms and Bunky
found himself in a loving embrace of those whom he missed so dearly, even
though he was abroad only for one night. Rodney and Plum were also in
this loving embrace, so happy to be back home. Bunky realised that there
were tears in his eyes.

"Aunt," he said, "I can easily explain everything. I am so sorry. I promise that it was the last time when we left the house through the window in the middle of the night. And Santa Claus . . ."

And here Bunky realised that he was still in the company of Santa Claus, the Elves, and the Reindeer.

" . . .Santa Claus is here!" he exclaimed, "And also our friends: Merino, Shetland, and the Reindeer! We travelled to the Faroe Islands on Rudolph's back!"

"Dear friends," Santa Claus addressed everyone, "please meet the Heroes of this Year's Christmas: Bunky, Rodney, and Plum!"

"Welcome home, Christmas Heroes!" cheered everyone, "Hooray, hooray, hooray!!"

As you rightly suppose, the Mice were the loudest again. Rodney and Plum were especially happy and surprised: Santa Claus called them "the Heroes" too!

Uncle Bill gave Rudolph the Reindeer a big hug. "I hoped so much . . ." he said, "I truly hoped so much that we will meet again!"

And then, Santa Claus joined uncle Bill and Rudolph and they greeted each other like good old friends do—even though the last time Santa Claus met uncle Bill was when uncle was very small and wasn't even an uncle.

"I wanted to thank you for the herbal pills for memory loss," said Santa Claus, "I feel like my old memories are slowly returning. But you, Bill, you are the person whom I always remembered! And if I am to be honest, you have not changed at all!"

It was true: Santa Claus could see uncle Bill's heart and it was still the same—childlike and honest.

Aunt Barbara nodded her head gratefully towards Santa Claus and Rudolph. "I am so glad to get to know my husband's good friends," she remarked.

In the meantime, the Mice surrounded Bunky, Rodney, and Plum and continued their wild dance with their tiny coffee mugs.

Sir Williams, Mr. Meow, and Mr. Elk initially participated in the overall joy. They had been immensely worried about Bunky, Rodney, and Plum and they were so relieved on their arrival. Yet, at present, they were standing quietly behind the Snowmen, gazing with reverence at Santa Claus, the Elves, and the Reindeer. Santa Claus knew their hearts like the palm of his hand and easily recognised their shame. He also recognised a lot of goodness in these hearts. He understood that it was just a temporary disbelief.

"Everyone should receive a hug from Santa Claus, even adults," he stated, patting Sir Williams, Mr. Elk, and Mr. Meow on their heads as if they were children.

"We deeply apologise . . .," said Sir Williams, seeing that Santa Claus knew what was on their minds.

"There is nothing to apologise for," smiled Santa Claus and, in a moment, Sir Williams, Mr. Meow, and Mr. Elk felt childlike and carefree again.

"What a beautiful feeling," observed Mr. Meow.

"Almost like I could fly!" Mr. Elk joined him.

"I feel so happy!" said Sir Williams in a trembling voice.

"The good, old Christmas is here once again," thought Santa Claus, reflecting on all the miracles happening in front of the Walms' house.

Something special happened again—something that made our Hero, Bunky, even happier than before.

"Breakfast everyone!" uncle Walm announced loudly, "Warm rice with stewed apples and cacao!"

"Finally, I am home!" Bunky thought.

What a joy it was to have breakfast in the living room in the company of Santa Claus, two Elves, and the Reindeer! All the nine Reindeer fit through the door and gathered around the table on which uncle Walm triumphantly placed a tray with his best breakfast. He was honoured that such magical guests would try one of his favourite meals. The Mice ensconced themselves on the table on Christmas napkins, whereas our resourceful aunt Walm offered them bottle caps which they could use as plates. Bunky the Christmas Hero was finally resting, sprawled on the sofa close to the table in the company of two other Heroes—Rodney and Plum. They were all very, very tired. Santa Claus received Great Grandma Walm's armchair and the rest of the company satisfied themselves with cushioned chairs. The living room was bustling with life.

Even though he was so tired, Bunky did not forget to throw a secret look at the portraits of his ancestors. They were smiling from ear to ear, carefully watching Santa Claus and other guests. Great Grandma Walm winked at Bunky, or at least this is what he thought she did.

"Unbelievable!" thought Bunky and began his breakfast on the sofa.

Usually aunt Walm would disapprove of eating on the sofa, but today the Christmas Heroes were allowed to eat wherever they wanted to have their meal. Bunky threw another glance at Great Grandma Walm's portrait and saw her winking again. Was it an illusion?

"Perhaps Great Grandma Walm is proud of us too," he thought and felt so tired that he almost fell asleep.

"Saving the world requires a lot of sleep afterwards," he resolved.

Great Grandma Walm nodded from her portrait. Bunky winked and decided to go to bed early. But how was it possible to go to bed early when so much was happening all around him?

Rodney and Plum couldn't stop yawning—it was a very long night for them too. The breakfast lasted longer than usual, as everyone wanted to talk with Santa Claus, the Elves, and his Reindeer. Uncle Bill was sitting between Santa Claus and Rudolph the Reeinder and his face was beaming with happiness. They had a very long conversation filled with the memories from those old days when little Bill encountered Rudolph and Santa Claus in his living room. Shetland and Merino were listening carefully, as if it was a Christmas fairy tale.

It was, Bunky thought, one of the most amazing breakfests in the history of his family. If only the Bunky Princess could see this gathering! One day, thought Bunky, he would tell her all about his adventures and all about this memorable breakfast! She would be so impressed!

"One day, when I will finally find her . . .," he mused.

"These herbal capsules for memory are doing wonders!" said Santa Claus, "I just feel like all my memories are coming back! I don't think that I would ever confuse any gifts again!"

"Perhaps these are not the capsules, but rather the fact that we are here altogether!" suggested uncle Bill, "All the happy past is here again!"

Bunky overheard their conversation and got up from the sofa.

"But Santa," he said, "it was probably the most fortunate mistake because, you know, I just *adore* the cookbook!"

This time he meant it with his whole heart. Santa Claus patted Bunky on his head.

"But Santa," whispered Bunky confidentially, "will you please take us for a trip next year too? Even if your memory is fully restored?"

Santa Claus looked at Bunky thoughtfully.

"I don't think that I would be able to travel on Christmas without the three of you—especially since we developed such a special bond and created so many memories," he responded, "but please, refrain from sharing our plans with your aunt and uncle at least until tomorrow—so that they have some time to get better after today's shock."

Bunky grinned at Santa Claus and returned to the sofa. He was sure that Great Grandma Walm grinned from her portrait too.

Conversations at the table lasted till noon and, finally, Santa Claus remarked that they should be returning to the North Pole.

"I don't want Mrs. Claus to be alarmed," he explained, but everyone kept protesting, especially Sir Williams, Mr. Meow, and Mr. Elk who experienced a spiritual return to their childhood years. They hoped to teach Shetland and Merino the game of pick-up sticks and worried that there wouldn't be enough time.

"Smile, everyone!"

Aunt Walm appeared in the living room with a camera. Bunky grinned from ear to ear.

Before leaving, Santa Claus decided to have a word in private with the Christmas Heroes. He took Bunky by the hand and Bunky took Rodney by the hand too, while Rodney embraced Plum. They took a path to the backyard were frost covered the boxwood with a silvery-white paint. It was the very same boxwood nearby which Bunky encountered Plum on the famous Christmas Eve—the Christmas Eve he would never forget.

"Here we are where it all started," thought Bunky, "Here I met Plum."

Yes, mysterious adventures usually start in the backyard. The world around them was very quiet, submerged in an elegant, festive kind of silence. Bunky, Rodney, and Plum remained quiet, trying not to disturb this special peace. Santa Claus spoke first.

"My Christmas Heroes," he began rather officialy, "I have to leave you here for the whole next year. Please be gentle and kind to one another."

The Christmas Heroes nodded their heads. After everything that had taken place, such promise wasn't that difficult.

"I've had the time of my life with the three of you," continued Santa Claus, "and I can say the same about the Elves and the Reindeer. Be sure that we will invite you for the next Christmas travel, my magnificent Christmas Helpers!"

"Hihi!" giggled Bunky joyfully, as he was already thinking about their next travel together.

"Ho, ho, ho!" rejoiced Santa Claus, "Now, I don't have a doubt that you will be good this year!"

"Yes," promised Bunky, "I will be good and kind, especially to my cousin Rodney and to my Plum, and to my aunt and uncle Walm. I will study well and improve in Maths and I won't add sugar to my tea. Not every day, but only on Sundays and on holidays."

"And, perhaps," added Rodney, "we could limit a daily number of cookies."

"Why would you do that?" asked Bunky in astonishment.

"We will be together throughout the whole year!" Plum howled happily.

"Of course!" exclaimed Bunky, "You and Rodney are my best friends!"

"Oh, cousin Bunky!" said Rodney, "I just thought the same! But I will have to leave soon after Christmas and return home with aunt Barbara and uncle Bill!"

"We will be writing to each other very long letters and Plum and I will invite you for the winter break!" decided Bunky, "What about you, Santa? What will you do now?"

"Well," smiled Santa Claus, "I will return home and Mrs. Claus will welcome us with dinner. She will probably be complaining that it took me so long, but she complains because she loves all of us. And probably when I tell her about our adventure, she won't be able to stop complaining. At the same time, I'm sure she will immediately invite you to visit us! Also, I think that I might take a nap—for a day or two. My Reindeer and Elves will be resting too and then we shall start preparations for the spring! You know, Mrs. Claus is very keen on cleaning the floors and washing carpets. She is always finding new carpets and floors to clean."

"Spring already!" wondered Bunky. Indeed, it was as if there were only three seasons: pre-Christmas, Christmas and post-Christmas.

"Now, my friends, I have some gifts for you!" offered Santa Claus with a spark of joy in his eyes.

"Gifts again!" protested Bunky, "We have already received our gifts and we have everything we need!"

"I would like to show you my gratitude," responded Santa Claus, "and you deserve a prize."

"A prize!" squealed Rodney. The word "prize" sounded very, very big and he felt very, very tiny. Even though Rodney was a very mature and responsible person, he was still much younger than Bunky and Bunky himself was still quite small. In Rodney's imagination, the "prize" was something very big—too big for such little creatures as him, Bunky, and Plum.

"Yes, a prize!" smiled Santa Claus, "Rodney, Plum, firstly I have something for you!"

Thus saying, Santa Claus fumbled in his pocket, visibly looking for something and, finally, he placed in front of them a simple bag tied with a red Christmas ribbon. Rodney felt no longer intimidated by the word "prize" and looked gratefully at Santa Claus—he liked simple things. Plum approached the bag and sniffed it carefully. It smelled really nicely—like gingerbread cookies and milky cupcakes. It smelled like Rudolph the Reindeer.

"Dear Santa, thank you so much! Shall we open the bag?" asked Rodney courageously. He felt that it was another Very Important Moment of this Year's Christmas.

"Is it for Rodney and Plum?" asked Bunky, but not because he was envious or disappointed, but only because he wanted to make sure to whom the gift belonged, so that he could participate in his friends' joy. Only within one night had Bunky learnt how to be selfless and how to be happy for others. Also, he had already delievered so many gifts that he could hardly think about seeing any new ones. Yet, the thought that Santa Claus had some gifts for them was making him happy.

"Yes," responded Santa Claus, "It is something for Rodney and Plum and you should definitely open it!"

Rodney's paws trembled, so Plum untied the ribbon.

"Oh!" squealed Rodney.

"Oh!" exclaimed Plum.

"I want to see too!" said Bunky, rushing to get a closer glimpse of the bag. He was astonished to see that it was empty.

Santa Claus was standing aside, smiling in a mysterious way. All at once, several tiny, flickering stars emerged from the bag and surrounded Rodney and Plum, only to disappear seconds later.

"But I dare say that it was empty!" observed surprised Bunky.

"Well, it is just like the magic bag with presents. It is enchanted," explained Santa Claus.

"What happened with the stars?" asked Rodney.

"They are here," answered Santa, placing his hand on Rodney's heart.

"The stars?" Rodney felt slightly confused.

"Well, they weren't precisely the stars. It was *happiness* in the shape of stars. My gift for you is joy. Now, if you like, you will be able to share it with anyone whom you meet!"

"Oh!" squealed Rodney, "What a truly beautiful gift!"

He ran to Bunky and took him by the hand. As soon as Rodney took his cousin's hand, Bunky felt something warm and peaceful in his heart. It was joy.

"Now you are all sharing joy. I wish you happiness through all year round!" rejoiced Santa Claus. Indeed, it was a gift like no other.

At last, Santa Claus addressed Bunky.

"Brave Bunky," he said, "here I have something for you to thank you for all the worthy deeds you have performed last night."

Bunky blushed once again but, obviously, no one could see the blush behind his blue fur. Bunky was often blushing, but it was usually entirely unnoticed.

"Dear Santa, it is really too much about me," he said sincerely.

"You have been travelling all around the world for me, even though it was probably the most difficult decision in your life," responded Santa Claus, reaching for his magic bag.

Deep inside, Bunky thought about his aunt and uncle Walm and agreed.

"Here they are!" Santa Claus announced, offering Bunky . . . a pair of golden skating boots! As he lifted them up in the air, tiny, magical stars glittered around them. Bunky felt faintly and sat down on the snowy ground. Immediately, he heard in his imagination aunt Walm's voice telling him not to sit on the cold ground. He got up and stared at the skating boots with awe and reverence.

"These are . . . for me?" he whispered.

"Of course, my dear friend!" confirmed Santa Claus, "It is the least I can do!"

Bunky could hardly contain his happiness. "If only," he thought, "if only the Bunky Princess could see them!"

"Can I wear them?" he asked eagerly.

"Right now?" asked Santa Claus, "There is nowhere to skate here, my dear, but if you like to try them on, do not hesitate!"

Bunky was thinking for a while and, finally, he grinned in a secretive way.

"I will try them on later in bed!" he answered.

Santa Claus appeared to be a little surprised, but didn't say anything, knowing that Bunky was a very unique individual.

"After all," thought Bunky, "aunt Walm has never told me not to wear skating boots in bed! She asked me not to eat in bed or not to wear dirty clothes in bed, but she has never mentioned skating boots in bed before, so it should be alright!"

"Thank you, dear Santa Claus!" said Bunky, holding both skating boots in his paws and feeling extraordinarily moved.

Santa Claus smiled sincerely and looked at his young friends with his usual peaceful kindness. Bunky, Rodney, and Plum reminded him of his own youth almost two thousand years ago. He felt instantly rejuvenated in their company. Today he felt as young as on that memorable day when, as a very small Santa, he climbed the highest tree in the neighbourhood and his family got worried how to bring him down! "These were the good, old days!" thought Santa Claus mischeviously.

After a while, they all returned to the house, leaving behind them footprints in the snow. The final time of parting was drawing near. In the back of his mind, Santa Claus was constantly thinking about Mrs. Claus and how she would become excessively worried if they were too late.

"Mrs. Claus doesn't know about the wonderful herbal capsules from uncle Bill and about all our adventures, so she might be really worried!" he reasoned with himself.

Still, he didn't feel like leaving the Walms' house. It doesn't mean that he didn't miss Mrs. Claus: he simply hoped that this amazing adventure could last longer, but he was also missing home.

"Perhaps next year you can stay here for a couple of days with Mrs. Claus, the Elves, and the Reindeer?" Rodney asked and aunt Walm immediately clapped her hands in approval. She wasn't even intimidated by the fact that the Reindeer would be probably staying in the living room.

"We would be thrilled to do so!" Santa Claus smiled, "But you should also visit us!"

"In the summer?" asked Rodney with a spark in his eye.

"Whenever you would like to visit us!" promised Santa Claus.

While they were exchanging these warm invitations, Bunky sneaked out of the house to see the Reindeer. Rudolph was standing a little aside, admiring the Snowmen who were still successfully blocking the light in the living room. Yet, it was impossible to be angry with the Snowmen: they both had such serene, happy faces and looked very innocent.

"These are unbelievably perfect Snowmen!" remarked Rudolph, as Bunky approached him quietly.

"Rudolph," said Bunky, "we shall meet soon again. We will!"

"Yes, my dear," promised Rudolph, "We will be delivering gifts world-wide next year too!"

Bunky embraced Rudolph's neck, placing his chin on Rudolph's nose. Rudolph had this very comforting scent of gingerbread cookies and milky cupcakes around him today too.

"I will miss you so much," continued Bunky tearfully, "You are so good and so fluffy. I have a little gift for you."

It was a sugar cube from the kitchen. It looked like a perfectly polished, giant snowflake when placed on Bunky's blue mitten.

"Aunt Walm disapproves of eating such amounts of sugar on daily basis, but today we have a special occasion," Bunky explained and embraced Rudolph again.

"I wish I could keep you in the living room," he continued, "I would cook for you and brush your fur every day, and also I would take you for sleigh rides."

Rudolph the Reindeer smiled.

"They would miss me back at home too," he offered.

"I understand," admitted Bunky. He really understood.

"This is the most delicious sugar cube I have ever received and you are the most amazing Bunky I have ever met," stated Rudolph and fondly touched Bunky's forehead with his nose.

"I don't know why I am getting so attached to everyone," said Bunky almost angrily, not because he was angry but because he didn't want to be perceived as a crybaby. But the truth was that Bunky's tears were a sign of his noble and sensitive heart.

"I think," observed Bunky, kicking a snowdrift with one of his boots in order to keep the tears away, "that I am so attached to all of you because you are so amazing and good, inside and out. You are so special and so genuine. You know, it is not every day that one meets Rudolph the Reindeer and Santa Claus, or even the Elves. And you also believed in me, even though I might have been slightly grumpy at times. Ah . . ."

Bunky burst into tears and embraced Rudolph again. He found out that Rudolph was also crying.

"Now," thought Bunky, "we look like two aunts who met after twenty solitary years of knitting stockings."

But these were all tears of joy. After a while, they stopped sobbing and began laughing. Bunky gathered some snow and threw a snowball in

Rudolph's direction. Then he found his pocket handkerchief—another one which he had received from Santa Claus, and gently dried Rudolph's eyes. It was easier for him than for Rudolph, since Rudolph had hooves and Bunky had paws.

"Perhaps we will meet again as soon as the summer arrives!" Bunky wondered, "In the living room I heard some conversations concerning the summer!"

Everything happened as fast as it usually happens during all unusual, magical events: Santa Claus, Merino, and Shetland hopped into the sledge, the Reindeer began running and soon they were soaring up in the skies, higher and further onwards, heading towards the North Pole. Bunky wondered if they would encounter the Northern Star and what would Mrs. Claus say on hearing about their adventures. They were all standing on the terrace, Mice including, waving tissues, scarves and even bedclothes—everything available at hand. Everyone wanted to bid Santa Claus farewell. The Mice gathered outside on a railing, fervently waving feathers.

Apart from Santa Claus, Merino, and Shetland, there was one additional passenger in the sledge who was admiring the Walmland Village from above for the first time in his life. It was Sir Williams. Santa Claus offered to drive him to his uncle's house, so that he could finally pay his long-awaited visit. According to the plan, Sir Williams would return by bus in a week's time. He was very excited to travel in Santa Claus's sledge and already imagined the surprise on Sir Laurent's face. He also wanted to see Lady Octavia and all the fluffy Alpacas.

Soon the sledge transformed into a tiny flicker on the background of the sky and completely disappeared on the horizon. Bunky turned around towards his family and saw their dreamy faces.

"But it really happened, it really happened!" he kept repeating as if hypnothised.

Uncle Bill placed his hand on Bunky's shoulder in a friendly and understanding manner. "You have my word for it, Bunky, and I assure you that you will see your new friends soon again," he offered.

"They invited us for the summer and we invited them to stay with us after Christmas!" aunt Walm reminded them. She was very enthusiastic about Santa Claus's visit.

"Then," said Bunky, smiling from ear to ear quite mysteriously, "you won't be too mad with us if I tell you that next year Rodney, Plum, and I are also delivering gifts with Santa Claus and Rudolph!"

Instead of being mad, aunt Walm was beaming with pride.

"That's great news, my little Bunky," she said, "but just promise me that you won't be secretly leaving through the window anymore!"

"Oh, aunt!" mumbled Bunky, "You would never let us go otherwise!"

"But now I allow you!"

"But it is different, since now you are personally acquainted with Santa Claus!"

They spent the entire afternoon on such and similar conversations. In the meantime, Bunky made three circles around the house to make sure that Santa Claus's footprints were still there and, afterwards, requested Rodney to pinch him, but Rodney denied to do so. In the evening, the three Christmas Heroes felt extremely sleepy. Rodney decided to sleep in Bunky's room, since he wanted to be close to his friends. Plum made himself comfortable among the soft blankets in his cosy basket and Rodney brought his pillow. Bunky was already in bed, wearing his golden skates. Each time he moved his legs, those tiny magic stars would float around the room.

"These are magical skating boots," he explained in a whisper.

There was a sudden gentle knock at the door. The door creaked open and uncle Bill appeared.

"I apologise," he said in a low voice, "I really couldn't fall asleep and I was thinking about the three of you."

"Oh uncle, please come in!" said Bunky invitingly.

Uncle Bill tiptoed into the room and sat on Bunky's bed, thus joining the whole company.

"I am very proud that you, Rodney, and Plum keep the family tradition alive," said uncle Bill, beaming with sincere joy, "As soon as I saw you with Rudolph the Reindeer, I understood everything immediately. It's been a very long family tradition."

"A very long tradition?" Bunky got interested in uncle's words and instantly sat on his bed, resigning from sleeping.

"Tell us about it, uncle," begged Rodney, "We cannot fall asleep anyway, even though we are so tired!"

Plum's ears perked up too. Rodney made himself comfortable in bed, supporting his chin with both paws. They were ready for a goodnight story. Uncle Bill smiled quite secretly.

"Yes," he said, "It is a long family tradition. Your Great Grandma Walm was the first to encounter Rudolph the Reindeer and Santa Claus on one Christmas Eve. Years ago, she told me this story in person."

"Ah, I knew that!" exclaimed Bunky rather too loudly but, thankfully, he didn't wake up anyone, "I could swear that Great Grandma Walm was winking at me from the portrait during our breakfast with Santa Claus!"

"That is highly possible," agreed uncle Walm in an amazingly simple way. Bunky loved his attitude.

"So what happened exactly, uncle?" inquired Rodney impatiently. He really wanted to know everything.

"Once upon a time, when Great Grandma Walm was a very litte girl, just like you . . .," began uncle Bill.

"I'm not a little girl," Bunky interrupted him. Uncle Bill began anew:

"Once upon a time, when Great Grandma Walm was very little, just like you are . . ."

"Yes, we are *very* little," Bunky echoed uncle's words in an approving way. He was satisfied with the new version of the story.

" . . .very little, just as you are," continued uncle Bill, "she couldn't sleep . . ."

"Just like us!" squealed Rodney, "We cannot sleep!"

"Shhh!" said Bunky.

Uncle Bill sighed and continued: "In short . . ."

"No, uncle, we would like a full version of the story," begged Bunky.

"Shhh!" said Rodney this time.

"Ah," said uncle Bill, "so anyway, she was very little and couldn't sleep and dreamt about a chocolate cookie . . ."

"Just like Bunky!" giggled Rodney.

Bunky pretended that he didn't hear him but, after a while, he decided to make a short remark: "Quite recently I cut down on sugar," he observed.

"Oh, my dear ones," began uncle Bill again, "I am trying to tell you the rest."

"But we are listening, uncle," said Bunky, "We are all ears!"

"She went to the living room in order to search for cookies left on the table after the dinner," continued uncle Bill, "There was a big window in the living room and she saw a Deer looking at her from the outside."

"Ohhh, it was Rudolph the Reindeer!" squealed Rodney.

"We all know that," groaned Bunky, "Shhh . . ."

"Well, it wasn't exactly Rudolph the Reindeer with whom you are acquainted personally, but Rudolph's father, also called Rudolph," uncle Bill explained, "Great Grandma Walm was a very brave little girl and she did not hesitate even for a moment to open the terrace door and let the Reindeer in. It was a very cold, snowy night and she thought that the Reindeer must be cold from standing outside. And then, the Reindeer introduced himself . . ."

"I am Rudolph the Reindeer!" exclaimed Rodney in excitement, trying to sound like Rudolph himself.

"Yes, and Great Grandma Walm believed him. She offered Rudolph cookies from the table and begged him to take her to the North Pole. She had been hoping to become a traveller since the age of two. And then Santa Claus appeared in the living room. Back then he was using chimneys in some of the houses, so he appeared quite of the blue. Great Grandma Walm managed to convince Rudolph and Santa Claus that she would be a perfect Helper and spent the whole night delivering presents all over the world . . ."

"Really?" asked Bunky, "Great Grandma Walm was the Christmas Heroine?"

"Yes," agreed uncle Bill, "She was a very brave girl and a very courageous and strong woman later on in her adult life. Just as women can be."

"Wow!" squealed Rodney, "What an amazing story!"

"I am so proud of Great Grandma Walm!" said Bunky, "Truly proud to have such an invincible woman in our family!"

"Your aunts are also invincible, believe me!" smiled uncle Bill, "Now, it's time for you to go to sleep."

"How can we sleep after hearing such highly exciting family stories?" asked Rodney, but soon they were all fast asleep, dreaming about their adventures, and uncle Bill got up from Bunky's bed and gently closed the door.

He went to his room where aunt Barbara had been sleeping for several hours, tiptoed to the window and gazed at the moonlit sky and frozen pavements of Walmland. Uncle Bill still didn't understand everything from the mysteries of life, but he deeply believed in the magic of kindness, goodness and hope. These three existed and could do wonders when put to good use—of that he was sure.

"Life," whispered uncle Bill, "The biggest adventure of all." And then he peacefully went to sleep.

10

Bunky Finds Ultimate Happiness in the Walmland Village

Bunky woke up with the golden skating boots on his feet. Naturally, he forgot to take them off before falling asleep.

"Ah, I was dreaming all night about skating!" he mumbled while yawning, stretching, and removing the boots from his feet. He placed them carefully underneath his bed, next to the precious blue notebook.

Rodney and Plum were still fast asleep. They were breathing in a peaceful and regular way like someone resting after a very long and tiring day. Bunky wrapped himself up in his dressing gown and tiptoed out of the room in order to shower. From there, happy and refreshed, he marched straight to the living room. It was still quite early but he didn't want to waste any time. He didn't want to waste a single minute from his life anymore, especially since the world was such a bright and hopeful place where magical events could really take place. On entering the living room, Bunky looked curiously at Great Grandma Walm's portrait and saw her beaming with joy. Even the wrinkles around her eyes disappeared, as if someone repainted her portrait overnight.

"She is happy," thought Bunky, "and so am I."

"I am proud of you, Great Grandma Walm," he whispered to the portrait.

Aunt Walm was already in the living room. Bunky noticed her sitting in Great Grandma Walm's armchair, reading *The Adventures of One*

Tiny Snowflake. On seeing Bunky, she put her book aside and smiled comfortingly.

"Dear aunt!" cried Bunky, "Good morning!"

"Come here, my little Bunky!" said aunt Walm, rising from the arm-chair and embracing him.

"I feel that from today everything will be always alright," said Bunky.

"Me too, my dear!"

She smiled and took Bunky by the hand and led him to the magnificent Christmas tree.

"I think that it has taken root," stated aunt Walm, "We will be able to plant the tree in the garden when the spring arrives!"

"Oh, it is truly great! I wouldn't like to watch our beautiful Christmas tree wither—especially after so much happiness it offered us!"

"Yes, my little Bunky. Look what I found here!"

Bunky knelt down underneath the Christmas tree and saw a beautifully wrapped parcel with a note: *For our Little Bunky—from your Loving Aunt and Uncle Walm.* His heart was beating fast as he was slowly unwrapping the box. There, on an ornate paper, he found elegant, blue skating boots with silvery blades. He became quiet. He gazed at the skating boots and thought that it was the most precious gift, as it was from his aunt and uncle—the two persons whom he loved so much. They wanted to make his dream come true against all the odds. He loved the skating boots from Santa Claus, but now he was also very moved by his aunt and uncle's thoughtfulness.

"It is fortunate that aunt and uncle Walm didn't see me receiving the golden skates from Santa Claus," thought Bunky with a sigh of relief.

"I am just so grateful that you are here," he whispered, "Thank you from my heart for the most beautiful skating boots! I do promise that I shall cut down on sugar and, also, I will be skating very carefully. These skating boots are just perfect!"

Aunt Walm patted Bunky's head.

"I am so grateful that *you* are here," she said quietly, "I was going out of my mind when you disappeared."

"I think, aunt, that I should tell you something about Great Grandma Walm and then something about a very kind Bunky Lady who lives here nearby with Mr. Cat," Bunky began.

They sat on the sofa. It began snowing outside again and Santa Claus's footprints entirely disappeared. Naturally, it doesn't mean that Santa Claus became less real. It was the same case like with dinosaurs—nobody saw them, but we all believe that once they were here . . .

๕๖

In the afternoon, Bunky was pacing the streets of the Walmland Village, wondering what Santa Claus might be doing at the present moment and whether Mrs. Claus wasn't too mad at him.

"Well, probably she isn't mad at all. After all, she is Mrs. Claus," he resolved.

In the early afternoon, they received a telegram from Sir Williams—he was sending them his warmest wishes:

> *I shall return by bus with a little delay—probably in two weeks'* *time,* he wrote, *as it is my heart's desire to work here on the liter-* *ary pearl of my life—"A Full and Detailed Guide to Perfect Life of* *An Old Bachelor." The climate here is magnificent for a spiritual* *task, therefore I decided to accomplish my work here, accompa-* *nied by my family and the Alpacas, many of whom being bach-* *elors themselves offer an unprecedented[1] opportunity and unique* *inspiration to create a literary work for generations yet to come!*

The telegram was read aloud in the living room and Mr. Elk and Mr. Meow nodded their heads in approval, vowing that they would be the first readers of this future bestseller.

Bunky was thinking about Sir Williams while carrying a box full of pasta and a box with an unparalleled dessert—a delicious chocolate cake. Aunt Walm lovingly prepared the boxes for Lady Amalia.

"Pet Mr. Cat from me, please," said aunt Walm, offering Bunky the boxes when he was leaving the house.

Today, Bunky was also wearing his beloved Christmas sweater with the squirrel and cotton snowflakes, a warm scarf, winter boots and these very comfortable blue mittens which always accompanied him during all his Christmas adventures. The Walmland Village was bright and thriving with life. It was this singular time between Christmas and New Year when everyone seemed to be doubly happy and busy. Bunky was happy too as he was marching on, stretching his head towards the sun.

"Have a good day, Mr. Bear!"

"Have a good day, Mrs. Bunky!"

---

1. Never done or seen before!

"How are you, Mr. Beaver?"

He spontaneously greeted all his neighbours encountered on the way, smiling at the thought that just two nights ago he had been secretly vis-itng their living rooms and admiring their Christmas trees. He reminded himself a silver figurine in the shape of a toothbrush in Mr. Beaver's living room.

Mrs. Amalia's house was situated slightly away from all the other houses in the Walmland Village. Surrounded by a vast garden, it was prob-ably one of the most beautiful places in the Village. Bunky wondered how it was possible that he had never seen Mrs. Amalia's house before—after all, he had been living in the Walmland Village through all his life! It happens quite often that there is a beautiful or well-known place in the vicinity of our neighbourhood and, yet, we have never visited it. This is exactly what happened in Bunky's case.

Bunky walked past the withered rosebush and rang Lady Amalia's doorbell. A little thrush nestled himself on a nearby tree and tilted his head, carefully tracking Bunky's moves. Then the thrush flew away, prob-ably hoping to enjoy his day at the pond. The pond was quite popular in the Walmland Village.

A ginger-coloured squirrel flashed through the garden and Bunky managed to see her velvety tail. There was a mysterious silence inside the house, so Bunky rang the doorbell again and, being slightly impatient by nature, gently knocked on the door.

"Mrs. Amalia, Mr. Cat, it is me, Bunky the Christmas Hero!" he cried.

There was a little noise on the other side and, as Bunky thought, a little laughter and, finally, someone opened the door. But instead of Mrs. Amalia, Bunky was brought face to face with a beautiful Bunky girl of his age. She was holding in her arms Mr. Cat who looked quite delighted. The girl had soft, green eyes with rich, black eyelashes. She gently smiled at Bunky and he immediately blushed and looked down at the stairs. She was wearing pink boots and the most beautiful, pink woollen dress.

"My goodness," thought Bunky, "it is the Bunky Princess herself!"

And he felt a sudden weakness in the knees. The world began swirling in front of his eyes.

"Ehm, ehm, ehm," said Bunky, still staring at the stairs. At last, the world stopped swirling and he tried to look at the Bunky Princess.

"Grandma, the Christmas Hero of whom you had told me so much came to visit us!" rejoiced the girl, inviting Bunky to step inside.

But Bunky completely lost his mind and ran down the stairs in order to hide behind the withered rosebush. It was exactly as in his blue notebook —he, as the Hero, was meant to emerge from the rosebush! The only difference was that the rosebush was withered, since it was still the winter time.

"Courage, courage, courage!" whispered Bunky and felt stupid that he ran down the stairs. He didn't want the Princess to think that he was uncouth[2].

"It's not what the Hero would do," Bunky thought and immediately emerged from the bush. Blushing and feeling dizzy, he bravely approached the girl and introduced himself.

2. Lacking good manners!

"I apologise for being indisposed for a moment," mumbled Bunky.

The mysterious girl smiled at Bunky even more beautifully and even Mr. Cat smiled at him.

"Dear Bunky," she said, "I am so pleased to meet you! My name is Rosalia."

And she gave Bunky her beautiful hand. Bunky took Rosalia's hand and gently shook it.

"I am very, very pleased to get to know you," he said, blushing all over underneath his blue fur, "I brought some delicious gifts from aunt and uncle Walm."

With trembling paws, he placed the boxes on the nearby table.

"Oh, that is so kind of them and so kind of you! My Grandma told me sooo much about you!" exclaimed Rosalia, taking Bunky by the hand and leading him into the living room. She carefully placed Mr. Cat on the pink armchair and he began purring in his usual friendly way.

"He remembers you!" smiled Rosalia.

"I must be dreaming," thought Bunky and grinned from ear to ear.

"I returned," he said bravely, "because I really loved Mrs. Amalia's and Mr. Cat's company. Now, I am more than delighted to meet you too!"

"Mr. Cat?" smiled Rosalia, "His name is Maurice, but I just love that you call him Mr. Cat! It sounds so noble and dignified!"

"Maurice?" repeated Bunky and immediately thought about his blue notebook and Maurice the Dragon, the Bunky Princess's pet.

"Can it be true?" he kept wondering, feeling like in a dream.

On seeing Bunky, Lady Amalia got up from her sofa and opened her arms.

"Welcome, young man! My Christmas Hero!" she greeted him warmly, as if they had known each other for more than a hundred years.

The house was smelling with tea and roses again. Bunky was invited to sit on the sofa with Mrs. Amalia and Miss Rosalia on both sides and Maurice on his lap. In the meantime, Mrs. Amalia decided that they should eat the treats from Mr. and Mrs. Walm together. She also prepared some aromatic tea and brought from the kitchen her delicious apple pie. Mr. Cat received a bowl of warm milk.

"Children," began Mrs. Amalia after the lunch, "this is the happiest Christmas time of my life! Maurice and I did not expect a single companion and here you are, making us so happy with your presence!"

Maurice, that is—Mr. Cat—purred in approval, as if confirming Lady Amalia's words.

Bunky was happy to hear that Lady Amalia addressed them as "children"—it meant that they were still quite little.

"Oh, Grandma!" smiled Rosalia, taking Mrs. Amalia by the hand. She had this endearing habit of taking by the hand those who were close to her heart. Grandma Amalia had told her so much about Bunky the Hero that he instantly became very dear to her. She was gazing at him with kindness and curiosity and Bunky kept hoping that his hair was combed properly and that he cleaned his ears very well. He wanted to look as presentable as possible.

"This is truly my best Christmas ever too!" he admitted.

"My Granddaughter Rosalia," said Mrs. Amalia, "will remain here with me for a long time—perhaps you two can become friends!"

"Very good friends, I should think!" Rosalia rejoiced. She was speaking in such an elegant way—just like the Bunky Princess.

"The best friends!" mumbled Bunky, blushing all over his face.

"The best friends!" Rosalia agreed.

On hearing this, Bunky felt dizzy from joy and saw ten Mr. Cats instead of the particular one, but it was only a moment of dizziness and, in a while, the one particular Mr. Cat returned to his proper place.

"Rosalia decided to move here also because she will be attending school in the Walmland Village!" remarked proudly Grandma Amalia.

"Oh, that is more than amazing!" cried Bunky.

"My dear young man, are you also attending the local school?" kindly inquired Mrs. Amalia.

"Yes, of course! In three years I shall be graduating from primary school!" said Bunky, visibly beaming with pride, "Currently we are studying decimals. There's not much about dinosaurs, but I am reading about them after school."

"I hope that you and Rosalia will be able to spend a lot of time together and that you will be visiting us here too!" rejoiced Grandma Amalia, "I feel that it will be one of the happiest years!"

"Yes, Grandma, I would be happy to show Bunky how to play the harp!" exclaimed Rosalia. In truth, she didn't have many friends, as she was the only child in her local neighbourhood. At present, she felt that she had encountered her best friend. She was gazing with admiration at Bunky, thinking what a polite and kind person he was. And to think that he was also Santa Claus's Helper, the Christmas Hero! But even without this title, she thought that Bunky was simply the kindest person. Apparently, Maurice enjoyed Bunky's company too. Maurice always approved of those who had kind hearts but, usually, he would hiss at those of whom he didn't approve. At present, he was relaxing on Bunky's shoulder.

"Are you playing the harp?!" cried the astonished Bunky.

"Yes!" she smiled.

"Oh dear," thought Bunky, "Just like in the novel! Perhaps I should start learning how to knit soon!"

Indeed, their friendship began immediately. Bunky decided to invite Rosalia to the Walms' house right away and Mrs. Amalia did not oppose, feeling happy that her granddaughter found such a special and well-mannered friend. Bunky could hardly wait to introduce Rosalia to everyone. He still wasn't sure whether it was his reality that mingled with the plot of his novel, or whether it was the world from the novel that entered his reality. He only knew that everything was happening for a reason.

"I met Mrs. Amalia for a reason," thought Bunky, "And Mr. Cat too!"

"You will see," he told Rosalia while they were walking through the Walmland Village together, "I will prepare for you my special meal which I call *Scrambled Eggs a'la Omelette*! And you will meet my best friends: Rodney and Plum, and my uncle and aunt, and everyone! Mr. Elk and Mr. Meow like playing the piano and they also enjoy singing, while Sir Williams is writing a book! And also my aunt Barbara and uncle Bill are so kind! I will share with you some amazing stories about our travels with Santa Claus!

Bunky kept talking excitedly and Rosalia was listening carefully. Bunky thought that she was the gentlest creature he had ever seen, apart from Rodney, Plum, and Rudolph the Reindeer, of course. She was walking very gently in her pink boots, gracefully whistling a well-known Christmas tune.

"You are the first girl I know who whistles in such an elegant way!" said Bunky with admiration.

"Oh thank you, my dear!" rejoiced Rosalia, "You are the most noble and kindest boy I have ever met! You will be my Christmas Hero!"

"Oh!" said Bunky and felt that the plot of his novel was turning into reality.

"And then, one day," continued exhilarated Bunky, "I will show you a Very Important Notebook which I keep underneath my bed. In this notebook I was writing our story . . . but will you believe me?"

Rosalia looked at Bunky curiously.

"I believe you," she said with uncle Bill's simplicity, "You know, Bunky, I often had these dreams about a castle and the Hero who looked like you and we had so many amazing adventures . . ."

"I know," answered Bunky seriously, "You will read about these adventures in my notebook."

As they walked, the sun illuminated their path. Passing nearby the pond, they saw Rodney and Plum playing in the snow.

"Hey, hey!" shouted Rodney on seeing Bunky. Plum began wagging his tail.

"Hey, hey!" rejoiced Bunky and offered hugs to both Rodney and Plum.

"My dear friends," he said in an official manner, "let me introduce you to Rosalia the Bunky. The Bunky Princess."

Rosalia bowed in an elegant manner and offered them her hands.

"I am Rosalia, Mrs. Amalia's granddaughter," she said simply, "I am so pleased to meet you!"

"Rodney and Plum are my best friends," remarked Bunky.

"Hooray!" shouted Rodney wildly, "It worked, it worked!"

Bunky stared at Rodney in surprise, wondering why would Rodney act in such a wild manner on such an important occasion.

"Why would such a mature and reasonable person suddenly resort to such wild screams?" he wondered.

Rosalia leant over in order to pet Plum. She really loved his deep, blue eyes. She really loved all animals.

Bunky took Rodney aside and asked: "Dear cousin, what do you mean by this?"

"Oh, cousin Bunky!" pleaded Rodney, "Please do not be angry with me! You have finally met the Bunky Princess! The magic worked!"

"Cousin, indeed," said Bunky, "I can hardly understand what happened today, but my heart is filled with so much joy!"

And then a sudden thought crossed Bunky's mind.

"Rodney, are *you* responsible for the appearance of the Bunky Princess?" he inquired.

Rodney blushed quite more visibly.

"Oh, cousin Bunky," he giggled, "I wrote a letter to Santa Claus in which I asked him to bring the Bunky Princess to the Walmland Village. When you were delivering the gifts to Mrs. Amalia's house, Santa Claus and I were doing some magic in order to make your wish come true. I learnt that the true magic comes from one's heart, so I was trying to imagine the Bunky Princess walking through our town in her pink boots, whistling a well-known Christmas tune and . . . here she is! It was very difficult, because I had to believe that something almost impossible could actually become our reality. But tell me, cousin, does she know how to whistle?"

Bunky was staring at Rodney and he was quite speechless. There was a look of surprise on his face. Finally, he smiled in the happiest bunky way.

"Oh, Rodney!" he rejoiced, "If only you knew how beautifully she whistles! And she plays the harp—just like in the novel! She remembers everything that we have lived through in the novel—she saw it in her dreams. And Mr. Cat is called Maurice, just like the pet Dragon in our story! Whatever you did, I am so grateful! You have no idea how grateful I am! I can only imagine how much strength you needed to have in order to bring the Bunky Princess here—to Walmland!"

Rodney gave Bunky a loving hug and looked at him seriously.

"But now," he said, "please, do not to forget about me and Plum."

"No, never," promised Bunky, "You are my dearest friends. Tonight I will share with you and Plum my collection of stamps. We haven't seen the stamps yet!"

"Yes, since Christmas began!" smiled Rodney.

"We had better things to do!" smiled Bunky, "I have some great stamps with dinosaurs and you and Plum can keep some of them!"

The time between Christmas and New Year was very happy for Bunky, Rodney, and Plum. As Bunky promised, he did not forget about his friends. Aunt Barbara and uncle Bill decided to spend the New Year's Eve in the Walms' house, so Rodney could stay longer with his cousin Bunky and his friend Plum. They were playing in the snow each and every single day, trying new recipes from the cookbook, reading books and admiring Bunky's stamps. Quite often, they would receive a telegram from Sir Williams and read with curiosity about the progress of his masterpiece. There were long and interesting descriptions of the Alpacas and Sir Williams' daily routine on the farm and, also, some passages about his new passion for gymnastics in the morning performed on the top of the local mountain.

But on every third day, the Bunky Princess, that is—Rosalia, would come to visit Bunky in the Walms' house, or Bunky would go to visit Rosalia. On such days, they would have very serious conversations about dinosaurs and then, usually, they would go skating on the pond. On such days, Bunky would be wearing his precious skating boots which he had received from aunt and uncle Walm. Rosalia would be gliding on a silvery surface of the pond in the beautiful, golden skating boots, leaving behind a faintly trail of stars. It was Bunky's idea—noble at heart, he decided to offer Santa Claus's skates to Rosalia. They would be skating and laughing until the evening, and then they would return to their houses, knowing that their next meeting would be coming soon. Finally, on such days, the Christmas star on the Walms' spruce would light Bunky's path back home and he would always return there with love and peace in his heart.

Acknowledgments

I would like to express my sincere gratitude to Anna Kędra-Kardela, Ewelina Prażmo, Maria Pirgerou, Christopher Stern, Bruce Gatenby, Gregory Papanikos and Ibrahim A. El-Hussari for the insightful comments, support and encouragement on the journey through the literary Walmland. Moreover, I am so grateful for the wonderful Wipf and Stock Team. I am also very thankful for my closest family's untiring support. A big 'thank you' to the Readers—it is an honour to encounter Bunky together with you!

Aleksandra Tryniecka

www.aleksandratryniecka.com